A BROKEN MIND

Travis A. Seabrook

Acknowledgements

I would like to thank my OG Patreon Subscribers. Thank you to Wanda at Fox House Publishing for helping me debut this novel. Thank you Stainart for capturing my vision and creating such a beautiful cover. And an even bigger more special thank you to my wife, Andrea for believing in me and supporting me through this journey from the first word written all the way through publishing. I love you. Dedicating this book to my mother, who blessed me with life and the talent to tell this beautiful story.

Contents

Chapter 1

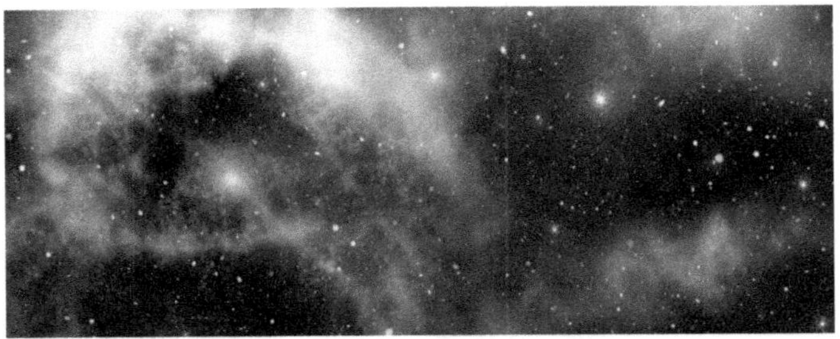

My therapist, Dr. Ricardo, said whenever I felt anxious after a night's rest, I should go to my favorite spot in my home and collect my thoughts. That favorite spot was in front of my enormous bay windows so I could look out at the city. It was so beautiful during the day, but even more remarkable at night. My condo overlooked the river and the edge of the city. I loved to people-watch—mothers strolling with their children, men gliding across the bridge on bicycles, and the rhythmic pulse of the city moving in quiet harmony. The train that passed by was a symphony of steel and momentum, roaring along the riverbank like a heartbeat I could rely on.

The air was always rich with the scent of damp earth and distant food trucks, blending into a sensory balm that made the chaos in my mind feel small, almost insignificant. Sometimes, I'd step out onto the patio and sit for hours, letting the world unfold before me, allowing it to ground me in its ordinary, beautiful noise.

I don't remember my dream from last night, but why did I wake up in such a panic?

A tiny voice in my head always made me question why I could never remember my dreams or why falling asleep at night felt impossible. Dr. Ricardo has me break down and psychoanalyze all the possibilities of why that could be. When I was younger, I used to have such vivid dreams, and for a long time, I thought I could predict the future. As a child, I would have these dreams where something would happen, and then later, what would happen in my dream would come to fruition.

It could be a small, fleeting dream—something harmless and easily forgotten, or one of deep significance, where time felt urgent and the details weighed heavily. Sometimes, I'd become consumed by it, hyper-fixating to the point of madness, desperately trying to unravel its meaning, as if decoding it could somehow unlock a hidden truth I was meant to understand.

Why was remembering my dreams so important to me in the first place? Were they supposed to uncover why I don't sleep or reveal something even more profound? I try not to talk to Lauren about these things because I'm sure she'd think something was wrong with me.

Psychic? Predicting the future in dreams?

She'd probably run for the hills. My dreams were one thing I'd kept from her since we had been seeing each other. It's something I would never have the guts to disclose to her.

Lauren was my incredible, beautiful, and down-to-earth girlfriend, and we'd been together for some time now. She had this effortless grace about her—gorgeous on the outside, with a soul that radiated kindness. By day, she nurtured young minds as a kindergarten teacher, and by night, she was the woman who loved me deeply and without hesitation. Lauren stands at a petite five-two, a sharp contrast to my six-three height, giving her a cutesy charm that never fails to make me smile. We're both thirty-one, but her youthful energy sometimes makes her seem years younger. Her naturally curly, strawberry-blonde hair frames her face beautifully, with soft ringlets that catch the light just right. Her warm brown eyes, which she always reminds me she gets from her brown-skinned father, are full of life. Sprinkled on her medium tan skin are delicate freckles, which she says she inherited from her white mother, that seem to dance across her cheeks and nose, giving her a uniquely radiant look. In contrast, my dark, curly brown hair is a wild explosion atop my head, often untamed. Considering we both come from biracial backgrounds, our parents are white and black, the blend of features we share makes perfect sense—it reflects the beautiful complexity that defines us both.

Lauren's style was comforting and cozy, always opting for a casual look, such as sweatpants or sweatshirts, rather than a formal one. Then, when she dressed up, she was stunning, knowing how to bring fashion forward. Her style fits her personality in more ways than one. She was very laid-back and an introvert, like me. In comparison, I'm more of a casual button-up with slacks and boots type of guy. I keep it very simple and demure. I was also very clean-cut, with no tattoos, only accessorizing with my left ear piercing, a cuban chain, and sometimes a watch.

I lived in the heart of Metrotown City, a ways from Sunrise Grove, where Lauren lived. I was a true city boy at heart and loved to hear the roaring of nightlife around me—the cars blaring their horns, the sirens of emergency personnel, and the screams of annoyed city-goers were my very own ASMR, which meant autonomous sensory meridian response, used to describe tingling or goosebumps in response to audio or visuals. Metrotown City was just another average city that never slept. It had tall buildings, lots of shopping districts, and public transportation. In fact, I lived in the best shopping district, better known as Holiware Square—a vibrant, high-end hub of luxury and exclusivity.Holiware Square was a special marketplace, full of fashion and influence. The streets had tall glass-front shops showcasing the latest styles from famous designers. Bright signs lit up the sidewalks below. And the best part was that my condo had the best view of it all.

Now, Sunrise Grove is a little suburbia. I only visit there when I go to Lauren's place. Sunrise Grove was a place to escape when my introversion peaked.It was a place where everyone knew each other by name, neighbors would ask you about your day, and genuinely care to hear about it. The neighborhood has sidewalks and cul-de-sacs, buses that drop kids off instead of public transportation, and more stop signs instead of stop lights. Sunrise Grove had trees—big, beautiful, different color trees that smelled like fresh pine. Smelling the fresh scent of honeysuckles that were nestled into the corner of every house made you feel at home.

The small town was home to single-family homes, its own cozy diner, a small family-owned coffee shop, and an eclectic bookstore that was Lauren's favorite place to visit. Sunrise Grove was always a place to escape if I grew tired of the city.

"Lanno, are you going to get ready or just stand there daydreaming?" Lauren's voice rang through me. I disengaged from my thoughts and turned towards her as I buttoned up my shirt. I stood before my huge bay window, as I always liked to bathe in the sun and let the fresh light soak into my caramel skin. Lauren continued her way from the bedroom to the kitchen and turned the coffeemaker on to make a fresh cup to start her day.

"Uh, yeah, I'm almost ready. I just have to brush my teeth," I say, shifting my focus from looking outside at her.

Lauren chuckles. "You might also want to put on some pants." She smirked as she went into the fridge and grabbed the creamer.

I look down at my legs, and I am only wearing boxers. "Right, right."

I headed to the bedroom, grabbed my jeans, and put them on.

Lauren returns to the bedroom and looks at me: "My man is fineeee."

I laugh and then shake my head at her as I grab a pillow to hit her with it playfully. She always made me feel good. Lauren enjoyed complimenting me and showing me off just as much as I did with her.

Lauren steps back and lifts her hands into the air, "You better not hit me with the—"

I smack her with the pillow and then smile innocently. She then runs full charge into me as I hold up the pillow to brace her impact.

"I'm supposed to be getting ready, and here you are trying to knock me over!" I've been gaslighting her since I started the fight.

"Oh, I'm distracting you, huh! Am I?" Lauren looks at me with the most surprised face. She punches the pillow playfully, and I cower behind it as if I were afraid of her five-two self. She punches the pillow one last time.

"Get dressed, sir." She demands as she puts a fist up to her eye, threatening me. I laugh again and throw the pillow back onto the bed.

We did little for most of the morning since I slept in late, but we had plans to meet up with some friends. We are a small, tight-knit group that meets at least once a week to try a new restaurant or distillery. As you grow older, the simpler things, like grabbing lunch, are how we have fun these days. Lauren quickly adopted my best friend, and I adopted hers. Our friends adore our relationship, often commenting on how well Lauren and I complement each other. I'd have to agree—we truly mesh effortlessly. We share silly, playful personalities, making every moment together feel lighthearted and fun. Whether cracking jokes, teasing each other, or simply laughing at the smallest things, our connection feels natural and filled with joy. She is very caring, nurturing, and supportive. However, she does have some insecurities, which I never understood because Lauren was a fantastic woman.

I walk to the bathroom and grab my toothbrush and paste. Quickly, I brush my teeth and finish getting ready so we can head out.

Lauren and I finished getting ready. I grabbed my coat and put it on, and Lauren did the same. We left the apartment and headed towards the garage to find my car. As we got into my truck, all I could think of was the delicious food we would eat at Deluth. Deluth is a local restaurant that is our absolute favorite. Since we have been exploring restaurants we've never visited lately, we revisited our go-to. I'm a huge foodie—I love eating, exploring different cultures, and sipping creative cocktails. My passion for food runs so deep that I'd gladly travel to try a new dish.

I work at a major tech company, and while it pays the bills handsomely, I might add, there are days I dream about leaving it all behind to travel the world and eat my way through every continent. One day, when I retire, I'll finally have the freedom to do just that—go anywhere, anytime, and follow my appetite wherever it leads.

Today, we met with Lauren's best friend, Fallyn, and my boy, Jah. Jah has been trying to get at Fallyn for some time, but I'm almost positive she enjoys the chase. Jah had just met Fallyn around the time Lauren and I started talking. Since then, whenever I tell him we're heading out, his first question is always the same: "Will Fallyn be there?"

Sometimes, I think they did mess around, and Jah got it bad for her now. Cause I've never seen a man stick around this long if a girl isn't giving it up, and whenever Fallyn flirts back, Jah eats it up.

Fallyn is a fiery Latina with tattoos and jewelry from head to toe—a walking work of art with a bold presence to match. She works at a tattoo parlor and wears her confidence like a second skin. Sassy, sharp-tongued, and fiercely loyal, Fallyn doesn't hesitate to stand up for the people she loves. If you cross one of her friends, she's coming for your throat—no questions asked.

Standing around five-two, she's slim with curves in all the right places, and her style is always on point. One thing about Fallyn—you'll never catch her without her nails done. They're always decked out, jeweled, and polished to perfection. Honestly, I don't think I've ever seen her without a fresh set.

Lauren always tells me stories about how she and Fallyn met in high school in Rockdale City, a few cities over from Metrotown. Rockdale City was a smaller city with a predominantly Latino demographic. Lauren's family had gone through a house fire and had to move outside of Sunrise Grove, where Lauren was born, into temporary housing until they could get back on their feet. It was a rough transition for Lauren, and it was even tougher for her to go through four years of high school being the minority. She was teased and bullied for that very reason; that was until Fallyn stepped in and stood up for her. Lauren would explain the nuances of being a teenage girl, how cliques were real, and that mean girls existed. A group of girls would always make fun of her size, or how she dressed, or laugh at how awkward she was. Fallyn would defend her, scold the girls, and take Lauren under her wing. They became best friends in those moments, sharing secrets and forming their own unique group of nice girls who accepted people for who they were. Eventually, Lauren would be accepted by everyone in the school, and the bullying would cease to exist. I tease Lauren now and then about how that's where she gets her spiciness from—the four years of culture shock. Lauren knows how to stand up for herself now and for others, but when Fallyn is involved, Fallyn is the protagonist of their story.

Now, Jah—he's tall like me,shorter at six-one, but a lot more muscular. He's got rich, dark skin and rocks a clean taper fade. Jah's always dressed in name-brand clothing and designer accessories, effortlessly blending style with swagger. He's the comedian of the crew, constantly cracking jokes—not the kind that puts people down, but the kind that leaves everyone in stitches over the most random, hilarious observations.

Unlike me, Jah isn't quiet or reserved—he thrives on conversation and lives for the drama of girl gossip. Anytime the girls talk, you can bet he's right there chiming in, sipping imaginary tea, and adding his two cents with flair.

Professionally, Jah is a boss in his own right. He runs a private security company and has been working hard to grow it from the ground up. He's at the point now where he's hiring more staff, assigning them to posts across the city. His team handles security for local businesses, and they're all certified to carry weapons—trained, professional, and reliable. You can tell he's proud of what he's built, and rightfully so.

Jah and I met in college, during our freshman year, at a party. He was mixing drinks for everyone in the kitchen, playing bartender as he cracked jokes with everyone who came up to him. I'll never forget what he said to me the moment I waltzed up to him for a drink.

"You look like a martini man."

It must have been my appearance—dapper, clean-cut, and my body language always screamed, laid-back and reserved. I was always a quiet guy who observed everything and everybody. I remember chuckling at what he said and giving him a nod as he served me exactly that—a martini.

It surprised me to be at this party. I had gotten invited by a girl in one of my classes and figured I'd step outside of my regular, daily routine and partake in the festivities. I'm glad I went because who knows if Jah and I would have ever crossed paths besides then? We stood there and talked for a while, and the conversation was seamless. We asked each other what we were studying and how we liked college, being both freshmen. Jah admitted to me that he was struggling with his classes and didn't think he'd be able to finish college, let alone the semester. He confessed his aspirations to own his own company, where he could protect and serve his community in the security business. I recall telling him he should always follow his heart and do what felt right in his mind. After that long conversation we had that night, I remember him texting me days later, saying he was going to drop out.

I remember feeling immense guilt, as though I had persuaded him to make that decision. He promised me that where I was a contributing factor, this had been on his mind for as long as he could remember, and now he had the courage to make some moves. Either way, I was proud of Jah for following his dreams and investing in himself, trusting that he could produce greatness.

"Hey babe, are you ok? You've been super quiet today," Lauren asks, breaking the silence between us.

We pulled up to the restaurant, and I parked the car. I sat back against the seat and looked at her. She grabs my hand, and I squeeze hers, then warmly smile.

"Yeah, I'm good."

Lauren gave me a look. "Are you sure? We can cancel going out and go back home."

"Nah, I'm good, seriously; I've just been in my head. You know, it's usually the same old—work, sleep, work." I lean over and kiss her lips to reassure her, and I feel her squeeze my hand back.

"Y'all gonna sit in there and make out or get out of the truck?" I hear a familiar muffled voice through my window. I stopped kissing Lauren and looked out the driver's window to see Jah waiting outside. He takes his index finger knuckle and taps it on the window. I smile even bigger and shake my head as I laugh.

"You goofy man, we're coming," I say as I open the door.

"I'm glad you opened the door because I was about to... only I never know how to open these boujee ass trucks." Jah looked around where the door handle would be, only not to find it.

"This? Bougie? Not even close." I responded to him. Lauren gets out of the car and walks around to us as Jah and I mess around. She gives Jah a friendly hug.

Jah hugs her back. "The beautiful Miss Lauren. How are you?"

She smiles. "I'm good, Jah. How are you?"

Jah steps back and starts looking around. "Oh, I'm good, I'm good. Just looking for your fine-ass friend, Fallyn."

Lauren and I laugh, shaking our heads at his shamelessness.

"Jah, please." Lauren says as she walks away.

We head towards the restaurant together, and through the window, we see Fallyn waiting for us. As we enter, Lauren tells the server we are with Fallyn, and they tell us we can sit with our party.

The restaurant emitted a warm, inviting ambiance, with beautifully carved wooden tables and sleek black chairs with plush red cushions. At the center of it all hung a breathtaking, handcrafted chandelier made from intertwining deer antlers—its lights strategically placed to create a soft, enchanting glow.

The moment you stepped inside, the air greeted you with mouth-watering aromas—rich with spice, smoke, and sizzling meats—proof that the chefs knew their way around a kitchen. And as the sunlight streamed through the windows, it cast a warm, golden haze across the space, wrapping everything in a comfortable, timeless glow that made you want to sink into the moment and never leave.

"Haaay boooo!" Fallyn yells as we come up to the table. She stands up, and they hug each other. Jah immediately takes a seat in the chair next to Fallyn. I sit across from Jah, and Lauren sits next to me on the other side of Fallyn. Right next to our table was a giant window where you could see outside. Outside, there was another smaller bar, designed to entertain the awaiting guests. There were also fire pits and a flower arrangement etched into the wooden perimeter of the patio.

"Hey, Fallyn, how are you doing, gorgeous?" Jah asks as he scoots a little closer to her.

Fallyn tilts her head and strikes a pose. "I'm good, Jah. How are you?"

I couldn't help but smile and turn to Lauren, who was doing the same. It was pretty damn entertaining how he swooned for her. He's a good guy, but always has a harem of women at his disposal. I know Fallyn must know this, and it's why she doesn't give him the time of day. As they continued to flirt and talk, I picked up the menu and looked through it.

Mmm, chicken and waffles are my favorite.

I feel Lauren's hand gently rest on my leg, her touch warm and reassuring. I turn to her, and she meets my gaze with a soft, knowing smile. Without a word, I lean in and kiss her—slowly, tenderly—letting the moment speak for itself.

"Ya'll are so damn cute!" Fallyn yelled. "I want some of that love, bestie."

Lauren blushes and responds. "You'll find it, girl."

Jah glances around, raising his eyebrows with an exaggerated expression that practically says, "What am I, chopped liver?" His playful smirk and dramatic head tilt make it clear he's only half-joking, fishing for a little attention of his own.

I laugh at him and then clear my throat. "Thank you, Fallyn."

"So, when y'all getting married?" Fallyn asks, catching me mid-sip of my water. I nearly choke, coughing slightly as I set the glass down.

"Oh my god, Fallyn, please." Lauren says playfully as she gently shoves her. I adjust myself in my seat, eyes all locked on me. My hands get clammy, and I rub them together. Lauren continues, "We just started dating, friend."

"Okaaaay, six months is a long time. I'm just saying. If you were happy and serious about each other, there would have been a ring on that finger." Fallyn taps her finger and gives me a bold look.

"Hey, I'm serious about her. I just—" I look around the table. "Marriage is serious. I want to, uh, I want to make sure we are both ready, yanno." I looked at Jah again, and my body language was super uncomfortable. Lauren's hand squeezes my thigh and then rubs it.

Jah blurts out, "Easy on Lanno, Fallyn. When are you getting married?"

"I don't have a man!" She looks at him and then pushes his chest as she laughs.

Jah laughs and then bobs his head. "Exactly, so go easy on my boy, easy on him."

Fallyn continues her banter. "Listen, I'm not tryna put Lanno on the spot, but look at Lauren. She's a ten. Beautiful, smart, funny. She's got a great career. She's the whole package."

Lauren gives Fallyn a death stare, her face red and blushing. "Oh my god, please stop."

"Alright, alright, I'm done, seriously. I'll ease up," Fallyn says with a playful smirk, her tone light but teasing.

The server comes over and asks us if we want to order drinks and if we are ready to put in our order for food. It was flights around the board, mimosas for the ladies, and harder drinks for the men. I got chicken and waffles, Lauren got an omelet, Jah got the rodeo steak and eggs, and Fallyn got pancakes. We stayed a couple of hours, ate, drank, and continued to converse the day away until we were ready to go.

It was Sunday, and I had work in the morning. So, Lauren headed back to her place for the night, and I would go home and prepare for my week. After we left the restaurant, I drove Lauren home, and once we got to her house, she hesitated to get out of the car.

I turn the music down in the car and look at her. "What's wrong, babe?"

Lauren sighs. "We never actually discussed marriage or moving in together."

I look back at her, then let my head fall against the car's headrest. In deep thought, I grew quiet. The silence hangs thick in the air, almost suffocating, as if even the vehicle itself is holding its breath.

I want to respond carefully and gently because the last thing I want is to hurt Lauren's feelings. The truth is, I don't think we're ready. Or maybe it's just me. Sometimes, our relationship feels like pure bliss—laughter, love, and light. But other times, we're clashing, struggling to understand each other through the noise of our disagreements.

How do I explain that without making her feel like I'm pulling away?

"I'm... not ready." I finally let out.

Lauren asked without hesitation, "Is there someone else?"

I sigh and shake my head. "This is what I mean, Lauren. I tell you I'm not ready, and you assume I'm cheating. Instead of just asking, "What can get me ready?" or "What's stopping me from being ready?"

"I know, I know—I'm sorry, babe. I don't know why I get like this. Ugh!" She hits the glove compartment and then stops talking. I turn and look at her, and she continues, "But Fallyn is right. We have been together for six months, and you won't even let me stay over at your place for more than three days in a row. What's next for us?"

"Lauren, Fallyn is single. Why are we taking relationship advice from her?" I push her hair out of her face, and my index finger knuckle goes underneath her chin. I lift her chin and then grab it gently, turning her head to make her look at me. "I don't want to rush anything, and I also want us to be in a good place before we combine our worlds."

She smiles and then leans into me, kissing me. I held onto the side of her face and kissed her back.

"I love you," she says.

My heart drops.

The words hit me like a wave—gentle, but heavy. My entire body tenses as I try to process them. I love you. Words she's never said before. Words I've never told her. Not out loud, at least.

I sit there, frozen in the moment. Part of me wants to say it back, to wrap her in reassurance and give her the response she's hoping for. But another part of me hesitates.

I smile and kiss her again, feeling her slightly pull back.

"What?" I say, my voice wavering.

She looked away. "Nothing. Goodnight, Lanno." Lauren opened the car door and got out. I watched her as she walked into the house, and then I drove off.

Shit! I completely fucked up.

Why did I not say it back? I asked myself this rhetorical question repeatedly, but even rhetorically, I still can't answer it honestly. I stayed in my head the entire drive home, beating myself up for not responding to her. I love you.

Because I did love her.

I step inside my condo, switch on the lights, and hang my jacket on the hook.

Standing there, I felt a surge of loneliness rush over me that I've always felt and never could explain. Maybe it was my apartment that expelled that energy. It was quiet—too quiet, considering the location where my building sat in the city. The inside of my home was very monochromatic—the walls were gray, and a ginormous black leather couch sat at the focal point of the room. In front of the sofa was a wooden coffee table with a metal rim that sat on top of a shag area rug.

I kicked off my boots and took off my socks, allowing my feet to lie flat against the cold hardwood floor that ran throughout my home. The kitchen is connected to the living room in an open concept with a huge chef island. The bar next to my kitchen was a staple of the floor plan, crafted perfectly in its nook for anyone to enjoy a drink at their leisure.

I placed a few pictures of my mom, Lauren, and friends intricately throughout the space. I loved art, so I made sure I had some black-and-white abstract art pieces.

Even though I enjoyed my spacious home, chef-style kitchen, and bedroom with a massive walk-in closet, I still felt empty.

Slowly, I approached my favorite bay window on the twentieth floor, which overlooked the city. I pulled out my phone and started texting Lauren.

You know I care about you a lot, right?

Quickly, I backspace and clench my phone. I can't send that.

"You know I care about you," I say, mocking myself. How stupid do I sound? I should have told her right then that I love her.

I returned to my sofa and sat down. Every few minutes, I would text her and then backspace it. Time slowly went by, and the hour got later. I watched the sunset as I continued beating myself up over how I responded to Lauren. Usually, I would already get an I miss you text from her, but nothing came through, which was completely understandable.

I picked up my orca-shaped bowl and lighter off my coffee table and sparked it up, taking a puff. I might as well try to get to sleep early. It was now eight o'clock, and I knew I would be up all night if I didn't start trying to go to sleep now. As I smoked my medical-grade marijuana that helped me fall asleep, I stared at my orca-shaped bowl.

Orcas were my favorite animal. They symbolize memories and sleep from my childhood.

I remember one specific time when I dreamt of orcas. I was swimming with them in the ocean. Hundreds of orcas were in the water, packed so tightly that it felt more like a prison than the boundless freedom of the sea. It was a powerful moment because I remember the emotion, fear, and deep-seated distress I felt while having this dream. The orcas were distraught and had nowhere to go. The water was rough and rugged, as if it had just stormed or was about to. In this dream, I could smell the copious amounts of salt in the water and the sharpness of the frigid temperature. I remember thinking how much I didn't want to be there. The overwhelming sadness and help-lessness made the dream unbearable. Their cries echoed through the water, resonating with a haunting intensity that seemed to vibrate through every wave. The sound was heart-wrenching, filled with fear and sorrow, each note carrying an overwhelming sense of desperation.

I am a huge animal lover, so this dream was terrifying. Once I woke from that dream, I remembered it, but did not understand its importance. Why was I dreaming of orcas? Was there something I needed to do? That is how much I trusted my dreams had some deeper meaning. That is how invested I was.

Something told me to turn the TV on, and when I did, the first channel that popped on was the news channel. Now, it is no surprise that it was on the news. As a child, our TV stayed on the news because it was my mother's favorite program. It was what was on the news that caught my attention.

Hunters in another country were killing hundreds of orcas for sport. The sheer fear, anger, sadness, and con-fusion shook me to my core. I had all kinds of thoughts running through my mind. Was this a coincidence, and did I foresee this happening?

I asked myself an even more complicated question—was I there?

In my dream, I do not remember being there as myself, at least not in human form. I remember being there and feeling all the emotions around me as if I were the orca.

I could go on and on about the countless dreams that turned into reality.

I felt my eyes getting heavier, and it appears the marijuana was working. In a huge effort, I managed to stand on my feet and make my way to the bedroom. I stripped out of my clothing and lay on the bed. As I sank into the mattress, my thoughts began to blur and dissolve, and I could feel myself slowly drifting off, pulled into the quiet embrace of sleep.

Chapter 2

My eyes slowly opened, and my heart raced.

Where am I?

It's not my condo. This home is entirely different. There were plants everywhere, and the entire room had indie vibes. The walls were brown, and a small black cat was lounging on the windowsill of a huge bay window that sat directly behind a brown sofa. I sat on the couch and continued to look around the openness of the apartment, as I could hear low-playing soul music echoing across the room from an old-school record player. In front of me were low-lit candles and incense burning. The only light illuminating the room was from the natural light that crept past the curtains and the low, dim string globe lights strung across the ceiling.

It smelled amazing, like jasmine and a deep vanilla scent. As comforting as my surroundings appeared, I sat up fast and looked around. Scared and confused, I stood up slowly from the couch and headed towards the front door, where I saw a bat in the corner. I grip it firmly and walk around the room slowly. I hear a soft voice in the next room, humming and singing. Footsteps approach, so I grip the bat and prop it on my shoulder like a batter. Finally, someone comes out, and I begin to swing—

"What the fuck!" She yells as she steps back and puts her hands in the air. I stopped mid-swing and looked at her. Standing before me was a chocolate woman with goddess locs. She was beautiful, tall, and slim. Undoubtedly one of the most beautiful women I have ever seen. She was wearing a black tank top and very snug red boxer shorts. She had long, pointy acrylic nails and statement rings around her fingers.

As much as I was nervous and unaware of where I was, I couldn't help but be hyper-focused on how she looked. She had stunning, big, beautiful, dark brown eyes and full lips. Her skin vibrated against the sun, which snuck into the room. Her energy seemed controlled and collected. It radiated calm, soothing, and warmth. I felt at ease with her presence, but I was still on high alert.

Holding the bat firmly in my hand, I yell back, "Who are you!? Where am I?"

There was a pause between us, and then she tilted her head and squinted at me. "Mahant?"

Her voice was trembling, fragile, and uncertain as a rush of emotions surged through me. Strangely, I could feel her energy shift as well.

I continue to hold the bat up and take a step back. "Who the hell is Mahant? My name is Lanno!"

She looked super puzzled by my question and stopped walking towards me. Her hands were still in the air, afraid of me. "Do you not remember me?"

I shake my head. "No, I don't remember—"

"Mahant, remember me." She whispered low, her voice more controlled and confident.

As soon as she said that, a sudden rush shot through my body, sending chills racing down my spine as my breathing grew heavier. My mind erupted with flashes of memories, vivid and overwhelming, as if my brain was on fire, trying to piece it all together. Images of us flooded in—lounging on the couch, walking hand in hand through the park, and sharing quiet moments that felt so intimate and familiar.

There were glimpses of us kissing passionately, dancing under soft lights, and making love, each memory hitting me with an intensity that was both exhilarating and terrifying. The clarity of it all was staggering, yet it carried an unshakable sense of unease. I tilted my head, my eyes locking onto hers as a name rose to the surface of my mind—her name.

"Imani?" I asked, surprised.

She smiled a little, nodded, then stepped closer again. "Yes, it's me, Imani."

How do I know her?

I lowered the bat and looked around the room, completely confused. The room was relaxing but loud, and my head pounded. The tip of the bat finally hit the ground, and with my other hand, I grabbed my head to control the vibration that led to an insane headache.

Imani continued to close in on me as she reached for the bat, taking it out of my hand. "Calm down, it will be okay. I promise I'm not here to hurt you."

"What is going on?" I asked, my voice laced with confusion as I looked around, trying to make sense of the moment.

She takes my hand, leads me back to the sofa, and sits down. I'm puzzled, disoriented, and lost. I don't understand what is going on. The last thing I remember was me in my condo, smoking and slowly drifting off to sleep, and now I'm here. In an entirely different room, in an entirely different home. The memories coming back to me slowly faded and did not rush through me.

I did not understand how I got here, though. That was what frightened me the most. I had just gotten into a spat with Lauren. Wait—

"Where's Lauren?" I asked.

Imani responded, "Lauren? I don't—"

"My girlfriend, tell me what's going on!" I interrupted, my voice now shaking uncontrollably.

I feel Imani's hands rubbing my shoulders. I can tell she's trying to relax and calm me down.

"You are really worked up this time around," Imani rubs me, her hands moving from my shoulders to my back, scratching. I take a deep breath, close my eyes, and breathe.

I must have been through this before. I didn't understand why bits and pieces of memory were slowly coming to me, fading in and out, but I couldn't process it. Some images that swallowed my mind were easy to put together because it was clearly myself and Imani. But other images were of different people. However, the feelings and emotions felt like they were mine. It was hard to explain, but it reminded me of my connection to the orcas. I can feel the emotional attachment to the memories, but I can't recall whose memories they were. It was as if they were mine, but I couldn't recognize the people. It seemed as though the people were me.

I exhale slowly. "I feel like I'm going crazy."

My leg bounced uncontrollably, and I could tell I was going into full-on panic mode. Imani slowly backs off, and I hear her getting off the sofa. I open my eyes and watch her disappear into her bathroom. She quickly returns with a pill bottle and sits down next to me. I watch her as she twists the top off, takes two pills out, and hands them to me.

I looked at her, laced with concern. "What are these?"

"It'll just calm you down a bit. It's anxiety meds." She explains.

I look at her and then take the pills from her. She gets back up and walks to her kitchen. She opens the pantry, removes a glass, and fills it with distilled water from the fridge. I watched her every move. It was almost like it was programmed, as if she'd been here before with me. My eyes slowly look around the room again, and I notice some photos of her in different places that look like Metrotown City.

Incense burned quietly, and candles flickered against the wind because of an open window nearby. I took it all in and tried to calm myself down, adjusting myself to shake this overwhelmingly uncomfortable feeling.

My heart raced, and I looked at Imani. "I don't understand what's going on."

"You just have to focus. It will all come back to you. Sometimes, it's slow and takes time. You forget completely, and then it all comes rushing back again, like now." She explained as her fingers slowly moved through my hair, pushing the tiny strands out of my face. On the edge of the sofa, I slowly stared deep in her eyes—those beautiful brown eyes were breathtaking. There was a gut-wrenching guilt that formed in the pit of my stomach—I've missed her. How is it possible to miss someone you are just now remembering?

I close my eyes again and breathe, fully accepting my fate, allowing the memories to flow through me.

"I don't know what's real anymore. I don't understand what's happening to me." I admit, with a brokenness to my voice.

Was this a dream?

Everything felt so real.

I looked down at my hands and slowly felt even more relaxed.

"Unfortunately, you will not be here long, and I don't have enough time to explain exactly what's going on, but

I promise I will explain everything to you when I can," Imani explains as she continues to play with my hair.

I look at her, confused. "I won't be here for long?"

Imani's eyes arch, expressing sadness in response to my question. Her hand caresses my face and rubs it gently. She lays me against her chest, and my eyes close for the final time.

"Shh, just close your eyes and rest your mind." She softly whispers, her voice soothing.

My eyes grew heavy, and an overwhelming wave of exhaustion swept over me. It was the strangest sensation, one that felt as though I was drifting off into a deep slumber while simultaneously waking up from a dream. It reminded me of those moments right before your alarm clock goes off in the morning, your internal clock ticking away to release you from the dream world.

I leaned against Imani, her presence grounding me. Was it possible to wake up and fall asleep at the same time? That's exactly what it felt like—an in-between state, surreal and consuming.

Finally, I drifted off to sleep, leaving Imani and waking up in my bedroom. The transition was a strange phenomenon—the completely dark void I entered and then emerged from felt impossible, almost like magic, like my soul re-entering my physical body from a dreamlike world that was real.

It was an intense dream, only it felt more real than me lying in bed now, staring at my ceiling. After a while, I regained feeling in my body, and I sat up. Slowly, my eyes traced every corner of my room, questioning if I was really awake. The curtains were opened wide, and the sun shone brightly through, dodging between the tall buildings just outside my window.

As I looked around my room, everything grew more familiar. The walls were dull and dark, and painted gloomy black, with more abstract art on each wall. My platform bed is still centered in the room, wedged between two night tables carved with expensive Brazilian rosewood and lamps on top. At the foot of the bed was another black shag area rug that would engulf your feet the moment you rolled out of bed.

I inhaled deeply, smelling the crisp notes of cedarwood, orange flower, and lavender mixed with a warm touch of vanilla. My heart rate was slowly leveling out, and I continued to control my breathing as my chest rose and fell quickly.

I frantically looked for my phone and found it in between the sheets of the bed. When I checked the time, I realized it was early, around seven am, when I usually got up and prepared for work.

It was also Monday, which meant therapy day with Dr. Ricardo. My body felt sluggish, and I was completely disoriented as I attempted to ground myself back from the dream world. Usually, it took me hours to recollect dreams, but this time it was different.

I remembered a lot—Imani's apartment, the scents, and all the memories of us that felt real and authentic. I even remember the name she called me—Mahant.

It rang through me, familiar but locked away like an imprisoned memory from a distant life I once lived.

Finally, I got out of bed and stood beside it, letting out a much-needed stretch and yawn. I looked down at my phone again and checked for any text messages, hoping there'd be one from Lauren.

There was nothing.

I sluggishly walked to my bathroom and grabbed a clean towel from the shelf to wash my face. After washing up and brushing my teeth, I left my bedroom and headed to the kitchen to make some coffee.

I needed to finish some work before my appointment, so after fixing myself a cup of coffee, I settled onto the sofa and opened my laptop. I tried to focus, but my mind kept drifting. The dream I'd had lingered like fog—thick and inescapable. It was hard to concentrate on emails and deadlines when every part of me was still tangled in the emotions of something that felt so real.

I kept questioning it. Was it truly just a dream?

Or had I brushed up against something deeper—something real in a way this world couldn't explain?

Reality blurred in ways that scared me. Was I going to bring this up in therapy? Or hold on to it like a secret, cast in the shadows of a realm that was only meant for me to understand.

Chapter 3

Disassociating again, that's the new normal for me.

"How are you sleeping?" Dr. Ricardo asks, breaking the silence in the room.

I break my gaze from the window and turn my attention towards him in his chair. I sigh deeply and yawn while stretching. I don't respond. Instead, I fidget with my watch on my left wrist as I glance around his office.

It was a small room, big enough for him and his patients to sit comfortably in and converse. There weren't many distractions besides the colorfully eclectic puppy art painting hanging on the wall behind him. His desk sat against the wall, nestled into the corner with a low-lit lamp on it. A planner sat underneath his laptop, next to a pen and a cup of steaming hot coffee. His office was big enough for his chair, another chair I sat in, and a chaise lounge for a more stereotypical therapy session.

The room smelled like cedarwood and lavender, giving it a relaxing and calming atmosphere. There were no windows, as his office was inside a room in a building with other services, and his company rented the space.

It was eleven-forty in the morning, and my therapy session had only five more minutes left. I don't remember having any conversation with Dr. Ricardo this time around. Did we sit here in silence for almost forty-five minutes?

Dr. Ricardo continues to ask another question without waiting for the answer to the first one. "Have you been taking your meds at night?"

I chuckle a bit and then look straight into his eyes. Dr. Ricardo stares back into my eyes and then adjusts himself uncomfortably. "I'm worried about you a bit, Lanno. Should I extend our session?"

"That won't be necessary," I finally responded, breaking my silence. "I'm just having vivid dreams again and don't know how to process them because they seem so real. Plus,

I fought with Lauren yesterday, and we haven't talked since."

"What did you fight about?" he asks, intrigued and happy that I was finally speaking.

I look at him and shake my head. "I fucked up. I didn't say I love you back when she told me she loved me."

I noticed Dr. Ricardo writing something down on his notepad. It always worries me when he does that.

"I promise I'm not writing anything bad." He says it as if he were picking up on my uneasiness. "I'm just making notes to remember our conversation so we can tackle it together." He looks up at me with his relentlessly trusting smile. "Do you not love her?"

"I do," I groaned, and my head fell back against the cushion as I looked up at the ceiling.

"Then why didn't you tell her?" He questioned, pushing me to internalize the question.

I sat for a moment in silence before answering, "Because my head is all screwed up. I don't know why I feel so foggy lately."

"Because of a lack of sleep, maybe," Dr. Ricardo suggested as he continued to write in his notepad.

"No, I've actually been sleeping. That's the problem; I've been..." I stop myself. I don't want to tell Dr. Ricardo about Imani.

Right now, he only knows that I self-proclaim myself as someone with vivid dreams that sometimes come to fruition in real life. I didn't want him to know that I recently had a vivid dream about another woman, with countless other memories that came to the surface from our encounter. I didn't even understand it enough to break it down to him. All I know is that I remember all these memories of me and Imani, and I don't know why.

I needed to find answers.

Dr. Ricardo patiently waited for me to continue. However, I was quiet, so he talked. "Well, it's good you've been sleeping, but it seems to be without the meds."

I turned to him, shocked. I've never had a good poker face. Well, if he had any doubts about whether I was taking my meds, my reaction just confirmed that I wasn't. I sigh and smirk a little bit at him.

"Listen, it's okay if you aren't taking sleeping meds and falling asleep at night without aid. There's nothing wrong with that. You know I'm no pill pusher. I only want what's best for you." He leans forward in his chair. "Just don't lie and say you are sleeping when you're not. If you are sleeping, that's good."

I wanted to bring up the Imani situation, but how would I without sounding crazy?

I sat in the chair, fingers laced, thinking. Finally, I spoke. "What if I didn't tell Lauren I loved her because there might be somebody else that I love?"

I see his eyes widen, and he reaches for his cup of coffee as if attempting to conceal his reaction. He takes a sip, sets the cup back on his desk, and taps his pen on his notebook. Proposing the question that way was the only way I could ask him about Imani without fully disclosing that this was just a dream. It made sense. The guilt in the pit of my stomach was unbearable. I felt as if I had been cheating on Lauren with a woman I'd only dreamt about.

Dr. Ricardo clears his throat a bit. "Well, I think you need to be honest with yourself. If another woman is in the picture, maybe you should figure out which one you care about more. Either way, you'll want to break ties with one before the other gets hurt."

Another question popped to the forefront of my mind. "What if one is far away? Distance can't bring us closer, but the connection with her is stronger?"

Dr. Ricardo thinks, then answers, "What it sounds like to me is that the distance needs to be closed because that's where your heart beats stronger."

I felt insane even thinking these thoughts, let alone asking the questions out loud. Was I losing my grip on reality? I wasn't even sure I believed Imani was real. But then again... maybe she was. Maybe there was a version of her out there somewhere—a real person who existed beyond the confines of my dreams. If I could see her so vividly in my sleep and feel her presence so deeply, wasn't it possible she existed in some form?

Maybe this dream wasn't just a dream at all. Perhaps it was a sign—an invitation.

I nodded at Dr. Ricardo and stood up. Our forty-five-minute session had ended, but my journey was just beginning. I had to figure out who Imani was... and, more importantly, where I could find her.

I stood up and then paused. "Thank you. I'm sorry I was so quiet today. Like I said, I've just been in my head a lot lately."

"Lanno, it's cool. I won't force you to talk. I want you to feel comfortable talking to me when you're ready. We've been having these sessions for years now. I'm here for you, man." Dr. Ricardo approaches me and pats my shoulder as I tower over him.

He's a short guy compared to me. There was not a single follicle on his head. However, he had a nice beard that I can sometimes be quite envious of. Dr. Ricardo is very progressive, and the reason he's been my therapist for years is because of how open and accepting he was to the idea of me being, well, unique.

I rushed home and spent some time on my computer searching for Imani. First, I started by searching through social media platforms by putting the name Imani in the search field. I then filtered through all the profiles of women with locs and dark skin. To no avail, I came up empty-handed.

Memories of us faded in and out of my head throughout the day. Suddenly, I remembered one of the pictures in Imani's home and knew it would significantly lead to finding Imani. It was a picture of a cute little coffee shop in the city named Tochi's Coffee Shop. I grabbed my phone and pulled up a search engine, typing in the shop. I was excited to see that it was only a five-minute drive from my home.

As I sat there, I thought about a stakeout. That's ridiculous, though, right?

My eyes suddenly redirected to my keys. I clenched my fist and then ran my fingers through my hair indecisively. I picked up my phone and checked the time. Damn, I've been at this search for three hours; it was almost three o'clock, and I lost track of time. If I were going to check out the coffee shop, now would be the time.

I grab my keys, hesitating only briefly before stepping out the door. My thoughts spiral with every step, looping through the same wild questions—What am I doing? Would she even be there? What would I say if I saw her?

Is she even real?

She has to be. That's the only explanation for why she showed up in my dream—so vivid, so visceral, it lingered in my chest long after I woke. The way she moves, the way she speaks—it all feels too real to be imagined.

As I drove, the city blurred by. I gripped the steering wheel tightly. Every streetlight and stop sign felt like a chance to turn back and admit this was a mistake, but I kept driving.

Once I arrived at the coffee shop, I parked and hopped out of the car to enter. It was such a cute coffee shop, and as soon as I walked in, a memory of Imani and I flashed in my head. It wasn't a memory of this specific coffee shop, but many shops we had been to together to order drinks. Whenever it was a coffee shop, she ordered an iced matcha latte with caramel drizzle and made me do the same. She always encouraged me that it was super tasty and I should try it, and eventually it became our signature drink. This warm, fuzzy feeling was everlasting, as it radiated through my entire body.

I went to a nearby table by the window and took a seat. I took out my phone to look busy and looked around. There were tons of people in the shop. Some placed their orders while others conversed, read books, or worked on their laptops. The shop had plants placed strategically everywhere to portray a hipster vibe. There were many options for regular seating, including tables, love seats, and chairs for a more intimate session, as well as an upstairs lounge with additional seating. The walls were yellow, and the barista and register sat in the middle of the coffee shop for people to come up to from any side. The aroma was strong, with perfectly brewed coffee beans, steeped tea, and freshly baked goods. Soft jazz drifted through the air, blending seamlessly with the guests' warm ambiance of laughter and lively conversation.

No wonder she loved this place so much. It matched her energy and almost looked as cozy as her apartment.

People came in and left, and time stood still as I waited. Hours passed every time I checked my phone or watch for the time. Soon, the shop became empty, and it was time for me to head home.

It didn't end there, though. I made this an everyday visit. Since I work from home, I take my computer to the shop when they open. I would order an iced matcha latte and sit there until the shop closed.

As hours turned into days and days into weeks, Imani never showed up.

I became so regular that when I walked in, Jessica, the barista, would say, "Morning, Lanno! Iced Matcha Latte, caramel drizzle?"

I'd nod, offer a soft "yes," ask her about her day, and then settle into my usual spot by the window. It had become a quiet routine—familiar, almost automatic.

After three weeks of this routine, I was exhausted mentally. I decided not to go to the coffee shop, so I paused the coffee shop stakeouts on Saturday. As I stared in the mirror in my bathroom, I almost didn't recognize myself. I had not been sleeping well or shaving, and then there was Lauren, whom I still hadn't spoken to since she told me she loved me. Responding to texts felt like a mere chore, so it was radio silence whenever Jah hit me up.

I stepped out of the bathroom and made my way to the balcony, a bottle of alcohol in hand. The cool air hit my skin, but it did little to calm the storm inside me. I sank into the chair, gripping the bottle tightly, feeling like I was on the edge of madness.

Chasing a girl from a dream. Being so consumed and obsessed with someone I had never even met before. Someone whom I've rendered was non-existent. I've given up on this search for Imani and what could be, and maybe

I will seek professional help on what I could be experiencing. Sometimes, I feared that my reality was blurring.

The night was chilly, and the sun was setting over the city's buildings. I took a swig from the bottle in my hand, and I wanted to scream.

A sudden knock at the door jolted me awake. I blinked, disoriented, realizing I must have passed out without even noticing. My head throbbed with a dull ache—ugh, I definitely drank too much. The half-empty bottle sat on the patio table in front of me. I shivered as the air on the balcony now felt colder than I remembered.

What time is it?

I reached for my phone and realized the time now was eleven o'clock.

When did I fall asleep?

Another knock—this time louder and more urgent—echoed through the apartment. I groaned, pushing myself out of the chair, my movements sluggish and unsteady. I staggered through the living room, each step a reminder of how much I had to drink, and made a beeline for the door.

"Who is it?" I yell out.

"It's me, Jah. Open up, man. I've been banging on your door for a minute now, damn." He yells back.

Finally, I reach the door, unlatch the locks, and open it up. Jah walks in on a mission, looking around my apartment.

Without hesitation, Jah starts his mouth, "What the hell has been going on with you? I gotta come all the way over here to check up on you because you don't answer your phone, bro. You're not responding to my texts!"

"What are you, my girl, now?" I obnoxiously respond as I close the door behind him and walk towards the couch. "By the way, come on in... sure."

I can feel his eyes glaring at me as I plop down on my sofa, my elbows on my knees and my head in my hands, trying to reduce the pressure in my head.

I hear Jah move from before me and head towards my kitchen. "Well, someone's got to be your girlfriend since you know... what you did to Lauren. Yeah, I heard! You left that girl cold. High and dry. Devastated."

"Enough, man, please stop. Who even told you what's going on between me and Lauren?" I asked, visibly showing I was annoyed.

"Well, I mean, she told Fallyn, and I happened to see Fallyn the other day, and she told me to knock some sense into your bitch ass." Jah rustles through my kitchen, opening different cabinets & drawers and then closing them, which sounded and felt more like he was slamming them.

"Dude, easy on the cabinets," I say, irritated.

"You need some water. You look like shit," Jah responds as he finally finds the cups, grabs one, and pours water into it. He swipes the pain reliever off the nearby counter and heads back to me. Standing in front of me now, he nudges me. Jah hands me two pills. "Here, take this, and you won't have a hangover in the morning."

I responded arrogantly, "Of course, I won't have a hangover in the morning. I have one now."

I take the cup and pills from him, then swallow the pain reliever with the water. As I finish all the water and lean forward to put the cup on my living room coffee table, I still feel Jah's eyes glaring.

"What, Jah?" I asked reluctantly.

He sighs. "The girl tells you she loves you, and you ghost her for three weeks?"

"I didn't know how to respond, man," I said, my voice low and defeated, the weight of uncertainty pressing down on every word.

"What the hell, Lanno? Maybe, uh, I love you back? You two have only been together for six months. The girl didn't ask for her hand in marriage. Shit, even if you had to tell a small lie, say something back," Jah adjusts himself, then rests his hand on my shoulder.

I get up and look down at him. "No, that's what I don't want to do. I don't want to lie and tell Lauren I love her when I don't know if I do."

I didn't understand myself. Just a few weeks ago, I was certain I loved Lauren—unshakably so. And now? I wasn't sure of anything. My thoughts were scattered, tangled in a web of doubt and confusion. The alcohol clouding my mind wasn't helping either; it only made everything feel heavier and messier.

"You either know or you don't. If you can't say "I love you" back, maybe Lauren isn't the one for you, broski," Jah looks up at me while shrugging. He hesitated, then continued. "You really look and smell like shit too."

I look away from him, sigh, and then rub my face.

Jah continues to keep talking as I process everything he's saying. I sit back down, and he heads to my bedroom. Everything is still foggy, but hopefully, the meds will slowly kick in. He's right, though. Maybe I should break everything off with Lauren for now, at least until I can get my shit together.

Jah returns from my bedroom with some of my clothes as he continues to ramble, but I'm too deep in my thoughts to hear anything he's saying. I'm thinking about Lauren and Imani. Where do I go from here? I'm chasing a dream that can't possibly exist when I should fix things with Lauren.

He hands me the clothes. "Lauren is at the Sky Lounge with Fallyn and Deja for Fallyn's birthday. I told Fallyn I'd come by and say happy birthday to her, and you're coming with me, so go take a shower and put these clothes on."

I stand up, grab the clothes out of his hands, and head to the bathroom. Me seeing Lauren would be an excellent opportunity to fix things with her—to fix my fuck up and stop being consumed over something that isn't real.

Jah sits down on the couch as I walk into my bathroom. I close the door and turn on the water to shower. Once I finish showering, Jah and I take a ride-share to the lounge.

My mind was weighed down by the thought of leaving Imani behind in that dreamlike world and trying to make things right with Lauren. The entire ride to the Sky Lounge, I replayed possible conversations in my head, trying to piece together the right words, the right tone, and the right apology.

As Jah and I walk into the lounge, my eyes dart all over the place in search of Lauren. When we reached the back of the lounge, my eyes finally found their target. My heart sank into my stomach, and I found it hard to swallow. There was Lauren, as stunning as ever. She was wearing a floral dress with heels. She had her hair out. All her curls were engulfing her face, framing it perfectly. Fallyn and Deja sat on either side of her in an open leather booth.

The lounge had a vibe—it was bursting with a strong, smoky oud scent, swirling delicately around the room and mingling with faint hints of sandalwood and amber. Stage lights targeted the DJ booth on the very far left of the lounge and the bar adjacent to it. Most of the light came from those two focal points. Every other part of the lounge was dark, with black walls and wooden trims. There was a DJ present, playing a smooth blend of hip-hop lo-fi that wrapped the lounge in a calming, laid-back atmosphere.

As we approached, I noticed her entire demeanor changed. I panicked and began to turn around, but Jah grabbed my arm and pulled me closer to where everyone was sitting. Jah sat down in the chair across from their booth, and I just stood there, staring deep into Lauren's eyes as she glared back at me.

"Hey ladies," Jah said to break the tension.

"Jah, who the hell invited Lanno?" was the first thing out of Fallyn's mouth. Deja looked shocked, and Lauren's eyes never broke from mine.

I felt so uncomfortable.

Lauren gets up and excuses herself from the booth, and I instinctively grab her arm as she tries to walk away. "Can we talk?"

"Oh, now you want to talk!" Fallyn interjects before Lauren could get a word in.

I look at Fallyn, begging for forgiveness with my eyes, and then back at Lauren. "Please, can we just talk? I promise I will leave you alone afterward if that's what you want."

Lauren replies sharply, "Yeah, because you're so good at that, Lanno."

I sigh and stare at Lauren. "Please."

"Fine." Lauren pulls her arm away from me and walks off, with me following close behind. She heads towards the bathrooms, where it's quiet, and turns around. She leans against the wall just outside the entrance of the ladies' room.

"Talk," she said firmly, her eyes locked onto mine with an intensity that made it clear—this wasn't a request.

I stand in front of her, barely a foot away, taking another deep breath to steady myself. My eyes never leave hers as I stare into their depths, searching for the strength to speak, but no words come. My throat tightens, and I clasp my hands before me, clearing my throat to ease the tension. The confusion swirling inside me is unbearable. My feelings for Lauren are undeniable, yet my relentless obsession with finding Imani has clouded them. But as much as I've let that fantasy consume me, I must face the truth that Imani isn't real. She's just a dream—a figment of my imagination, haunting me in the quiet hours of the night. And here, in the reality of my life, is Lauren—the woman I love, the woman who's stood by me. I care about her deeply, with every fiber of my being. It's time to let go of the dream, focus on what's real, try to fix what's broken with Lauren, and leave Imani where she belongs—in the past.

"I should have said I loved you back because I do." I finally say, breaking the silence between us.

I hear her suck her teeth, and then she lets out a dry laugh. "Don't pity me, Lanno, that's bullshit!"

"Lauren, listen to me, it's not bullshit. I love the shit out of you; I do." I reach forward to touch her face, but she slaps my hand away.

"Three weeks, Lanno!" she shouted, her voice crackling with frustration. "I haven't heard shit from you in three weeks!"

"I know, and I'm sorry! I fucked up so bad, Lauren, but I don't want to lose you." I try to reach out to her again, and I feel another slap on my hand as she pushes it away.

There was a massive lump in my throat, and I could feel my heart beating a million beats a minute. I see a tear running down her cheek, but she wipes it away.

I stared at her for what seemed like forever, and I watched helplessly as more tears just continued to stream out of her eyes. She wouldn't look at me anymore, and it hurt me to see her like this.

"Babe, what can I do to fix this?" I pleaded with her to find a resolution. "How can I fix us?"

She remained quiet as she wiped away her tears. "I don't think this can be fixed. My heart was crushed three weeks ago, and I feel like I've already mourned us."

After wiping the last tear, Lauren adjusts herself and looks back at me again.

"I'm sorry," I apologized. "You definitely didn't deserve what I did to you, and even the aftermath of me not talking to you for weeks is a shitty thing to do to someone you love. I'm so sorry, Lauren."

I step closer to her and try to connect with her again physically. My arms slowly wrap around her, and she lets me in this time. I can feel her melting into my embrace as I hold her tight. My lips pressed against her forehead, and slowly, we rocked back and forth. I can hear her crying getting more intense as she lets it all out into my shirt.

I pulled her away just a bit, and my hands pressed against her cheek, making her look up at me.

"Shh," I say softly, wiping her tears away. I leaned in slowly, closing the space between our lips as she looked up at me.

"I can't do this right now, Lanno. I'm sorry." She pulls away from me and walks into the bathroom, locking it. I stand there momentarily and debate whether I should walk away or try harder. I didn't know what to do. Women often say they want a man who would go to the ends of the earth for them, and I would for Lauren—without hesitation—but I don't know how to make things right. The weight of my thoughts feels unbearable as I press my forehead against the cool surface of the bathroom door and let out a heavy sigh.

"Lauren, please," I pleaded, my voice low and strained, barely more than a tortured grunt. It carried the weight of desperation, the kind of raw emotion that comes from deep within. However, the space between us echoed in silence.

I sigh and walk away, heading straight out of the lounge, and I stand in front of the building. Coming here to see Lauren was stupid because I knew I shattered her heart into pieces. I pull my phone out of my jeans pocket and text Jah.

Hey man, sorry, but this was a mistake. I'm going to head back home.

I called for a ride-share and headed home.

On the drive home, I sat silently, deep in my thoughts, allowing them to cloud my judgment. Maybe Lauren not taking me back was for the best. I believed what was for me could possibly be hidden away in a distant dream. Somewhere in the back of my mind, the guilt of being with Lauren while dreaming of another woman made me sick to my stomach.

However, the true question always came back to Imani being real. How could I know for sure? My mind always felt like it was on fire, consumed by an endless swirl of thoughts that left me in a constant state of confusion. I couldn't find clarity, no matter how hard I tried. Should I make another attempt to win Lauren back and face the possibility that Imani is nothing more than a fleeting dream—a figment of my imagination or a longing that will never manifest? The choice weighed heavily on me, each option pulling me in a different direction, leaving me stuck in a loop of uncertainty.

Once I got home, I sat on my sofa and stared off into space for hours. My eyes began to get heavy, and surprisingly, my thoughts weren't so loud. I started thinking of Imani and whether my dreams would take me to her again. And as those thoughts ran rampant, I smiled. I was eager to fall asleep, hoping to be with her and get some answers. Answers were what I needed, but the feeling I felt while with her was indescribable. It was true that my heart yearned more for Imani, a figment of my imagination. But just the mere feelings and passion that welled up in me when I thought about her made this so real. I felt myself slowly drifting off to sleep as curious thoughts of her danced through my mind.

Eventually, I was at peace.

Chapter 4

There was a distant yet familiar voice whispering in the background.

"You've gotta want it hard enough for it to work, or it never will." She said out loud.

My eyes slowly open, and I look around.

The voice continued. "You must be able to clear your mind and be in a state of peace."

The room has changed again, and I'm no longer in my apartment. Everything is a blur as I try to gain conscious-ness and open my eyes.

The room was recognizable, with plants everywhere, and the walls were brown. Gradually, the record player's music became louder, this time playing calming meditation music.

"It's Zen. Your mind is clear, and your heart is pure. You believe you can do anything impossible because you're here now and present in this moment." That familiar voice spoke again. Finally, my eyes focused, and there she was, Imani.

I sit up real fast on the couch and look at her. "Imani?"

"Hey, babe! Good morning!" Imani replied, her voice was gentle and happy.

I glanced around again, trying to steady myself and make sense of my surroundings. The world felt vivid and alive, each detail sharper than expected. The sunlight bathed me in a golden glow, its warmth wrapping around me like a gentle embrace. I could feel its energy sinking into my skin, as if it were infusing me with life.

The rays danced against my arms, creating a soft shimmer that caught my attention. My skin radiated beneath the sun's touch as if reflecting the light into the world. I closed my eyes briefly, letting the heat seep into me, grounding me in the present. The sunlight wasn't just warmth—it was reassurance, a reminder that I was here, alive, and part of something greater.

How surreal it felt to be with Imani again. However, I needed to get straight to the point, not waste time.

"Listen, I need answers," I say to her, slowly sinking my body into the sofa.

Imani smiles as she sits on the floor in front of me, Indian style. She gets up on her knees and crawls over to me, kneeling before me, and gently places her hands on my lap.

"Ask away," she says, then winks at me.

I look down at her and can't get over her beauty. Every time I look deep into her eyes, memories of us flash through my mind. I get an overwhelming feeling, but it's also warm and cozy. Her smile lit up the entire room, and her chocolate skin radiated as the sun cast upon her. She brought me an inexplicable comfort—I felt at home, as if our connection stretched beyond this lifetime, spanning multiple lives and countless moments that I can't fully remember but somehow felt deep within me.

There's a familiarity in her presence, an unspoken bond that defies logic and time as if our souls have crossed paths over and over again.

"Where am I?" I finally asked.

She answers without hesitation, "You are in my apartment in the Spalling District."

I give her a sarcastic smirk and squint my eyes at her.

The Spalling District sat within the city limits, only a fifteen-minute drive from the glitzy, high-end Holiware Square. But the two couldn't have been more different. While Holiware catered to luxury and status, Spalling was a vibrant mosaic of cultures, a place where the city's heartbeat pulsed with authenticity. It was our international district, a hub where ethnic traditions thrived and were celebrated openly through food, art, music, and community.

"How did I get here?" I ask.

"Now that's a good question," Imani responds. "That may be a little bit harder to explain."

I continue to ask my questions, "Is this real?"

She pinches my arms, and I jump back and pull away.

"Ow!" I wince as I look at her. She had a mischievous look on her face. I guess that answers that question. "Imani, I went looking for you in the coffee shop, and you never came."

"The coffee shop?" She tilts her head and looks at me, confused.

I explained further. "Yes, Tochi's Coffee Shop, you always get the iced matcha—"

"Latte, with caramel drizzle," Imani cuts me off. "Mmm, yes. Tochi's Coffee Shop. You must have seen the photo on the wall and gone looking for me. Unfortunately, that would have never worked in your world. You're blurring timelines together."

My face goes blank, and I look at her, confused. "My world? Blurring timelines?"

She smiles softly and takes my hands in hers, holding them with a firm, reassuring grip. "Lanno, look at me," she says gently. "What we're about to talk about—it's going to be the hardest part. But I need you to trust me, and more than anything, I need you to believe what I'm about to say."

I get nervous, but I still feel more comfortable with her than I did weeks ago when we had our last interaction.

"You're special, so very special. There are things you can do that you won't understand right now, but in time, you will understand and be able to master their abilities." She scoots closer and grips my hands tighter. "You remember you once told me about a boy who had a dream about orcas,"

I pulled back from her because I wondered how she could know about my dream about orcas.

"You are the orca," Imani says, her voice calm but full of conviction.

"What the hell are you talking about, Imani!" I yell, pulling my hands away from her as I stand up off the couch. "I feel dizzy."

Imani gives me a look and sighs. "In your dream, you were the orca. However, these are not just dreams, Lanno. You are remembering real-life memories of previous lives."

I laugh nervously and shake my head. "You sound crazy!"

"Wow, thanks, I'm the crazy one. You want the answers, and I'll give them to you, but don't call me crazy." Imani replies sternly with one eyebrow raised, and her look intensifies.

I stop my nervous laughter and look at her. "Look, I'm sorry, but that's impossible."

Imani sighed deeply and threw up her hands. "Let me just rip the Band-Aid off. You can jump."

I tilt my head and stare at her, even more confused. "Jump?"

"Yes, jumping. It's what you're doing right now. You're in a different timeline," Imani explained further.

I stare at her, but I don't say a word. And here I thought I was crazy, but no, she has completely lost her damn mind. My palms were sweaty, and I still couldn't catch my breath.

Imani finally broke the silence, her voice steady yet filled with a quiet intensity. "When you dream about the orca, it's déjà vu, fragments of what you experienced in another existence, echoing back to you now. You should start to remember your life as an orca soon; it'll all come back to you."

"This is maddening," I finally said with a nervous chuckle. My chest rose and fell quickly, and I was having a full-blown anxiety attack.

"Also, you couldn't find me at the coffee shop because I'm in a different timeline than yours. What it sounds like, however, is that our timelines are a bit similar." Imani grabs my arm and pulls me back onto the sofa, and I look at her. I take a deep breath and feel her hand rest on my arm. As I felt her hands on me, slowly, the anxiety washed away.

She continues to talk as she caresses my chest, my shoulders, and down my arms.

Imani coaches me through breathing. "In through your nose and out through your mouth, slowly."

She explains that I can go to infinite timelines or dimensions if I focus hard enough and know where I want to go. The initial wave of emotions was overwhelming, crashing over me like a relentless tide. My mind raced, trying to process the gravity of everything, but the intensity of it all left me feeling numb. After a while, the storm within me began to settle. My breathing slowed, my heart steadied, and I could sit quietly, letting the calm wash over me like a soothing balm.

I focused on Imani, and her presence quickly grounded me in unimaginable ways. She was the calm in the storm that brewed inside of me, the constant in my life in the universe. I could feel her energy coursing through me as if it were my own. She felt so familiar, so I allowed her to speak.

"It may seem like a dream to you," she ignited the conversation. "But imagine there are worlds out there, infinite worlds that break the barrier between our current presence and what could be. We can tap into other realms while meditating or sleeping, and by opening our third eye and crown chakra. Our mind is the bridge to other timelines."

She describes the role of DMT, or dimethyltryptamine, a naturally occurring compound released during sleep.

"DMT isn't a drug, but like a door or a gateway to other timelines, dimensions, and other realms," she continues. "The more aware you are, the easier it is to connect to these infinite possibilities."

I remember once coming across a video that said we only experience DMT twice in our lives: when we are born and when we die. I recall hearing about DMT and investigating it further, but I couldn't remember how it worked in full. Imani explained that DMT is in plants and some species. She said some of those species are human and can tap into switching realities outside of birth or death.

We spent most of the day talking for hours. She decided to cook me some food, and we sat in front of the couch, discussing all the possibilities of jumping. After a while, it started to seem interesting that this was possible. But I must admit, during our conversation, I couldn't help but question whether any of this was real or if I was dreaming. It was as if I were having one of those dreams where you know you're dreaming, but you continue the dream anyway. That's how this moment felt—beautiful yet impossible.

She told me I was over a century old and always had trouble remembering and jumping, but she didn't say why. Imani also told me that we were soul-tied for eternity. She explained that we had always sought each other out, and sometimes it took decades to find one another, but we always ended up together. Imani said she lets me explore different lives and experiences without getting tangled in them. But often, it's hard for her to stay away.

After hours passed, I noticed how cozy we had gotten. I sat on the couch, my head leaning back against the cushion, and Imani lay across the sofa with the back of her head in my lap. She would expressively talk with her hands while explaining to me the infinite possibilities of jumping and where we could go.

Imani stared deep into my soul, "I would show you right now, but it's getting late, and I'm sure you will wake up soon."

"I want to stay. I want to know more," I say, taking her hand and lacing my fingers with hers.

She smiles and looks at me with her sultry eyes. "I want you to stay too."

"How do I stay, Imani?"

Imani freezes up a little and doesn't say anything for a while. She just continued to play with my fingers with hers, and then a tiny smile crept back onto her face.

"Just remember, when you're ready to fall asleep every night, just lie in bed and clear your mind. Focus on where you want to be and who you want to be with, and go to sleep. The good thing about this timeline is it's almost identical to the one you're in now, so it should get easier to jump to." Imani explained.

My eyes closed, and I started to feel extremely sleepy. I began to drift off, my body surrendering to that now familiarity of the pull of sleep, but waking up simultaneously—a strange, surreal overlap of realities.

"You will remember this time, Mahant. Focus your mind." Imani reminded me.

Her voice grew more faint. As I slowly drifted to sleep, a strange sensation began to overtake me. It was as if I were caught between two worlds again—my body, heavy with the pull of slumber, and my mind, fluttering on the edge of awareness. I could feel myself tossing and turning in my bed, each movement stirring a faint awareness within me. I was back in my apartment, and the sun was creeping through my blinds. I picked up my phone, and it was ten-fifteen in the morning. I looked around the room, and it was quiet.

Too quiet.

"Imani?" I called out.

Silence.

I got up out of bed and went into the living room. It was just me, and I was all alone again.

I felt empty and hopeless, as though I was missing a massive part of my identity. For the next few hours, my mind and body went on autopilot. I decided to drink my sorrow away and lounge on the sofa, hoping to fall back to sleep. The time had gotten away from me, and I would get up and pace around my home with the bottle in my hand. Minutes turned into hours as the day flew by. The sensory overload consumed me entirely. Every thought, feeling, and emotion tied to Imani and our conversation surged through me, overstimulating my mind. She told me to relax my mind if I wanted to get back to her, and I realized that I was doing the complete opposite.

These feelings were so infuriating, twisting and turning within me like a storm I couldn't escape. It all still felt like a dream that I was fabricating into reality. I wanted to believe I could jump into a different world and be with someone my soul yearned for.

Was this all in my head? Was it real?

It's almost impossible to put into words the depth of the connection I felt when I was with Imani. It wasn't just emotional or physical—it was something far more profound and seemed to exist beyond what I could fully understand.

Being near her was like tuning into a frequency that resonated within me. I could feel her presence coursing through me, from the roots of the hair on my head to the tips of my toes, as though my body was a conduit for her energy. It wasn't just warmth or comfort, but an electric, almost magnetic pull that made me acutely aware of every part of myself.

Whenever she touched me, vibrations radiated throughout my body and entered my core. When Imani spoke, her voice danced and played a harmonic symphony to my ears. Her scent was what I imagined heaven would smell like—a perfect blend of warmth, comfort, and something inexplicably divine.

The memories of us would flood my mind, and oh, how peaceful they were. We were together for ages—dancing, singing, and existing for centuries. Our bond was unbreakable. Whenever I'm with her, I feel invincible, like I can conquer anything. As the energy flows through me, I can feel a shift. My mind sharpened, and every thought was more precise and more focused than ever before. My body feels different, too. Like every muscle and cell charged with newfound power, I was stronger and more resilient. There's a strength within me now, a quiet confidence that rises from deep inside, making me feel as if nothing is beyond my reach.

This sensation is unlike anything I've ever experienced. It's raw, tangible, and undeniably real. It's as if every fiber of my being is responding to something greater than myself. This feeling can't be faked. It's far too intense and authentic. There's no other explanation but the truth of what Imani told me. She must be real, and the words she shared with me and our connection are not mere illusions. They are true, and I can feel every part of me resonating with them.

All I wanted to do was be with Imani. So badly that I even forget about Lauren. Just yesterday, I told her I should have said I loved her. It was just yesterday that I thought I did love her. But the feeling I get when I'm with

Lauren is nowhere near the same as when I'm with Imani. I can't continue to lie to myself and hold back. I'm almost glad Lauren didn't forgive me and allow me back. She deserves a man who can love every ounce of her—someone who is present and can assure her and release her of all her insecurities. Maybe somewhere deep down, Lauren knew I was not completely all in with her. Maybe I was lying to myself and just there with her for the moment. This decision is for the better—to allow the separation between Lauren and me before I involve myself entirely with Imani.

There is an unsettling thought in the back of my mind.

How do I get to Imani? How do I stay in her world?

Is there a trick to being undeniably loyal to her dimension? I must find answers. If only I could fall back asleep.

I looked at the clock. It was almost seven o'clock, and I had not eaten all day. I put the bottle on the coffee table and rested my elbows on my knees with my head in my hands. I scratch my head and then roll my fingers through my hair.

I've questioned my sanity a lot over the past few weeks. I've been drinking more and going out less. Self-care is nonexistent, so there have been few showers. Eating seems like a chore, and sleeping is a challenge. I've avoided speaking to my therapist because I can't hide or discuss what's been on my mind. I could never confess what I've been experiencing lately. They would put me in a mental institution. Doctors wait for excuses to drug people up and hide them away.

I'm not crazy. I'm just special.

There are people with extraordinary abilities in this world, such as mediums and psychics. I possess an uncanny ability to jump between timelines while sleeping. I've gathered that it's like I'm astral projecting into another almost identical realm I live in now. I need to master staying there or moving between other timelines as easily as Imani makes it seem.

During our long conversation, she mentioned seeing infinite worlds and possibilities. She's able to not only go linear within the same year but also forward and backward in time. Being unable to move through space and time was merely a construct of a limited human brain. We would be limitless if we unlocked a specific part of our brain. Imani has mastered it, and now I need to as well.

But how do I master it? Right now, all I know is to focus my mind before I go to sleep at night and picture exactly where I want to be. I can't even master that. How on earth will I stay with Imani? I had more questions, and I needed to see her again.

Time continued to pass as I paced around my apartment. I went to my fridge to make myself a sandwich because I was starving.

I took my phone out of my shorts and checked the time. It is now eleven o'clock. I grew increasingly excited as the time approached when I could finally fall back asleep. I planned to stay focused and at peace tonight before falling asleep. After eating my sandwich, I went into the bathroom and took a hot shower. Exiting the shower, I wrapped the towel around my waist and entered the bedroom. I took some boxers out of my dresser drawer and stepped into them, putting them on.

My bed was calling me, and I was eager to lie down and enjoy its embrace. I got into bed and pulled the covers over me as I lay on my back. I stared at the ceiling and then slowly closed my eyes. My thoughts were so loud. The memories of Imani and me, from her scent to her touch and everything in between, rattled through my mind.

I was not focused. I was not relaxed.

I needed to find a point to focus on and take my mind from its elevated state to a calm and collected mind.

I fluffed my pillow and adjusted myself to get more comfortable in bed. I started to think about what Imani could have done today in my absence. I sigh deeply and keep my eyes closed as I try to force myself to sleep. Maybe

I shouldn't push myself. Perhaps I should think of happy thoughts.

This was harder than it looked.

I breathe in deeply, hold my breath, and slowly exhale. I picture Imani—her smooth, moisturized, dark chocolate skin and her smile that could brighten up an entire room. I know she's waiting for me on the other side, and I can't wait to see her again. I want to know everything and anything about us. I wanted to know when we first connected and what her favorite memory of us was. A slight smile formed on my face as I lay in bed. My breathing started to slow down and level out. There was a short skip in my heart with the mere thought of her, and then it began to relax. I felt excitement coming over my body as I lay in bed.

To help me focus, I allowed a memory of us to come to me. We were in a park having a picnic. The sun shone brightly in the crisp, cool air—a perfect fall day with the trees beginning to show their vibrant reds, oranges, and yellows. The scene was picturesque. The fresh aroma of fruit from our picnic, mingling with the cool breeze, sparked my senses. I smiled, remembering how we'd snuck a bottle of wine into our thermals, drinking in secret like giddy teenagers. It was such a blast—her laughter echoing through the air, her radiant smile lighting up the moment, and the way the sunlight kissed her skin, making her look ethereal.

The memory felt vivid, as though I was reliving it all over again. I could still feel the playful intimacy of feeding her grapes and strawberries, the way she giggled as our fingers brushed together. We watched people running through the park, tossing frisbees with their dogs, and the world around us seemed to pause, enveloped in a peaceful stillness. We spent hours enjoying the simple day. At one point, I looked over and saw her lying on the blanket, eyes closed and body relaxed under the tree's shade. I couldn't help but admire her beauty as she slept peacefully, as if she were part of the calm scenery.

There was another distant memory that crept into my mind. We took a trip to a place called Treedom in one of the timelines we were both in. In a secluded, forested part of the world, towering, ancient trees stood with an almost magical presence. Their trunks were so massive and their branches so wide that they seemed to touch the sky, creating a canopy of green that shielded the ground below. The natives of this land had found a way to live in harmony with these giants, carving out homes within their massive forms.

The trees were hollowed out carefully to create a space inside for the natives to live. Inside the trees, steps led up to the interior, and then another hole was cut near the branches, where entangled ropes were hung securely to create a link between other trees, allowing them to move freely. It was an intricate city of dwellers on land and in the sky, living in harmony with the beauty of nature. While we visited this forest, we learned to be foragers, hunters, and cooks, as we lived off the resources the land provided us. As foragers, we carefully sourced plants, mushrooms and truffles to make spices. Each group of natives taught us something different. My favorite was being able to hunt for our food, trapping small furry animals, or fishing for the best catch. Then I remembered, Imani took over when it came to cooking. She effortlessly concocted a meal that was as beautiful as it was delicious, with everything we had collected for the day.

There was a lot to learn from the natives—unity and the balance of nature. Every plant, animal, and every life had a story. There was no mass production of food; they respected the life and offerings from their higher power. They would whisper a prayer every time a life was taken, and every time a meal was eaten.

One specific memory of Treedom was when Imani and I meditated in the Sacred Tree of Ahani. The Sacred Tree of Ahani was a tree from which the natives sourced wisdom. The tree was massive, the biggest one in the entire forestry jungle. It told the tale of how the Earth blossomed from the universe.

All you had to do was sit quietly in the sacred ancestral grounds, nestled beneath the sprawling canopy of the ancient tree, and connect your inner soul to its deep, sprawling roots. You could feel the Earth's heartbeat pumping and coursing through your own as you connected with this powerful, living, and breathing relic. As you connected to this tree, you could hear whispers of the universe coursing through you, healing the mind, body, and soul. The air felt lighter, and everything around you ceased to exist when connected to Ahani. Although nothing else mattered when tethered to Ahani, everything mattered all at once. The feeling of being connected to every living species in the entire universe, feeling their happiness and sorrow, was overwhelmingly beautiful. It was magical.

It was peaceful.

As I reminisced about all the distant yet exhilarating memories, my eyes became heavy, and my mind was at ease. I was slowly starting to fall asleep. However, as I felt my eyes getting heavy, my heart simultaneously began to beat more slowly. The turmoil that kept my mind ablaze was finally passing through. That familiar feeling of peace came over me, and I knew I was on my way back to Imani.

Chapter 5

I am pleased with myself, I must admit. Time has passed rapidly, yet at the same time, it has also stopped. Over the past few weeks, after our second exchange, I've successfully jumped to Imani every night. It's all about relaxing your mind, lowering your heart rate, and clearing away all distractions. I learned so much from being with Imani, but I also needed to know much more.

I've learned that I can be a different being in every timeline, and I'm not always human. So, when I dreamt of the orca, that was my soul in another timeline that I now remember clearly. I recalled being born into a timeline with Imani, and we explored the expansion of the oceans as these intelligent orcas—building community with our kind, breeding, and having a family pod. It was beautiful how the memories slowly came back to me, creating a sense of peace that swept over my body, allowing me to gain a deeper understanding of the universe.

Imani explained a lot to me during my multiple visits to her place. She also said that if I focused hard enough, I could go to different timelines. She said we could explore other timelines together once I mastered jumping to this one. Imani told me some beautiful worlds were out there—places that would shock me at first glance. I longed to see these dazzling realms, radiant and alive, where colors spoke louder than words and emotions pulsed in hues beyond human comprehension. These worlds defied the laws of reason, bending and breaking the rules of reality.

Imani spoke of lands where gravity was a mere suggestion, where the sky didn't rest above but spiraled around, enveloping you in its infinite embrace. Birds sang in sweet melodies as rivers of molten gold shimmered in endless cascades.

She painted these worlds with her words, each syllable a brushstroke that sketched vivid scenes on the canvas of my mind. I believed every detail, clinging to her tales as though they were promises of a hidden truth.

We even discussed my soul's name, Mahant. When I was born, the universe created that name for me.

The more I saw Imani every night, the more I wanted to sleep and not be in my world. The less I went out, the more I called out of work. I couldn't get enough of her. Her presence relaxed me, calmed my nerves, and caressed my soul.

I also loved it when she touched me.

The tips of her fingers would send sparks that radiated like lightning throughout my entire body, coursing through my veins straight to my heart.

I snapped out of my daze, looked around, and realized where I was—back in Imani's apartment. Sounds of water running in the other room erupted through the apartment, and I remembered that she had said she would go and shower. I sat on the sofa with a cup in my hand. A small smile appeared as I thought about how great it felt sitting in this room, waiting for her. The water turned off, and I got excited to know she'd appear from her bedroom at any moment.

Every visit with her was new knowledge, and I wondered what was on the agenda for the night. As she took her time in the bathroom, my mind drifted again. I get goosebumps around her, and I wonder if she feels the same way. She talks about our cosmic bond and how long we have chased each other around the timelines. We've shared intimate moments—lying together, caressing one another, and holding each other close during my visits. But despite the intensity between us, she always kept a careful boundary, keeping our physical connection in check. The glimpse into the memories of our intimate moments coursed through me, and I craved her touch. I love it when I can feel her energy and aura engulfing me. It was unfortunate that she stopped there, never allowing us to kiss.

My thoughts get interrupted by the bathroom door opening. Out comes Imani in just a towel.

I try to swallow away the large, anxious lump in my throat. Staring at Imani, I can still see water droplets from her hair rolling down the side of her neck. With her dark chocolate complexion, it was almost as if actual chocolate was dripping down her body. She mouthed something, but I was too locked in on her, wrapped in the towel, to notice or hear what she was saying. Her hair dripped with water, and her hand tightly gripped the edge of the towel so it would not fall from her.

Oh, how I wanted it to fall.

Her beautifully manicured, painted white toenails and bare feet tiptoed against the wood flooring. She was so perfect. My eyes wandered upward, irresistibly drawn to her lips. Full, luscious, and impossibly soft-looking, Imani's lips were made to be kissed. I could almost imagine the warmth, the softness, and the electricity that might linger at that moment. And yet, why hasn't she kissed me?

I should have been allowed to touch her if we had been together for years, but this barrier still stands between us.

"Babe!" Her voice broke through my thoughts, sharp and startling. "Can you hear me?"

My heart jolted. Imani caught me staring too long, as though she could hear the storm of thoughts behind my silent gaze.

I nervously scratch my head. "Sorry, yeah?"

She chuckles a little bit. "Are you okay?"

I grab the pillow beside me and place it in my lap, covering myself.

"Yep." I swallow and wipe my hand down my face, keeping my composure together.

She walks towards me, reaches onto the coffee table, and grabs her body oil.

"Don't worry, I got it," she says as she smirks, side-eyeing me. She tucks the towel into itself and sits on her coffee table directly in front of me between my legs. She looks at me.

"Are you sure you're okay?" She asks again.

I look up at her, and my heart beats even faster. I wanted to rip the towel off her and ask for forgiveness later.

"Yeah, I'm good, I'm good," I respond as I clear my throat.

"Good! I want to take you to my favorite place," she says, her voice bursting with excitement.

My eyes widened. "What's your favorite place?"

"It's a pho spot called Pho Them." Imani opens the body oil and begins to moisturize her arms slowly.

I watch every move she makes intensely. "I'm down,"

Imani responds, "Good!"

She continues to massage a deep jasmine- and vanilla-scented oil into her skin, working it in as much as possible. My eyes lock on her every move as I get remarkably quiet. She's concentrating, moving her hands meticulously from her arms to her neck and along her collarbone. Imani then changes positions and continues to her feet and ankles, slowly maneuvering up her still, very damp legs. She hikes the towel up just a bit to access her thighs—the oil sweet and fragrant, like a late fall day. I'm concentrating, realizing we both are locked in.

She slowly lifts her head, breaking her concentration from lathering her thighs inches away from me, and looks into my eyes. It feels like time has stopped, and every movement she makes seems to last forever, as if she is playing in slow motion.

Imani gave me a cute smirk. She then turns around and gently drops the towel, revealing her back.

As I sat there, infatuated, she handed me the oil bottle. "Do you mind?"

I swallow the excess saliva and take the oil from her. "Not at all."

I squirt some oil into my hand and then hesitantly touch her shoulder. I slowly started to work it into her skin, and she sighed deeply. I can feel her melting and relaxing into my touch. I put more oil into my other hand and rubbed it all over her back, massaging it in even deeper now.

She tilted her head and whispered. "That feels great, babe. Thank you."

All I wanted to do was wrap my arms around her from behind and nuzzle my face into her neck. I ached to inhale every part of her—to lose myself in her essence and never let go. My hands moved from her shoulders up the sides of her neck, squeezing a bit. Her head tilted back a little, then to the side; she reached up and grabbed my hands.

"Easy, cowboy," she says in a playful tone.

I quickly let go and sat back against the sofa.

What the hell just came over me?

I apologized. "I'm so sorry."

Imani turns halfway around, looks at me, and smiles. "It's okay, babe, really."

She sighed deeply, and her eyes got big as she tried to compose herself, then she looked away. I can feel my chest rising and falling rapidly. She does this thing when she's thinking, putting her finger to her mouth and biting on the tips of her nails. I must have thrown her for a loop.

Imani stands up and clears her throat. "I'm going to get dressed, and then we can leave."

She walks to her bedroom, and I sit on the couch, looking defeated. The blood was definitely not rushing to my head, at least not the right one. I can't believe I just did something so stupid. My head falls back against the sofa, and I close my eyes as my chest rises and falls fast.

After what seemed like hours, Imani emerged from the bedroom. She wore a burgundy shirt tucked into her black jeans and an awesome-looking biker jacket. Imani had her long locs up in a messy bun and platform boots to give her even more height. She had this alt-girl look going on, and I dug it.

Once she was back in front of me, she did a few cute poses so I could check out her outfit. I laughed because she was such a goofball. Imani grabbed my hand and pulled me off the couch so we could leave and grab some food.

Leaving her apartment would be the first time I've been out and about with Imani since I've been coherent enough to remember and jump freely. During the past few weeks of jumping, we stayed in her home, and for hours on end, she would refresh my memory of trips we've taken and worlds we've visited.

Our worlds were very much identical. Imani says this doesn't happen often, and the universe can create identical worlds when soul ties tether to each other strongly—worlds where the times, dates, and people are the same. However, there was always one thing that was different, if not many.

After our short walk there, we finally arrived at the restaurant, which was quite different from your average pho spot. It gave more new-age hipster vibes, and I loved it. There were plants everywhere, with black walls and a ton of art hanging up along them. There was a nice-sized bar when you walked in, and some smooth, upbeat tunes were playing. It was a vibe. As we sat down, the waiter brought us some water, and then we ordered drinks. I got a dirty martini and a glass of wine for Imani.

"Imani," I called out to get her attention.

She turns and looks at me, then smiles.

I hesitated but carefully said, "You're beautiful."

She strikes a pose and lets out a chuckle as she flattens out her napkin in her lap. "And you're handsome, babe. In this life and the next and all the ones before."

I smile at her, "I still have so many questions."

"I know, so ask away," she insists, gesturing for me to continue.

So, I continued, blaring with curiosity. "What was your favorite timeline?"

She bites the tip of her fingernail and looks up at the ceiling. "Oh, it would absolutely have to be Utopia, when we took a roadtrip with our friends to Treedom, Winterdon, excetera."

I smile and pick up my water, taking a sip. "Ah, Utopia. It's still coming back to me in bits and pieces." I lean forward and ask, "So, what was your least favorite timeline?"

"There are a lot." Imani looks around uncomfortably and laces her fingers together, resting them on the table. She then locks eyes back with mine. "You don't get to remember a majority of the time."

Hesitantly, I ask, "Did something happen? You know, to make me forget?"

She adjusted her body in her seat, and I could tell she was uncomfortable discussing whatever happened.

I proceeded, "Imani—"

"Are you both ready to place your orders?" The waiter interrupts.

We both look up at him, and Imani smiles. "Yes, I will have the ramen bowl with the chashu pork. For the appetizer, can we have the spring rolls with the peanut sauce?"

"Of course, and you, sir?" The waiter turns to me.

"I'll take the pho with meatballs and beef ribs." My eyes stay locked on Imani as she hands the waiter the menu and avoids eye contact with me.

The waiter takes the menus. "I'll bring that out to you shortly, thank you."

I don't understand why it's so hard for her to trust that I can handle whatever she's been withholding from me. At first, when she told me everything about different timelines and being able to jump to them, it all sounded unbelievable, but now I believe her. I trust her and know she has my best interests at heart. Imani continued to look around the restaurant, and I continued to stare at her until she finally engaged with me.

I wonder what she was hiding and how scary it is.

"Imani," I start up again, my voice low and deep with a calmness to it.

She finally looks at me and rests her hands in her lap.

Imani changes the subject again: "Let's talk about something else. I think you're finally ready to jump to a different timeline. I can teach you how."

"Oh?" I perk up.

Her eyes widened. "Ooo! We should try tomorrow and see if we can jump to Troterion."

"Troterion?"

"Yes, Troterion," she says, excitement ringing from her voice. "It's an entirely different planet. It's remarkable. I don't want to tell you too much because I want you to see for yourself."

I laugh a little in disbelief. "A whole other planet?"

Imani nods and takes a sip of her wine.

Impatiently, I asked. "Why tomorrow? Why can't we go now?"

"Well, you've noticed you've been able to stay longer and longer. That's a good thing. You can't stay forever, but you are staying longer. So, we will have more time tomorrow. You'll have to go back shortly after we eat." Imani explains as she sets her wine on the round wooden table.

"You've got a point," I say as I take a sip of my martini and smile at her.

We waited for our food to come out, and as we waited, we ordered more drinks. As the night got later and the drinks came quicker, I started feeling tipsy. Imani and I talked for hours on end about all the memories slowly returning to me. We ate our appetizer and food for the next couple of hours, which was delicious. After we finished, we walked to Imani's home.

The walk home was longer than expected because the blind lead the blind, with lots of laughter, slurring our speech, and stumbling in the streets.

We finally returned to her place, and I walked through the front door. Imani closed and locked it while a force from deep within told me to make a move. I felt like not only had I been waiting for a chance to do so, but she must also have been waiting too.

Imani turns around after locking the door, and I stand silently before her.

Everything was quiet.

All I could hear were the soft sounds of her breathing. I walk closer to her, and she takes a step back, her back against the door now. I take my hand and slowly guide it down her face as she looks up at me. My thumb grazes over her bottom lip and presses into it a little. I can feel her chest rise and fall against my chest, and then I watch as her eyes close. The tips of my fingers move off her lip, and my hand drops to her jaw, gripping it firmly. She lets out a sigh, and then her eyes open again, this time full of lust. Her gorgeous, dark brown eyes glared at me, looking into my soul. I've felt this feeling before—it was achingly familiar, like a whisper from a memory I couldn't quite place.

I tilted her head back and leaned down, my lips inches away from hers.

"Liquid courage, huh?" Imani whispers, then smiles big.

I say nothing. We just continued to stand in front of her door. The only light that crept between the blinds was from the moon, casting a shadow of us like a silhouette in her apartment. I feel her hand move between us, pressing against my chest and softly rubbing. My lips get closer, grazing over hers slightly. Imani's eyes closed, and she sighed.

"If you're going to kiss me, just do it already." She murmured barely above a whisper, her voice low and inviting.

I grip her jaw more firmly, press my body deeper into her, and pin her to the front door.

"I don't want to leave you just yet."

Imani whimpers, "I know."

"How do I stay then?" I asked amid this heated connection.

"Ugh!" She scoffs and presses her hand into my chest, pushing me away. "Stop asking or trying to get something out of me, something that isn't possible."

Imani walks away from me and heads to her kitchen. I rested my head against the door and hit it with my fist.

I turned around and watched Imani as she grabbed a cup from her cabinet and got fresh water from the fridge. "I'm sorry."

"Don't you think if I knew of a way for you to stay, I would just be like, hey, this is it, stay, Mahant!" She yelled at me, frustrated.

I walk over to her, defeated, and sit at her island bar on the opposite side of her. She was upset with me, and I ruined such a perfect moment.

I pleaded with her, "I'm just a little drunk, okay, but I'm sorry. I just don't want to leave you, Imani. And I need to know if there's a way to stay so I can do anything and everything possible."

"There's not, so stop asking," she demands, her voice stern and cold.

However, I continue to press the issue, "There's got to be."

"There's not!" Imani screams, then slams her glass down and glares at me. "Leave it alone, Mahant!"

The room gets quiet, and I look at her. Her eyes continue to beam at me, and then she takes a step back and breathes. She starts shaking her hands and arms vigorously as if she were shaking bad energy away.

"I'm sorry," I say again.

Imani sighs deeply, "You know, it's fine, it's fine, it's fine."

I stand up and walk around the island towards her. I wrap my arms around her waist, and she runs her fingers through my hair and then grips it. I hold her tight, and we stay in this moment for a while, quietly embracing one another as we rock back and forth.

"I'm getting a bit tired," I whisper to her. That feeling of waking up slowly was taking over me.

Imani takes my hand and leads me to her bedroom. She grips the bottom of my shirt, pulls it over my head, and then stares at my chest. I watch her as she drags her index finger along the crevice of my sternum down past my ribs. Imani stops, removes her jacket, tosses it to the side, and unbuttons her jeans. I watch her as she slides them down over her hips and then steps out of them. Imani then takes my hand and steps backward to the bed, and she sits down in front of me. Her fingers move to my belt as she unbuckles it and unbuttons my pants, pulling them down. She grabs my hand and pulls me into bed with her.

I pulled the covers over us and lay down beside her. As we lay on our sides, we stared at each other. I didn't know what to say or do. I did not want to make another wrong move or say something bad. Her hand pressed against my chest again, and she slowly rubbed it.

I spoke to fill the quiet, "You know—"

Before I could get another word out, Imani pressed her lips into mine and kissed me deeply. Her eyes were closed, and as I kissed her back, my eyes closed as well. Her lips were impressively soft, like two giant pillows that seemed to envelop my mouth and entire being, cradling me in their tender embrace. It wasn't just a kiss but a moment that consumed me, pulling me into a world where nothing else existed. The warmth of her lips melted into me, setting every nerve on fire.

Her hand, delicate yet firm, left my chest and moved upward, fingers grazing my skin until her hand draped around my neck. She brought me closer with a gentle yet deliberate pull, drawing me deeper into her kiss. My arm instinctively wrapped around her waist, holding her tightly against me as if letting go would break the spell we were weaving. Her body was soft, warm, and alive against mine, fitting perfectly into my embrace.

Sparks danced in the air between us, invisible but tangible, as electricity coursed through every inch of my body. Each second felt infinite, as though time had surrendered to this moment's intensity. My heart pounded in my chest, its rhythm syncing with hers, and I could feel the energy radiating from me like waves on a shore.

She tasted fresh, clean, like mint plucked straight from the garden—a sharp, rich, creamy scent of vanilla that lingered on her skin. Her warmth seeped into me, and her soft body was otherworldly. Every sensation—her taste, aroma, and touch—fused into a perfect symphony, leaving me utterly intoxicated and lost in her.

I did not want this moment to end. However, my eyes were growing heavier by the second. Our lips broke free of each other, and Imani released gentle sighs of pure bliss, each carrying her joy's quiet melody.

"Mahant, trust me this time, ok?" she whispers.

I pulled back from her and stared at her. I nodded, kissed her forehead, and then closed my eyes.

Half asleep, I responded, "I promise."

Sleep took over like an unbreakable force. I couldn't fight it, so I succumbed to the fight and slowly drifted off, back to the realm that started to seem more distant than familiar.

Chapter 6

There goes that sound again. It's the most hated sound in the world to me.

My alarm.

It reminds me of another day I must endure without Imani. It was depressing and excruciating. I hated the feeling of being away from her, even if only for a day. What was this burning desire? This obsession. It almost feels like a sickness ravaging through the tiniest crevices of my inner being.

My heart ached.

There was no way I was taking Imani's word for it, trusting that she was telling me the entire truth. There had to be a way to stay in her world, but for now, I am stuck here.

I tossed and turned in bed, not wanting to wake up, but I knew I had to. I sit up in bed and loudly sigh away the stress. I always had these stifling thoughts of Imani and being with her forever. I counted the seconds, the minutes, and the hours until I could go back to sleep. Sometimes, I even tried to make myself nap, but that never worked.

I looked around my bedroom and noticed my place was a mess, and I had let myself go. I finally got out of bed, my flat feet pressing against my cold, hardwood floors as I stretched. I started picking items off my floor to clean up a little bit. I almost looked unrecognizable as I reached the bathroom and looked in the mirror. My beard grew significantly in the past few months, and my hair was messy.

I picked at my beard as I looked in the mirror and sighed. I leave my bathroom and return to the bedroom to look for my phone. I picked up the blanket off my bed and moved my pants in search of it. Finally, I found it.

I had three missed calls from Jah and a text from Lauren.

I read the texts and realized that Lauren wanted to come over and look for something she thought she left here. She texted last night and said she'd be over by ten-thirty, which is now.

Shit!

I rushed to pick up more stuff off the floor and made the house look somewhat presentable. It had been a month since I last saw Lauren at the lounge, and I was nervous about how this interaction was going to go.

Suddenly, there was a knock at my front door.

I hurried to the front door, arms overloaded with clothes, and tossed them behind it in a frantic heap. When I flung the door open, there stood Lauren. She wore an oversized sweater and matching sweatpants, the logo printed down the legs adding a pop of style to her cozy look. She wore white sneakers, and her hair was pulled up into a messy bun, a few strands falling loosely around her face. She looked effortlessly beautiful, comfortable, casual, and completely herself.

"Hey, Lanno," she greets me, her voice soft and comforting.

I responded, "Hey..."

We both stood there awkwardly. She was outside the door, and I was inside, wearing only sweatpants, socks, and a T-shirt.

"So, can I come in?" she asks, waving her hands around confusingly.

"Oh shit, yeah... sorry, come in." I open the door wider, and she walks in. Lauren stops in her tracks and looks around my apartment. I stood next to her and looked as well. It looked worse than I initially thought it was. There were dishes everywhere, trash on the floor, garbage piled up, and laundry everywhere. Many bottles of alcohol were on the coffee table and counters. I looked at Lauren, and she bawled her fists up in front of her chest and bounced them off each other, but she was silent. It was so loud in the room, but nobody was saying anything.

She finally turned towards me. "Lanno, are you okay?" she asked, her face painted heavily with concern.

I was surprised. Lauren sounded like she genuinely cared about my well-being after what I had done. I'm sure seeing my apartment in shambles concerned her as well.

A calming sensation minimizes my nerves when I'm with Imani, as if the world slows down and the chaos inside me settles. But when I'm here, depression sets in, and I'm the worst version of me. How do I tell the woman whose heart I just broke that I don't want to be in this timeline anymore? If Lauren and I were together, I'm sure I wouldn't have lost myself in such a deep depression. She grounded me in a way that made me feel whole and gave me the strength to hold myself together. Without her, I'm unraveling. I was lost for words and didn't know how to respond, so I lied.

"Yeah, I'm fine," I say, not very convincingly. Lauren stares at me and nods very slowly as she squints her eyes. She does that when she's trying to read me. "Seriously, Lauren, I'm cool."

"You're lying." She responds sharply, cutting right through me.

It quieted for a minute. Lauren turned to me, gave me a big sigh, and then came and wrapped her arms around my waist.

I freeze up.

"What are you doing?"

She mumbles into our embrace. "Listen, you're a dick for ghosting me for three weeks, but I don't hate you."

My arms entered the air, not hugging her back as I stood awkwardly. She knew I'd been going through it, and I could tell that she was worried about me.

"Uhh," I let out, emitting nervous energy.

I finally wrap my arms around her and hug her back.

"Have you been sleeping okay?" Lauren asks as she hugs me tighter.

I sigh into her hug and then nod.

She clings onto me, "That's good."

She finally let go and started walking around my apartment, looking for whatever she had left behind. I watch her intensely as she puts her belongings in a small bag she has with her. I returned to the couch and sat down as I watched her. I tried to think about what I could say to her, but nothing crossed my mind. So, I sat there quietly. I still cared a lot about her. I hurt Lauren, but I wanted to make amends without further breaking her heart.

"I really am sorry, Lauren," I finally say, trying to break the stillness in the room.

She stops in her tracks, and time continues to stand still. The room got completely quiet, and the air was thick. I swallowed the huge lump and waited for her to say anything.

I continue to word vomit to break the silence, "I know I hurt you, and it kills me every day. I really do love you and hate that I ruined us."

She sighs, "It's hard to believe that you love me. You make me question if I'm enough for you. I don't understand how you couldn't say it back until after the fact. You had to think about it for weeks while leaving me high and dry. That doesn't sound like someone who loves me."

She turns around and looks at me and shrugs her arms. I get quiet and think carefully about what to say to her next. Trying to choose between the two, I was at an impasse.

Before, I believed it was good that Lauren didn't give me a second chance, but deep down, the magnitude of losing her was challenging. How could I throw away six months of building a relationship with Lauren? It may not seem like I cared about Lauren, but I do love the shit out of her. She grounded me well in this world and kept me together. My consciousness screamed at me from within to fix our relationship, to mend what was broken.

I watch as Lauren slowly approaches and sits on the coffee table in front of me. We sit in silence for what seems like an eternity, my leg bouncing nervously.

"I felt like I couldn't breathe for weeks after I said I loved you. I waited for you to text or call me, but you never did. It was like I lost my best friend." Lauren explained on the brink of tears, her voice cracking with every spoken word, and then her voice elevated towards the end through the crackling, and I knew she wanted to yell at me. I didn't want to fight with her, though. I hated our fights because they would get so heated. However, I knew Lauren was holding back. She continues, "Even though you hurt me, I want to forgive you, Lanno." Her hands were in her lap, fidgeting with her fingers as she stared down at them.

"I want you to forgive me, too," I responded. I sit on the sofa's edge and grab Lauren's hands out of her lap. She squeezes my hands tightly and then lets go.

Lauren points her finger at my face and gets serious. "If you hurt me again, I—"

"—I won't. That's the last thing I ever want to do." I interrupted her.

Lauren continues to point at me as she yells, "But you did! You ripped out my fucking heart and said, Fuck you, Lauren, for weeks."

I could tell she was getting angrier with every response I gave her, so I stopped responding and let her vent. Lauren sighs and then looks away. Her eyes grow red as she tries to hold back tears.

"What the fuck are we supposed to do now, Lanno?" She whispers as one tear drops from her eyes. She hurries and wipes it away. "Ugh, I want to forgive you so bad, but I also want to just—" Lauren reaches towards me and grabs a fistful of my hair, and with her other hand, she balls it up and motions to hit me. She finally lets go of my hair and stares deep into my eyes. Her hands then push against my chest hard.

"Three fucking weeks, you asshole!" She yells at me.

I fall back a little, then sit back up straight.

"That's good, let it out." I encourage her. Lauren slams her hands into my chest again, this time harder. Repeatedly, she continued to hit my chest. Finally, I grab her wrists and hold her hands down, but she resists.

"Lauren, listen! I'm sorry," I pleaded.

"You keep saying that. I'm sorry, I'm sorry. I know you're sorry, but what now?" She asks again.

I paused for a moment, my heart elevated, and my breathing grew more intense. What was happening? Seeing Lauren and listening to how I hurt her made every nerve in my body seize. For the past four weeks, I've been with Imani in another timeline, happily, but now all I wanted to do was fix things with Lauren. My heart ached for her, to mend her broken heart and promise to love her as I knew I did. Her question played repeatedly in my mind. What now, Lanno?

"Forgive me, Lauren, please," I beg.

Lauren tries to pull away from me, but I continue to hold onto her wrists.

She yells, "Let me go!"

But I don't let her go.

Instead, I continue to hold onto both her wrists. I pull them behind her back and lock them together, then I scoot closer to her, my butt on the edge of the sofa, and look at her deep into her eyes.

"Calm down and listen to me!" I scream at her. Lauren freezes in my grasp as I continue speaking, my voice demanding but gentle. "I'm sorry I hurt you and ghosted you for weeks. I'm a fuckup, I fucked up, but I do love you, Lauren, with every fiber of my being."

I felt like a dog, unfaithful even to myself, but there was no denying it anymore—I loved two women. The realization hit me like a wave crashing against an already crumbling shore. I didn't want to lose either of them, and the thought of choosing felt like being asked to carve away a part of my soul.

When I'm with Imani, she encapsulates my entire soul, my entire being wrapped in her fingers like a spell. She was someone I've come to realize I had spent eternity with, reliving the moments I remembered, which came back to me and made me whole. Imani made me whole. She was a force, grounding me and loving me with everything that she was—her dedication, chasing me across the universe, protecting me, and loving me unconditionally.

Then there was Lauren, a bond that had grown so profound in such a little time. She was a woman who created warmth, a blanket of comfort and ease, simply by existing. Maybe there was a way to have them both in my life. Their love was a force to be reckoned with. They loved me with all that they were.

Is it possible to love two people at once?

The question lingered, heavy and unanswered, as if the universe was mocking me for daring to ask. It was as if social constructs had power over the love the universe had blessed.

Lauren looked at me, and we stared at each other for a while. She was quiet, examining and searching for any glimpse of uncertainty in my eyes. Her chest quickly rose and fell as I watched her eyes dart from my eyes to my lips.

Before I could fully process what was happening, Lauren leaned up toward me, her movements achingly tender. Her eyes locked onto mine for a fleeting moment, and then, with a quiet urgency, she pressed her lips deeply into mine. The world seemed to stop, every sound fading into the background as her warmth consumed me.

Her kiss was everything—soft yet passionate, gentle yet commanding. It felt as though all the unspoken words, the lingering tension, and the emotions we'd both buried had finally erupted to the surface. My heart raced, and I kissed her back without hesitation, surrendering to the moment. Slowly, I began to let go of her hands. However, as soon as I did, Lauren shoved her hands back into my chest and pushed me away. I responded by grabbing her neck quickly and squeezing it. She reacted by biting her bottom lip and then continued to look at me.

"I hate that I've missed you so much," she confesses.

I stare at her. "I've missed you too."

There was nothing but raw, unfiltered truth in my words to Lauren. I missed everything about her—how she carried herself, the quiet strength behind her sweet, nurturing nature, and how she cared for me. She had a warmth that enveloped you, a genuine kindness that left a lasting impression on your soul. She wasn't just good to me—she was good to everyone. She'd give the shirt off her back without hesitation if you needed something, even at her own expense. She'd step in if she saw someone struggling, no questions asked. She was the kind of person who spent her holidays volunteering at soup kitchens, giving her time and energy to people who needed it most. She regularly donated to cancer research, children's hospitals, and special needs organizations—not for recognition but simply because she believed in helping others.

When I first met Lauren, it was at a campaign my job was doing for schools around the community. We donated to predominantly Black schools in the city, and a few teachers brought children in to meet people of color in the tech industry. We wanted to show Black kids that they can grow up to be managers, IT specialists, and executive officers. The kids were so fascinated to hear that they could even be CEOs.

The moment I laid eyes on Lauren, her energy pulled me in. Her aura was the calm in the quiet storm that lay hidden in me. I loved how she laughed and how her smile could brighten up an entire room. We also shared many things in common, like our love for the same genre of music and movies. She matched my introversion, and she always wanted to keep me happy and do the things I loved. We loved the little things, like being at home, wrapped in blankets, and eating popcorn while binge-watching shows. I enjoyed my time with her, so I couldn't just let her go, ruining six months of building a relationship with her.

My arms move down, wrap around her waist, and pull her into my lap as I sink into the sofa. Lauren straddles me and wraps her arms around my neck as she deepens the kiss. There was electricity that sparked out from us and roared across my apartment. I could feel the tips of her fingers creeping up the nape of my neck and rolling through the back of my hair, gripping it tightly. My hands moved from her waist, and I grabbed her hips so that I could pull her deeper into me.

It started to heat up—our make-out session was hot and heavy as if this were the first time we had ever been in this moment. Lauren reached down, grabbed the hem of her sweatshirt, and pulled it over her head, revealing herself in just a bra.

I laughed a little, "You had nothing on under that?"

Lauren laughs and then nods at me.

I wrap my arms back around her and squeeze tight, then press my lips into her neck, nuzzling her. I rock us side to side as I kiss her and then slowly turn my kisses into soft suckles against her neck. She sighs and lets out a small moan.

"I've really missed you," she says to me again as she pulls away to look me in the eyes.

I smiled as my nose pressed against her jaw, inhaling her scent. "You smell amazing... like sweet tangerines and coconut, and I've missed you too, babe."

My arms squeeze her torso as I stand up off the sofa. She squeals and wraps her legs around my waist, holding on. I walk into the bedroom and gently toss her onto the bed. She grins at me devilishly and slowly backs up as she grabs the edge of her sweatpants, pushing them off her hips. I climb into the bed with her, and we spend the next couple of hours making up. It was "I hate you" sex with a lot of "I love you too." It was rough, passionate, and forgiving. Even though Lauren was a tiny girl, she handled every bit of me.

After we finished, I was tired. My body exerted a lot of energy, and I needed to nap. I should be able to take one since I felt so relaxed and at peace. Lauren knocked out right afterward, and I looked over at her sleeping peacefully next to me. She was so beautiful, and I was lucky to have been able to fix us. I rolled over on my back and closed my eyes.

Whispering to myself, I tell myself to relax my mind and release all negative thoughts and energy. I had to think of where I wanted to go and who I wanted to be with. My mind immediately began to think about Imani. How would I tell her that Lauren and I were back together? How was I going to tell Imani that I loved her, but I also didn't want to lose Lauren? Even though I had all these heavy questions on my mind, I was still peaceful because I felt in my heart that I made the right decision to fix things with Lauren.

Slowly, I began to fall asleep.

Chapter 7

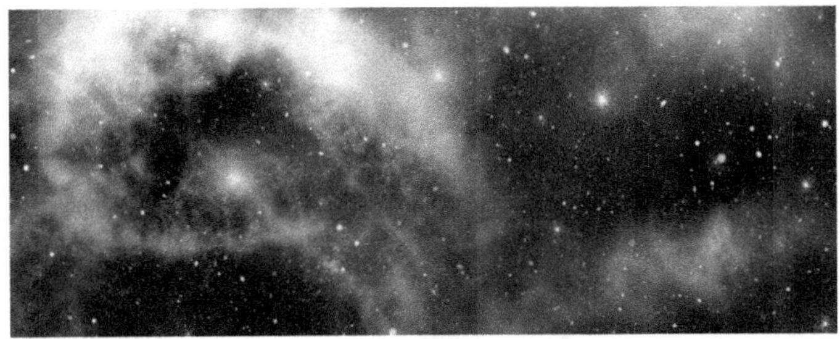

This conversation might be the most complex one I will have with Imani. I didn't expect to visit Imani during a nap, but it made sense. I relaxed my mind, opened my third eye and crown chakra, and fell asleep. Of course, I was back in her very familiar apartment. My eyes slowly opened, and I looked around to see where she was. I figured talking to Imani about Lauren would be easier than vice versa for some reason. But something still deep inside told me that Imani was going to be pissed off. I was in her bed this time, so I climbed out and headed towards the living room. What was I going to say to her?

Before I left her bedroom, I noted how cozy it was—just as comfy as her primary area in the living room. On her dresser, there were pictures of her and what I supposed were her mom and dad in this timeline. Even her cat had its very own photo resting perfectly against a jewelry box. Her bedroom had more warmth to it than mine, with a soft, gentle haze from her dim-controlled lights and the brown walls that continued from the other room. I smiled at the comfort it provided me, knowing I was back in her realm with her.

I finally entered the living room and approached her.

Imani gets startled as she's seated on the sofa, "Mahant?!"

I looked utterly defeated, like a man carrying the weight of the world on his shoulders. My posture slouched, and my face was hollow with guilt. I must've looked pitiful. The truth painted my face like a work of art.

"Are you okay? What's going on? Are you hurt?" She asks as she's touching all over my body.

"I'm fine," I inform her with a low, guilty tone as I sit down next to her.

She stares at me and continues to chew. She had been eating a bag of chips and watching TV before I interrupted and scared her with my presence.

Imani grabs my face and turns it, making me look at her. "Hey, baby. What's wrong—"

"—I slept with Lauren," I confess instantly.

The room gets quiet. I remove my face from Imani's grasp and stare forward, no longer having the guts to look in her direction.

Imani crosses her arms, and I can see her head tilting out of the corner of my eye, trying to process what I just said. There was a knot in the pit of my stomach, and my entire body froze up. The tension in the room felt thick.

What was she thinking? What was she going to say?

Finally, I heard a chuckle that grew into a loud, roaring laugh. I frowned and turned my head towards her, looking as she laughed hysterically. Imani grabbed her stomach and bellowed a laugh that echoed across the room.

With a single eyebrow raised, I asked, "What the hell is so funny?"

She's now lying across the couch, trying to contain her laughter. Imani sits back up and then stands up off the couch. "Ugh, sorry, this is so funny. You should see your face, babe. You look like you've seen a damn ghost! You made me worried."

I'm so confused. "What's happening?"

"Mahant, you've fucked Lauren, I'm sure, a dozen times as Lanno. I really couldn't care less." Imani tells me with a nonchalant tone.

I squint at her, "Wait—"

"—No, wait, you really thought I'd be mad?" She continues as she reaches to her coffee table and grabs her lighter, "Mahant, you've fucked hundreds of people across the timelines."

Imani walks to her bookshelf, grabs an incense, and lights it. She then waves around.

I sat there in sheer shock. Here I thought Imani would be pissed off, and she is completely okay with it. I was panicking for no reason. I know I felt it may be easier to talk to Imani about Lauren, but this was unexpected.

Imani comes back towards me and kneels in front of me. She rests her hand on my thigh and looks up at me. "Listen to me, babe, we are bonded for life. There's nothing that can come between us or anyone. But you're also allowed to live your life how you want to. With me, with Lauren, with anyone in this entire universe. You can have sex with Lauren all you want. It really does not bother me one bit, ok?"

I was shocked and dumbfounded. I stayed quiet for a while, and Imani waited for me to say something. I scratched my head as I thought. So, having two girlfriends or an infinite number of girlfriends was completely fine because there were multiple timelines for me to live out my life.

"She must have really put you to sleep." Imani finally breaks the silence and speaks. She starts to rub my legs. Imani playfully admits, "Our sex is better."

I look at her quickly, with a shocked look on my face. What a shady response.

"Is that so?"

"Hey, I'm just stating facts, but you're not ready yet for that conversation." Imani lifts herself using my knees and stands before me. With the most devilish look, she turns away and picks up her lighter again. I stand off the sofa and grab her wrist, making her turn back and look at me.

"You're not even supposed to be here just yet. You're not supposed to be asleep until tonight, so we can jump." Imani complains, trying to change the subject.

"So you truly don't care about me messing around?"

Imani stares deep into my eyes. "Mahant, babe. Truly, I don't care. There has always been someone else, and it's much more complicated than you think."

I tilt my head, confused, and say, "Tell me why it's complicated."

"Well, for starters, you and I are in completely different timelines. However, because I'm your soul tie, your direct link to me allowed you to jump to me in this timeline," Imani explains, then continues, "I don't exist in the timeline you're in with Lauren, so it makes sense that you found someone else to cling to. It's okay for you to do that. There aren't that many rules to this." Imani spoke, her voice steady, though she avoided making eye contact with me.

I was confused—yet curious, so I continued to ask more questions: "Why don't I know the rules? What are the rules?"

She lights each one of her candles and a couple more incense, then responds to me, "Because you never follow the rules, Mahant. There is honestly no point in telling them to you, but I wouldn't stress this one. You can love who you want. You must start opening your mind up more to understand our universe. I'm going to tell you more tonight, I promise. But you're springing this on me right now when I haven't gotten a chance to condense it to explain it to you fully."

I pressed her again, my voice firmer this time, questioning her as if I hadn't heard what she had just said. Her words lingered between us, but they weren't enough—they didn't satisfy the gnawing frustration building inside me. "What exactly are soul ties, and how do you create them?" I asked.

Imani let out a frustrated groan before finally responding, her tone sharp but tinged with an underlying seriousness. "You don't create them—the universe does. Soul ties aren't something you can force or manufacture. They are connections forged across time and space, bound by the deepest, most intense bond imaginable. Soul ties are two beings whose souls are intertwined, destined to love and understand each other unconditionally. They are, in essence, one."

She continued to explain how soul ties aren't limited to just one person. You can have multiple soul ties with different people throughout your life. These connections can manifest in various forms—sometimes platonic, like a deep friendship that feels like it's existed for lifetimes. Other times, they're romantic, intense, and consuming, pulling you toward someone in ways you can't fully explain. Each connection is unique, but all are deeply meaningful.

However, a twin flame—that was something else entirely. A twin flame is the other half of your soul, split across time and space. It's a bond that goes beyond even the deepest soul tie. Twin flames don't just complement each other—they reflect each other like two mirrors held face-to-face. The connection is stronger, more unbreakable, and often far more intense. It can be beautiful and chaotic, challenging you to grow in ways you never thought possible.

I didn't ask, but I wondered if Lauren and I were beginning to be soul-tied. I felt a deep connection to her—a connection not as strong as Imani and me, but it was there.

"You need to wake up, Mahant. We had plans tonight, and you taking a nap will give us less time tonight." Imani pleads with me.

I sigh and go back to the sofa to lie down. I'll ask Imani more questions when I come back later. I started to clear my mind in hopes of waking up. Jumping back and forth between these two timelines became easier the more I did it. There was that familiar feeling I would get when I was waking up and falling asleep simultaneously. I was slowly drifting off and shifting back to my timeline, where Lauren would sleep next to me. It was the strangest feeling ever, almost nauseating, but after doing it many times, you get used to it.

I finally woke up back in my apartment.

Lauren was still asleep next to me, completely naked. I lay in bed and stared at the ceiling, thinking about everything Imani explained on my short trip. I wish there were a way I could talk to Lauren about all of this. A big part of me wanted to be open and honest about everything I'd been experiencing for the past couple of months. However, a part of me also knew Lauren better than that. She would freak out, then contact Dr.Ricardo and have me admitted. I would break her heart all over again. How could I tell her I was in a relationship with my twin flame from another timeline?

It all sounded ridiculous.

I still sometimes question my sanity.

I got out of bed and headed to the shower to clean off. The air was cool, but as soon as I hopped into the shower, it's hot and steamy water soothed my skin. I loved my hot showers. I continued to think about soul ties and Lauren as I scrubbed my body.

Once done with my shower, I grabbed the towel and dried myself off. I stepped out of the bathroom dressed in grey sweatpants, a T-shirt, and socks, then grabbed my phone off the nightstand and walked into my living room. Quietly, not to disturb Lauren as she slept. Even though I cared about Lauren, I still felt this retching feeling in my stomach. This feeling was of me still trying to figure out how to stay with Imani. I didn't believe it would be enough to jump between both worlds for the rest of my life. The connection between Imani and me was too strong, and I still had this depressing feeling when I wasn't with her. Lauren made me happy and alleviated some of the darkness, but I questioned whether it was enough.

I went to my bar and grabbed the bottle of alcohol and a glass. Steadily, I poured a nice amount and then topped it with some olives, my favorite. I felt much better mentally now that Lauren and I were back on good terms. Between Lauren and I being on good terms and knowing how to jump to Imani successfully, I was semi-fulfilled for now. My lips pressed against the cold glass, and I took a sip. I grabbed my laptop and stepped onto the balcony, eager to soak in the crisp spring air. Settling into my chair, I placed my glass on the patio table beside me, the cool breeze brushing against my skin. Crossing my ankles comfortably, I rested the laptop on my lap, ready to lose myself in the moment of quiet and productivity.

However, my phone buzzed and distracted me. It was Jah.

So are you going to stop dodging me or nah?

I decided to text him back since I realized that I've been a shitty friend and haven't been responding to his texts for a couple of weeks.

Sorry, man, life's been crazy. Sup, broski?

I rested my phone back down on the table, not long before there was another ding. I picked up my phone and read the text from Jah.

Don't broski me. Where the hell have you been??

I chuckle to myself as I read it. Yeah, I didn't think that would fly over Jah's head. Everyone around me was always so concerned about how broody I could get. Especially Jah, he knows I can get closed off from the world and start drinking more. Jah has seen how I tend to enter a depressive state.

I text him back.

I've been… soul-searching. Lauren is here, sleeping.

I stare at my phone and see text bubbles immediately.

WHAT???!!!

I laugh and reach for my glass to take another sip of my liquor. I bet Jah didn't see that one coming. Jah texts again.

Bro, I'm happy as fuck. You both had me worried. I'm glad you two fixed things.

Another text from him.

Did you all make up yet?

I knew what he meant by that question, so I smiled and texted him back confidently.

Oh yeah, we made up alright. – Inserts smirk emoji

We continued to text for a few minutes and decided to catch up later this week. I finally put my phone down and opened my laptop to catch up on some much-needed work.

I'm a senior program manager at my job, and when I wasn't in meetings all day, I created learning and development content. I put out a lot of fires at my job with our production team, but it paid the bills.

I did a few work tasks for the next few hours and wrapped up for the day. I heard my balcony door slide open, and I turned to look back. Lauren, sloppily dressed in one of my buttoned-up shirts' steps outside.

"It's so cold," she says softly, in a low, raspy, sleepy voice.

I laughed, "Of course, it's cold, baby. You're wearing just a button-up." I smile and reach out to her, grabbing her wrist and pulling her into my lap. She giggles and plops down.

"It's my favorite shirt of yours," she confesses.

I lean in and kiss her lips softly as she begins caressing my face and then plays with my beard.

"How'd you sleep?" I ask.

Lauren does a big stretch and then curls into my arms, burying herself into me to get warm. "Really good. My body is so sore, though."

Sarcastically, I apologized. "Sorry."

Lauren punches my shoulder softly and laughs with me. "Mhm, I'm sure you are, big guy."

I rest my laptop on the table and pull her deeper into me. She wraps her arms around my waist and hugs me tight.

"You have no idea how much I've missed this," she admits. I rub her back gently. My head rests back against the chair, and I close my eyes.

I missed this, too.

Having Lauren close to me and spending time with her was one of the greatest feelings I've ever felt in this lifetime. I wanted to hold onto and cherish these moments forever. She made me so happy and content and helped me be able to focus. My brain wasn't on fire when I was with her.

The weeks that we didn't talk were stressful. I get in my way often when I'm so focused on one thing that I become obsessed and allow it to consume me. This wasn't the first time I had let something like this happen in our relationship, but it was by far the most significant. It was so catastrophic that it prevented us from mending our relationship for weeks. My obsession with figuring out who Imani was and how I could get to her world left room for nothing else.

I turned and looked at Lauren, pushing a strand of hair out of her face. "Hey, we should get dressed and head to our favorite spot."

"Ooo, The Cozy Fork?" Lauren sat up straight in my lap. I could tell how excited she had gotten just from her gripping my arm.

I laugh and nod, "Mhm, let's go and grab some food."

"I do have an appetite." Lauren tapped her lip with the tip of her finger playfully.

"Good," I whispered. "Go get dressed."

Lauren stood up and walked back into the apartment. I got out of the chair and grabbed my laptop so that I could head inside and get ready as well. Lauren took a quick shower, and then she put back on the clothes she came in. I wanted to match her style, so I dressed down—wearing a baseball cap, a long sweatshirt hoodie, and blue jeans with boots.

After we were both finished getting dressed, I grabbed my car keys, and we left my apartment. We entered the garage, climbed inside the truck, and left the carport to head to the restaurant, which was only a fifteen-minute drive. I found some off-street parking once we arrived. I parked, and we got out of the car and entered the restaurant.

The Cozy Fork was Lauren's favorite place to go when she had a craving for food. She loved the concept of the restaurant because the menu changed every day, so you had to catch them on specific days you wanted certain food items. It was a cute hole-in-the-wall—right in the heart of the city, tucked inside a tall building. The restaurant was on the top floor, and it also had a rooftop. They were always busy and had a long waiting list, but it was worth the wait. The restaurant's idea of a revolving menu also included an around-the-world menu, where they specialized in different cultural dishes.

Lauren and I were greeted by the host, who told us the wait would be at least an hour for the rooftop seating. We sat down in the waiting area, and Lauren snuggled up against me, wrapping her arms around my arm and resting her head on my shoulder. I responded by kissing her forehead gently. As we were waiting, both of us scrolled through our social media accounts to pass time, and we chatted here and there. Finally, our table was ready for two, and we followed the host to the rooftop of the restaurant.

The atmosphere in the restaurant was nothing short of enchanting. Soft, low-dimmed lights cast a warm, amber glow across the space, making everything feel intimate and inviting. The blend of luxury and comfort was seamless. The air buzzed with calm energy, and the music was the perfect finishing touch—smooth jazz-infused lo-fi drifting through the air, wrapping itself around conversations like a warm blanket.

The rooftop, however, was even more breathtaking—with straight overhead arched pallets, allowing the moon's glow to cast a subtle invitation through its spaces. There were fire pits in the middle, an open section for people to get comfy and have meaningful conversation while keeping warm.

Then around the perimeter was seating, where you could overlook the city that roared with life. A bar was off to the side as well, where multiple bartenders cooked up cocktails and served them to casual drinkers. And lastly, hints of plant life to boost endorphins were scattered across, deliberately fit into all the right places where people sat and enjoyed themselves.

Once we arrived at our table, Lauren immediately grabbed the menu and looked through it. I grabbed the drink menu to see what kind of bubbly I could get.

"Oh, they have the garlic parmesan stuffed cabbage rolls." Lauren announces as she taps the menu.

I smile at her and then set the drink menu down, already knowing what I wanted to order. "That sounds tasty. Are you getting that?"

Lauren scrunches her face, "I think so... Ooo, but they also have oxtail plantain egg rolls, and that sounds so delicious."

"Okay, how about I get the egg rolls, and you can try some of mine and have your cabbage too?" I bartered with Lauren, waiting for a response as she left her mouth slightly open, thinking.

"Deal!" She placed down the menu on the table and looked up at me, giving me a warm, inviting smile.

"You're normally not this excited for food. But it's good to see you happy." I tell her while putting my phone into my pocket.

She strikes a cute pose and then giggles, "I know, I'm just in a good mood, and I'm starving. I haven't eaten all day."

I nod and look at her. She was glowing from head to toe.

"You're so beautiful. I love you." My words cut through the loudness of others talking, music playing, and the sounds of the city.

Lauren looked at me and blushed, then she hid her face behind her arm. Butterflies stormed through my stomach when I said those words, but I really meant them. With everything in me, I loved this woman and was happy we were here together, at this moment.

Nothing else around me existed—everything else faded into a blur. My eyes were locked on her, and in that moment, she completely stole my breath away. Lauren reached forward and grabbed my hands, rubbing them with her fingers as she looked me deep in the eyes.

"I love you, too."

I gripped her hand tight and stayed present, hoping this moment could last forever.

The waitress finally came over and introduced herself while we held hands.

"Hi, I'm Hannah, and I'll be your server today. Do you want to start with some drinks or appetizers?"

"I'll take a martini, and I believe we are ready to order." I look at Lauren, and she nods her head as she bites her lip and picks up the menu again.

Lauren orders first, "I'll have the garlic parmesan roasted cabbage and a glass of wine."

The waitress keys in her order on her pad and then looks at me. "And you, sir?"

"I'll take the oxtail plantain egg rolls, please, thank you." I ordered and then handed the waitress the menu; Lauren did the same.

A breeze came through, and Lauren shivered, so I stood up and walked over to the other side of the table and took a seat. I wrapped my arm around her and held her close. Lauren placed her elbow on the table and then her chin in her palm as she looked at me. I leaned in and gave her a kiss, and she kissed me back softly.

I pulled away from her and looked into her eyes. "Hey, I want you to have something." While I reached into my front sweatshirt pocket, Lauren studied me, wondering what I had. I took out my keys and glanced back at her. Slowly, I began to take the extra key to my apartment off the key loop, and as I did it, I noticed her eyes widened.

As soon as the key was off the ring, I held it in the air and smiled at her, "I'm going to give you the extra key to my place. It's yours, and you are welcome to pop up at any time, babe."

Lauren covered her mouth and did a squeal and then waved her hands, "Okay, calm down, girl. Are you sure?"

"Yes, I'm sure," I laughed as I handed it to her. She hesitated to take the key, but I insisted, "Take it."

Her dainty fingers grabbed ahold of the key and clenched it in the palm of her hand. "Aww, babe, thank you." Lauren leans in again and kisses my lips.

"You're welcome, baby." I responded in between breaks of giving her short, sweet kisses.

The server returned to our table with our drinks and set them down in front of us. Lauren picked up her wine glass and held it in the air, looking at me. I reached for my glass and held it up.

"Here's to progress." Lauren toasted her glass, clinking it against mine.

I responded, "Here's to love."

We both drank after the toast and then set our glasses back down on the table. Lauren's hands rested in my lap so that she could get them warm, and I wrapped my arm back around her.

Our food finally came out a bit later, as we sat and talked. The plating was so well done, we ate with our eyes before we even picked up our forks. Both dishes were seasoned and cooked to perfection, and we gave our compliments to the chef before I paid for the bill and we left.

Lauren had to work and needed to head home, so I dropped her off at her home in Sunrise Grove. I gave her a goodnight kiss and then made sure she got into her home safely before driving off and heading back home.

Excitement buzzed through me at the thought of jumping to Troterion when I visited Imani tonight. I was ready to get to bed so that I'd have a good amount of time to be in other timelines. I found myself rushing through my nighttime routine, eager to get to bed, not out of fatigue, but anticipation. Sleep wasn't just rest anymore—it was a gateway.

The sooner I closed my eyes, the sooner I could slip into that space and have the time I needed to explore, to reconnect, to live in the in-between. I wanted to be fully present, well-rested, and grounded before entering such a complex and vibrant dimension.

And knowing Imani would be there to help guide me and anchor me made the anticipation even more intense.

131

Chapter 8

I sat up on Imani's sofa and allowed my eyes to focus. The room was dark except for the lit candles through-out the apartment. Imani had her string bulb globe lights dimmed to a very low setting, her coffee table pushed to the side, and big, fluffy blankets spread out on the floor in front of her brown sofa. Imani was sitting Indian-style on the blanket, staring at me with a beautiful smile as she quietly observed me. This time, the music playing was the sound of singing bowls coming from her stereo through a streaming station.

"Hey, you," she finally greets me.

I smile at her, then stand up and approach her as she sits with excellent posture. She gestures and pats the floor so I can sit in front of her. As soon as I sit, Imani locks her eyes on mine. She reaches and grabs my hands, pulling them towards her.

"Are you excited?" she asks, her voice laced with curiosity and a hint of anticipation.

I nodded my head and stared into her gorgeous eyes. "Absolutely."

She looked more beautiful than ever today—her face immersed in her long, thick locs that were down this time. She wore a loose mustard-colored crop top and black leggings. She changed the piercing in her nose to a hoop that hugged her nostril instead of a stud. There were even more earrings in her ears and rings on her fingers. She had different-colored crystals and layered necklaces hanging from her neck. I recognized the evil eye, rose quartz, and the Eye of Horus.

Imani breathes deeply and then exhales slowly through her mouth. Her eyes close as she continues to breathe in and out. "Close your eyes and do as I do."

I closed my eyes and began to match her breathing. Breathing in deeply, she would hold it and then exhale through her mouth.

We repeated that for five minutes before I opened my eyes and peeked at her. "So…"

She opened one eye and saw mine open. "Shh, close your eyes and just focus on your breathing."

"For how long?"

Imani laughs and then opens her eyes. "You know—you're a pain in my ass."

She leans forward and presses her thumb into my forehead, holding it there. She then takes her index finger and thumb and slides them across my eyelids to make me close my eyes.

She coaches me, "We have to breathe this one through."

Her hands return to my hands, and she continues holding them.

She proceeds, "There are so many benefits to breathing exercises. Breathing helps you focus and center your thoughts. I need you to remember a moment in time when you felt you couldn't breathe."

I begin to speak, "I—"

"Shh," she interrupts. "Just listen and think about a time when you felt the air escaping your lungs, and there was nothing you could do but accept fate. Continue your breathing. Breathe in slowly, hold it, then release."

I thought hard and long about what she was saying while focusing on my breathing and her voice as she coached me. However, it was even more complicated than it sounded. How was I supposed to concentrate on my breathing but think about me not being able to breathe at the same time? I tried to focus as hard as I could. My eyes closed, and I gripped Imani's hands tightly. There was nothing else I would rather do at that moment than do what she said, so I listened to her. Minutes passed, and soon, I lost track of time as I focused on breathing and losing my breath simultaneously.

Imani's voice was distant yet consistent: "Remember, you can do anything that feels impossible."

My chest rose and fell, each breath growing heavier, the pressure tightening, and pain flowing through me. Slowly, my breath thinned, slipping from my grasp. I inhaled harder, but my thoughts grew hazy, edges blurring like smudged ink.

My fingers loosened, slipping from Imani's grasp as I clutched my chest, and panic flickered across her face. Without hesitation, she caught my hands again, gripping them tightly, anchoring me, and refusing to let go.

"You're almost there. You have to keep breathing. The air will feel tighter, but you must focus your mind on breathing once you start to feel as though you can't. Remember, the first time you felt this, you passed out. But after, you saw it through. It should all be rushing back to you now—the memories, the colors, the void." Imani reminded me.

She was right. Images of vibrant colors and crisp, sweet air of something otherworldly began to rush back to me. Memories flashed through my mind, like the first time I remembered Imani weeks ago. It was all familiar, and I didn't understand, nor could I explain what I was seeing. All I know is that it was so beautiful, but the more I remembered, the thinner the air got. I started to feel as though I couldn't breathe at all. I tried to pull away from Imani as I gasped for air, but I couldn't even speak because the air was so thin. Imani's hand rested against my chest.

"This is where you will have to breathe," she demanded.

For some reason, I couldn't catch my breath. Panic crept in, tightening around my chest. Time stretched, each second dragging endlessly. Then, my vision blurred. The soft hum of the singing bowls faded, and the flickering of the candles disappeared into the void. Even Imani's voice grew distant, swallowed by my pounding heartbeat.

What was happening to me?

I gasped, but no air came. My lungs refused to obey as darkness crept at the edges of my mind. I tried to fight it; I tried to open my eyes, to take just one more breath.

Was I dying?

This felt like death.

My body shifted forward, heavy and unresponsive, but before I could collapse, Imani's hands clamped onto my shoulders, trying to hold me up. But I was sinking, slipping away.

Breathe, Lanno. Breathe, Lanno. Breathe, Lanno!

I kept saying it repeatedly, screaming at the top of my lungs. But nothing came out. The veins throughout my body were constricted, and it felt like someone wrapped their first around my heart and squeezed. Even my lungs were on the brink of collapsing. This unbearable pain and experience were going to be the death of me.

More memories poured in as I slowly started to feel myself fade away. I felt like I wouldn't wake up and return home to Lauren.

This meditation session was a mistake.

"Try to focus on the memories." Imani's voice said faintly in the background as my vision grew darker.

The vibrant images I once saw of water so blue, trees vibrantly colorful, and droplets of rain also began to disappear. The smell of sweet nectar and the sounds of creatures from another world, lost within the darkness. I tried so hard to bring those senses back to me, so I held onto what Imani told me to do—focus on my breathing and the memories. I was panicking and not staying present in the moment, my mind cloudy and jaded, distracting me from jumping. I tried to clear my mind to think of how grateful I would be if, at this moment, I did not die. I tried to remember what breathing felt like and even wanted to taste it. I relaxed my mind and focused harder, capturing the true essence of meditation, grounding my thoughts, and holding onto where I wanted to be. Realigning my crown chakra—grabbing a hold of my inner peace, dissolving myself of the anxiety and worry that coursed through me.

Then, everything went dark, but now I could finally breathe again.

It felt soothing but very quiet in the darkness, and the pain I was feeling was completely gone. I looked down at my hands, and I could see them with no blur or haze in my eyes. I turned around and looked behind me, and everything was black, engulfed in darkness—a vast and endless void that swallowed me whole. It pressed in from all sides, thick and suffocating. I couldn't tell where my body ended and the abyss began—there was no up, no down, no sense of time or space. There was weightlessness and silence, except for the faint echo of my fading thoughts. It wasn't just the absence of light; it was the absence of everything. I grab my chest and rub it. I was so happy I could breathe again, but where was I? I looked in front of me again.

"Imani?" I called out.

Silence.

What would Imani say if she were here? I sit down Indian style and close my eyes, breathing in and out to focus. The visions I saw before this massive, dark void felt so warm and inviting that I began picturing them again. I held onto not just what I saw, but also the aromas and the emotional connection to the familiarity of being there before.

Although everything as far as my eyes could see was dark, even this darkness was familiar, yet intimidating. I sat there for minutes, focusing on my breathing, until suddenly, through my eyelids, I could see light. I opened my eyes, and I saw colors all around me. Imani was sitting before me, smiling, and I could hear harmonious sounds echoing around me.

Everything was finally coming back to me.

I was in a cave—the walls stretched endlessly, shimmering with colors I couldn't name, as if they were alive, breathing with me. But what truly stole my breath was the sky—or what should have been the sky. Instead of open air, massive chunks of land, with vast bodies of water above me, floating weightlessly, rippling with unseen currents. It defied every law of gravity I had ever known, yet here it was, undeniably real.

Strange creatures soared through this liquid sky, weaving effortlessly between the waves and in the air. They weren't birds, not like the ones back home. Their bodies were round, almost like living orbs, with impossibly long necks. Their wings, detached from their bodies, flapped independently, moving with an elegance that was impossible. Hundreds of them filled the space, each one painted in a palette of brilliant, almost blinding colors.

And the smell—oh, the smell was overwhelming. It wasn't just one scent but all at once, crashing into me. It was bold and intoxicating, sweet like honey yet crisp and fresh, like the first breath of morning air. It was as if I could taste the colors, the light, and the essence of the world around me. My senses blurred, tangled together in a way that made no sense, yet I felt everything more vividly than ever before.

I tried to grasp it, to make sense of this impossible place, but words would never be enough. Even if I told someone, they would never believe me.

The air around me was thick, almost suffocating, until I was able to finally work through it and allow for the shift in the atmosphere to adjust within my lungs. Once familiar with my breathing techniques, I wanted to harness the air and stow it away in my pocket. It was different from any planet I'd ever been to. I took in my surroundings, in awe at the water droplets that fell from the sky islands but levitated before hitting the ground. Sometimes the water dissolved right before my eyes. There were even mountains across the horizon, fused in with a thick fog that looked like cotton candy. A mist that I could smell from miles away due to a heightened sense of smell and the dramatic aroma they emitted—fresh, clean, purified air.

I finally and slowly stood to my feet, still in awe. I look around and take everything in. I could see the entire planet from this cave on a mountaintop. Everything was so breathtaking. There were giant orbs in the sky, and hundreds of planets you could see in the distance, thousands of miles away. The trees were colorful with different hues—pinks, purples, vibrant oranges, reds, and greens—gigantic trees that touched the sky and small trees that I would tower over. Imani hangs onto my hand, taking it all in as I stand there.

There was a feeling of recollection—I've been here before—this was Troterion.

I realized my body was different from Lanno's, though. I was a distinct being, much larger and taller. My skin was blackish-blue, and scales filled my arm with tribal markings.

I stepped back and let go of Imani's hand once I realized my arm. I then look at both my hands, rotating them around as I examine them. I was now a hybrid form, part reptilian and part human. I had to be standing at least thirteen feet tall. I turned from side to side and realized I also had a long tail that had beautifully placed scales running along it.

"Tza'ku!" I say as I rotate my arm around and examine it. I realize that when I say "whoa," it comes out in a different language, but I understand it. I looked up at Imani in shock.

"Yeah, Trosthu. It's the language of the Troke people. We are Troke, and the language is a form of Light Language." Imani explains with great wisdom. Light language often follows a rhythmic, melodic, or tonal pattern rather than structured grammar, and it's deeply personal. Some beings experience it as channeled sounds, tones, or gestures, while others recognize it as an ancient, soul-connected dialect.

"Holy shit! I'm speaking and understanding another language!" I let out a cry in excitement. I can hear Imani laugh as she stands up and comes closer to me. I look at her and continue speaking. "This is so trippy."

I finally tried to take a step, and I stumbled a bit.

Imani grabs onto my arm and holds me up. "Easy. You haven't been here in a very long time. You're going to have to get used to gravity, or lack thereof. The air is also different here. Hence the breathing activity."

I take another step, and my leg floats in the air. I force it down firmly against the ground, then try my other leg, and it does the same thing.

Repeatedly, I lifted my feet and walked. Imani laughs, her voice echoing through the cave. I turned to her and laughed as well. "I feel like I got a stick in my butt."

"Well, you're definitely walking like you do. You should try jumping."

My eyes get big as I turn around and think about it for a second. I then leap, my feet lift off the ground, and I begin floating in the air.

I screamed excitedly, forcing my feet back to the ground. "Oh my god! Did you see that!"

I turned back and looked at Imani, who now had a massive grin. Imani then walks over to the edge of the cave and leaps off. She slowly floats through the air and then starts to descend the cliff. I unsteadily run over to the edge and watch as Imani lowers to the bottom. Once she lands on the ground, she looks up and motions for me to come down. I got nervous because it was a steep fall from the top of the cave to the ground, but I took a step back, then leaped forward off the cliff. I floated through the air and slowly glided down the cliffside, allowing the cool air to wash over me as I fell to the ground, like I was falling through soft pillows.

Once I landed, I regained my balance and looked over at Imani. "That was awesome!"

Now that I was on the ground, my eyes darted, taking in the familiar landscape. The plants were different from the ones back home, vibrant in colors of blues, greens, and yellows. Waving in the wind, releasing pollen that sparkled like glitter. You would think inhaling it would make you sneeze, but this pollen was different—it enhanced all your senses. I could taste the sweetness of the particles, feel every single fiber gently caressing itself around me, and even hear and see the shimmering glow. It was magical.

I reached out, my fingertips grazing the petals of a near-by flower. They were soft, like velvet, its texture sending a gentle warmth through my skin. Around me, tiny, irides-cent insects fluttered through the air, their wings catch-ing the light in dazzling bursts. Their presence felt oddly familiar, and as they hovered close, a sweet, delicate scent filled the air—honeysuckles, that's what they reminded me of. The realization stirred something deep inside me, and memories of me being in this place gradually came back to me.

Imani touches my shoulder. "It's beautiful, isn't it?"

I looked over to her, and although my memory was still hazy, I smiled because this place made me feel so happy. It was serene and peaceful—nostalgic yet new. I nodded at her and then closed my eyes to breathe in the crispy, sweet air, which felt, tasted, and smelled refreshing. I inhaled, and the air entered through my nose, caressing the follicles and filling my lungs, then exhaled slowly, allowing it to exit gracefully.

Imani reaches up and pulls down a star-shaped object from one of the nearby trees. She smiles and holds it out in front of me.

"It's called Umni," she says. I tilt my head and then reach out hesitantly to grab it from her. She continues, "Just think of it like fruit. It's edible; try it."

The Umni was about the size of her hand and had different shades of red and purple, with a stem coming out of it from where she plucked it from the tree. I slowly put the Umni into my mouth as I watched her, and her eyes gazed into me intensely as I took a bite. It tasted mildly sweet, creamy, and highly refreshing.

I couldn't help but notice that Imani could not stop smiling. She loved that I was having a good time.

As she spoke, Imani continued walking down the path. "Nothing here can hurt you. It's so peaceful and abundant."

I followed behind her, realizing how magical everything was around me—the trees emitted energy as if they were alive and breathing, the plants had their own scent, like the creatures of the sky, and the insects that buzzed around the dirt felt alive, vibrating in their own way.

In awe of everything, I asked, "So, we're Troke people?"

"We are," Imani answers. "There's a huge community of the Troke, one civilization that gets to live off this beautiful land. They are all at peace—no war, no famine, or disease. The Troke people live for thousands of years until they ascend to another life. We are baby Troke, and we aren't that old yet."

I continue to follow Imani as she shows me around. The more we explored, the more I remembered visiting Troterion in every timeline. It had been so long ago, and many memories were slow to return to me. Imani was able to explain how the Troke people lived. They were among the most enlightened beings and have been living on this planet for thousands of years. She explained that before, when I could jump more freely through timelines, this was one of my favorite places to go. The cave was where she would find me sitting in the sun or basking in the moonlight. Imani told me that my favorite thing to do was breathe in the air of Planet Troterion and that my favorite snack to enjoy was the Umni, which is why these were the exact things she wanted to introduce me to as soon as we touched down here. In hopes of helping resurface all the memories I lost.

I still didn't understand why I had lost or suppressed so many of my memories. Either way, I was happy that when I was with Imani, she could revive those core memories. I wondered what else I had forgotten.

Imani and I found a waterfall while on our walk, where gravity elevated the water to the sky instead of the water freely falling. We sat by the waterfall and listened to all the sounds around us. It was quiet between us for a long time, but I was at peace as long as I was with her. We sat in that moment and enjoyed it. Around the waterfall, plant life stretched along the coast of the river, a river that seemed to move in reverse as the current pulled it up the waterfall. Imani pointed out the Trollips—a beautiful blue and yellow plant used in native dishes as spices that grew as far as the naked eye could see. She even pointed out the Doxtails, which were a kind of fish that swam past our feet and were a delicacy to the Troke people. Even the fish were colorful and alien-like, with long tails and sleek, birdlike fins that could take them out of water for hours at a time. It was a unique ecosystem of species that existed beyond planet Earth and human comprehension. What took me by surprise the most was the smell of the river—sweet and salty, like candy mixed with a savory dish you could both taste and smell. I slid my hand into the waterfall and felt it flowing up between my fingers, and it was naturally warm and refreshing against my skin. I wrapped my hand around the water and pulled some towards me as it floated in the air and drank from it.

Imani watched me closely, smiling. I scooted closer to her with the remaining water I had left and allowed her to drink. She inhaled as I watched the water float between her lips and into her mouth.

"Mmm, sweet and refreshing," she lets out.

"Thank you for bringing me here. Everything is so vivid now, and I'm remembering more." I thank her.

Imani smiles and looks at me. She rests her hand on my chest and nods. "What do you remember?"

I take a moment to think as I let the remaining water float out of my hand and up to the sky. So many thoughts came to me. It wasn't just Troterion, but other places Imani and I have been to. Imani explained to me that not only did the Troke people ascend higher than any other beings in the timelines we visited, but Troterion also had energy-balancing properties, which means that once you've reached Troterion, it repairs your mind, body, and soul. The atmosphere was healing. So, if you were sick with any diseases or impaired in any way, Troterion would restore your inner being to its higher form.

Different names came to me—Bayzo, Thomas, Imogen, and Celeste—but as clear as the names were, my mind was still a little foggy, so I wasn't quite sure who they could be. There were so many different timelines that Imani and I had been in together that it was hard to remember them all. It came to me in bits and pieces, but it was a lot clearer than before. I even remembered my age. Imani didn't embellish its actual reality, but I was close to a thousand years old, just like Imani—952 years of living, to be exact, for us both.

It wasn't just a dream anymore; this was real, and it was all coming back to me in waves. Imani and I have been soulmates for hundreds of years, evolving and experiencing different forms across the universe—falling in love, having children, and building memories that I had somehow forgotten or lost.

Imani congratulated me, "Getting to Troterion is tough, but you did it, babe. You got through the void because you focused and centered your mind."

The void—that dark, empty space that I almost succumbed to—was a space that lived between the physical worlds, where space and time don't exist or travel. It can be scary and dangerous if you get stuck in it.

I felt Imani's tail hit me, and I smiled back at her. "I don't think I will ever get used to the tail."

I felt alive, more confident, and more assertive. With most of the memories flowing back to me, I felt invincible.

I was limitless.

Planet Troterion was healing me at a rapid rate. Just being here for hours strengthened my inner core.

The best part about this experience was that I was able to remember, but deep down, one question haunted me to no end.

Why did I forget?

We spent the remainder of the time exploring Troterion and enjoying its atmosphere until it was time to leave. We made our way back to the cave, and once we reached it, Imani looked at me and then lunged back up to the top. I followed her lead and jumped back up, my body floating effortlessly through the air. Once I reached the top, I realized that the moonlight was just as remarkable as the daytime. We sat Indian style in front of each other, and Imani held onto my hands.

"It should be much easier to get back," Imani assured me.

I confidently responded, "I know."

Imani smiles big and then closes her eyes. She takes a deep breath, holds it, and exhales slowly. Again, I followed her lead and did the same thing.

Minutes passed as I continued to focus on my breathing, uninterrupted. Slowly, the smells escaped me, and the brightness of all the moons and stars disappeared. I felt a moment of sadness, but that slowly disappeared because I knew I could easily return. My breathing evened out, and I felt a familiar room encompass me.

Before I could open my eyes, Imani spoke. "We're home."

I finally opened my eyes and noticed we were back where we first started—in Imani's living room, on the floor, with tons of candles and blankets surrounding us. It was dark outside her windows now, and I knew it would be time for me to wake up and return to Lauren. I stare into Imani's eyes, and she smiles back at me.

What a trip.

A refreshing and relieving trip to Troterion, my soul's home and heaven tucked away into the universe. Just from the brief visit, I have most of my memories back, and now I can fill in most gaps. I sat there quietly as Imani slowly let go of my hands and sighed deeply. She shook her hands to get rid of all the excess energy that had built up from jumping and the shift in timelines.

Imani looks at me and smiles again. She leans forward, rests her hands on my knees, and stares into my eyes. I hesitate, then press my lips into hers, kissing her deeply. Our auras began to radiate across the room, and I could feel her more than ever now—her body, her touch, and her soul were on fire.

The room felt like it was heating up by the second, as if the sun itself were pounding at her front door. A vivid blue light shimmered around us, casting an otherworldly glow that made the air thick with intensity. I was overwhelmed—every breath felt heavy, every second stretched thin. Even the thought of kissing her now made my chest tighten, like I was on the verge of combusting from the pressure building inside me.

What was this feeling?

I pulled away from her, and she looked at me.

"I can tell you remember almost everything now." She expresses.

I sigh and slowly nod, "I do."

"Eka'ra shi'lo, Mahant." Welcome back, Mahant, was what she said in Trosthu, and then she smiled.

I looked down at my hands and saw a blue aura surrounding them. I then looked at Imani, and there was a blue aura around her as well.

Imani must have known I was trying to understand what was happening, because she began to explain. "Our energy, it's a blue aura from being twin flames. You can see it, and you will be able to feel any emotion I ever feel."

I smile slightly, "When the universe created us, it made us blue for inner peace and a deep spiritual connection. We can read people's auras, but when it comes to you and me, we can feel each other. I remember now. It's always been a tense connection between us."

I am more confident now. I felt as though I had reached a higher form of enlightenment, as if I were more grounded and open. Troterion made me understand the true beauty of my life and the power of reincarnation. Being born into different timelines, different worlds, and as distinct species was only the beginning; remembering it all was the true gift.

It also unlocked this hunger to stay with Imani even more. I wanted to be one with her. The ravenousness I craved, wanting to devour her body and soul. I wanted her in every way. The thoughts that traveled through my mind were indecent but extremely powerful as I continued to stare at her intensely, not breaking eye contact.

She was right; I could feel her emotions, and now everything is heightened. Imani seemed nervous as I stared deep into her eyes, but in a good way.

She catches her breath, "Stop looking at me like that."

I couldn't take my eyes off her. I wanted to see her—truly see her—for everything she was. I searched for her face, her expression, trying to peer past the surface and into her soul, as if understanding her essence would anchor me in this moment forever.

Imani clears her throat and then pushes her hair out of her face. She adjusts herself and then looks back at me.

With my voice low and heavy, I speak, "Am I making you nervous?"

She bites her bottom lip. "Maybe, but I've missed this confident version of you."

I leaned in to kiss her again, but she gently pulled away, her eyes searching mine with a mix of hesitation and something unspoken lingering in the air between us.

Imani warns me, "Trust me, you don't want to do that again. You're really not ready."

I sigh and sit back straight. "I can handle it."

Imani shakes her head and then lies back across the blankets while still sitting Indian style. She inhales deeply, then exhales as her eyes close, and I watch her intently.

"You're the one who seems like you can't handle it." I tease.

Imani giggles and clears her throat, "If you say so."

"Hey, so I should be able to jump to Troterion whenever now, right?"

She continues to lie down with her eyes closed, concentrating on breathing. "What, don't you want to come see me anymore?"

"Of course I do. It's just—I feel like the more time I spend there. The more I will remember."

"I'm just teasing. Of course, you can jump straight there. If you focus your mind, you can jump to any timeline you have been to before." Imani sits up and scoots closer to me; her energy intensifies as she gets closer, our auras melding into one again.

I wrap my arms around her. "You can feel that too, huh?"

She nods, looking at me, her eyes now full of lust. "You've got to go back now."

I shake my head, "I don't want to."

Imani sighed and then gave me a look. "You have to, babe."

Imani pulls away from me, tucking her hands into the creases of her thighs, creating space between us. She begins to gently rock back and forth, her breaths deep and deliberate. It's clear she's grounding herself, focusing intently on her breathing. I can't blame her—if she's feeling even a fraction of the energy surging through me, then this moment is overwhelming. I lean in again, drawn to her like a magnet, desperate for connection—but once more, she turns her head and pulls away, her body trembling with restraint.

I continued to pressure her, "How do I stay?"

Imani tilts her head and then shakes it as she glares at me. "Why are you so persistent? Why can't you leave it alone?

What's wrong with just jumping to me for a little while and going back?"

I get quiet for a moment and think about what she says. She had a point.

Why was staying with Imani so important when I could jump to her whenever I wanted? It's not like I wasn't able to see Imani at all. I blame my hyper-fixation and the inability to lose focus on things I felt I needed to accomplish.

"Fine," I say, defeated.

As much as I did not want to admit it, I was tired and had no energy to fight. We had spent most of our time in Troterion, and I wished there was more time for Imani and me to intertwine our souls. We both felt this unworldly connection, and I wanted to explore it. She didn't think it was a good idea and that I was not ready, nor did we have enough time to. The feeling of getting close to or touching one another was out of this world. The energy around us seemed to gravitate into the inner core of our bodies, and it felt magnificent.

I stood up and made my way to the sofa to lie down. Lying on my side, I watched as Imani scooted towards me and sat inches away from my face. She reached her hand out and began to play with my hair as I closed my eyes and drifted off to sleep. As sleep pulled me under, I made myself a silent promise—next time I saw Imani, I wouldn't hold back. Her body, her presence, her essence—I would claim all of it.

She would be mine...

Chapter 9

I decided to give meditation a try on my own today to clear my crown chakra, practice my breathing, and speak positive affirmations, as Imani instructed me. It was only me in my apartment, and the only sound I could hear was the playlist Imani told me to put together for meditation purposes. It was time for sleep, and I wanted to try to jump to Troterion by myself tonight.

That was the objective.

I was nervous, scared, and worried that somehow, I'd mess it all up and end up in the void again. Thankfully, I remembered everything Imani had taught me: to speak positive affirmations into the universe and think clearly. Not to allow those thoughts to remain stagnant in my mind or create an unnecessary barrier. Her voice imprinted itself on my mind, urging me to stay present in the moment, clear my chakras, and breathe. As I lay in bed, my five hundred and twenty-eightHz music played in the background—creating a relaxing environment around me, allowing me to close my eyes, inhale through my nose, and exhale through my mouth, slowly. In this moment, I was more confident, more aware, and awakened into a space where I knew I could jump into another timeline. I had the power and control to expand my mind, opening it to infinite possibilities. Fueled by this power, it created a sense of serenity and calmness that swept over my body, allowing the astral projection state to come forward. While I meditated and slowly drifted off to sleep, I could feel my body lifting and transitioning into another space. A space of familiarity—roaring clouds, beautiful colors, and a shift in the atmosphere that called on me to adjust my breathing. I could feel my body transforming, my lungs growing larger, and my hands and arms rippling with dazzling colors and scales. It was a magnificent feeling, merging between two completely different realms, in another timeline on another planet entirely. Seeing the transformation before your eyes, while feeling the shift of the world around you, is a phenomenon no normal human being could ever fathom. I was blessed to have these abilities.

Finally, the world opened up, and Troterion welcomed me with open arms. This time, I was not in my typical cave but in a meadow. Dozens of colorful flowers danced around me, some floating right above the ground, with their pollen majestically whistling through the wind. They smelled out of this world—sweet, citrusy, and warm, stroking the follicles in my nose, corrupting my senses. I inhaled deeply to savor its essence before rolling over, off my tail and onto my side. The sound of the insect buzzing around created a unique symphony only Troterion could offer. Stretching as far as the eye could see, this meadow continued. I basked in all its glory, soaking up the warm rays, allowing the heat to caress my human-like reptilian body. I sat up and opened and closed my legs, feeling the chilled dirt and warm flowers creating this otherworldly hot and cold sensation against my skin. The moment I touched down on the planet, my mind unleashed a powerful wave that rippled throughout my body intensely. I could remember more memories, and the name Thomas came back to me even more now. I remembered a little more about my timeline in Utopia, and I was Thomas. I would come to Troterion as Thomas often and bask in this meadow. This meadow—a powerful ancient field of healing, ancient grounds to this planet and all who visit it. It restored the balance of nature all around it, expanding its healing energies into the universe. Troterion Meadows was a treasure, stories of it told and whispered across the universe for as long as time, and also a place I called home.

More memories poured into me, and I could feel my mind getting stronger. I stood up and inhaled deeply again, enjoying the sensational atmosphere and allowing the flowers' pollen to enter through me, as they were the healing properties that made this meadow so powerful. I wanted to venture off, revisit, and explore Troterion, taking in all its beauty. I walked for what seemed like hours until I finally reached the perimeter of the meadow and found myself at a lake. This lake, like all other water on Troterion, had water droplets that flowed upward towards the sky. The lake was gorgeous, so clear that you could see the bottom of it effortlessly, and bright blue. Around the lake were large trees and wildlife. Animals that were similar to ours but very different, like the Amilo—seemingly close in resemblance to a deer but bigger. On four legs, with longer hair and two horns that sat on top of its head. Its eyes were massive, glistening yet warm. They were gentle creatures—herbivores that I remembered only ate the Nolten plant that grew from the lakes and gathered around the shoreside. Out of all the timelines I'd recalled thus far, Utopia was the one where I visited Troterion the most as Thomas. Observing the Amilo and their daily routine was a favorite. Being able to slowly gain their trust and walk alongside them through the forest that lies beyond the lake and meadow was magical to me. Slowly, I walked into the water, and its sauna-like temperature soothed me. Instantly, I could feel my blood rushing and my bones growing stronger from within. Imani was right; all of Troterion had healing powers. Everything you touched or ate would grant you strength, solace, and energy.

As soon as I got deep enough for the water to reach my chest, I lay back and floated on my back, looking into the sky. Troterion was remarkable—everything, from the giant pieces of floating land to the levitating precipitation, and the planets and stars aligned, was uniquely stunning.

I floated there for as long as I could take the temperature of the water, basking in the sunlight and listening to the sound of the ripples entering and exiting my ears. When I got out of the water, I sat by a nearby tree, where the Amilo were grazing nearby. I shook off all the excess water out of my ears when suddenly, the sound of a branch breaking came from behind me. I turned around quickly and noticed a Troke kid standing a distance away from me. His posture was tense and defensive, as if he were about to take off. I threw up my hands and slowly got off the ground. Carefully, I made my way towards him as his stance remained startled and scared. However, as I approached him, his demeanor changed, and he stood straight up, confidence beaming out from him.

"Hello," he spoke in the most melodic-sounding way, with tones and vibrations only someone who spoke light language could possibly understand. It was low, calm, and inviting—a harmonic kindred tone. It was Trosthu.

We stood before each other, and before I could even respond, I bowed halfway down, bending one knee but making sure I didn't touch the ground—an instinctive gesture that the Troke people do when greeting an elder because this was no kid, but a Troke who's lived many millenniums ten times over. He touched my shoulder, accepting my bow, allowing me to stand before him.

He continued to speak in Trosthu, "You are a jumper. Welcome to Troterion."

I nodded my head and looked down as I towered over him. He had more tribal markings on him, and he didn't look older just by looking at him, but somehow I just knew he was.

I was finally able to create a melodic movement with my tongue and speak Trosthu. "I'm Mahant, what's your name?"

"I know you are Mahant. I am Kaelun, the keeper of sacred knowing. You don't remember me, do you, Mahant?"

I closed my eyes and inhaled deeply, trying to pull memories from my core. There were distant fragments of Troke people, a community fueled by love and wisdom—a place of harmony, known to be the most beautiful village of all of Troterion. Then a face and a name came to the forefront—it was Kaelun's face.

I remembered.

Kaelun and I were friends. Whenever I visited Troterion, he would bring me to his village, and I would spend hours there with his people. We would swim in the lake, forage for food, dance around the fire, and then tell stories of the universe all in one trip. So many memories rushed through me, bringing tears to my eyes as I stood in front of Kaelun. I felt his hand touch my shoulder, and he pulled me in for a unique form of hug, where only our shoulders touched each other. My hand wrapped around his head, and we embraced for a while.

"Eka'ra shi'lo, Mahant," Kaelun whispered, low and welcoming.

Kaelun let go of me and turned around, heading towards what I remembered to be his village. It was close by, just on the other side of the forest, so I followed behind closely.

As we got close to his village, I realized the trees quadrupled in size—they were massive. Giant trees, which the Troke called Dock trees, stretched across the plain. The trees were carved out on the bottom, creating hut-like homes for the Troke people. Then, within the trees, rope-like floors were installed, with additional huts surrounding them. It reminded me of Treedom, when suddenly, more memories came to me—a story of how the universe created the same trees in different timelines, allowing them the same power. Kaelun told me many stories, and the story of the Dock trees was one of my favorites. It was amazing to me how glimpses of memories of previous lives came back the more I stayed on Troterion.

My mind was healing miraculously.

We arrived at the village, and I took everything in—a fantastic view of Troke life. There were no kids here; everyone was hundreds of years old and had reached the highest form of enlightenment, thus being the only way their body could truly transform into a Troke species. Different-sized Troke walked through the village—some carrying Doxtails, others with baskets of Umni. There were even domesticated Amilo helping to transport other goods or services. The scent of the trees was reminiscent of fresh pine and honeycomb. Around the trees were the same flowers from Troterion Meadows, and finally, a name came to me. Lassotills—the flower of spiritual healing. They emit pollen that can enter your bloodstream and cure diseases.

As we walked through the village, Kaelun noticed how in awe I was, taking everything in.

"You, Mahant, always look so thrilled to be here." His voice hummed in Trosthu. "You look at the Dock trees and are captivated by them."

I smile then sigh happily, "They're so beautiful. They remind me of—"

"Treedom, I know." Kaelun cuts me off. "They are the same trees from Treedom. The same sacred land—it's all connected."

"It's all coming back to me in fragments, Kaelun. My mind has plagued me." I admitted, my voice low and broken.

Kaelun continues his walk through the village. "I see your future, Mahant; your mind will be plagued no longer, but you must have patience, and you must trust your heart."

Kaelun was always wise and warm. I trusted him and his words of wisdom. Finally, we arrived at a gathering of sorts. There was a massive fire, and Doxtails were being roasted on pits. Kaelun grabbed two Umni and tossed one to me. It was perfectly firm and dark, and when I bit into it, the sweetness of the fruit burst in my mouth like an explosion.

I loved Umni—it was my favorite part of Troterion. As I ate the fruit, I watched as a small group of Troke danced around to music played on their parchellos—a long, spiral, flute-like instrument that you blow into. Another group of Troke were getting tribal markings imprinted on them, while others watched and cheered them on. We were in what seemed like the community center of the village, where everyone gathered to enjoy each other's company. A lady Troke walked up to Kaelun and me and offered two fish.

"Grilled Doxtails?" She offered, holding out both of them in front of us.

Kaelun looked at me as he took the offered fish. "This is Kaiya; she is the best cook in all of the village."

Kaiya smiles and hands me the fish. I take it from her, and she stares at me blankly, waiting for me to take a bite. I look over at Kaelun and then back at her as I sink my teeth into the perfectly grilled Doxtails. The meat of the fish was so tender, flaky, and deliciously flavored. It was charred to perfection, and the natural spices elevated its taste, making it the tastiest fish I had ever eaten.

"Mmm, this is so delicious!" I complimented her passionately. I meant what I said, and my body language and gestures suggested that I was not lying. The food weakened my knees and almost made me collapse by the sensation it created on my taste buds. Everything was fresher, healthier, and more delicious on Troterion.

Kaiya's tail immediately wagged as she perked up to my responses. She bows down slightly and then scurries off to offer her delicious meal to others.

Kaelun and I continue to stand by the fire and take in our surroundings—unspoken words between two friends enjoying the company of each other again. The crackling of the fire was music to my ears, creating a sense of ease within me. Troke laughing, speaking Trosthu in an ethereal, almost unreal dialect, was beautiful.

I was proud of myself for successfully jumping to Troterion by myself, without any effort. Whenever I was not with Lauren or Imani, here is where I wanted to be—my true home between timelines.

As it got later, I started to get sleepier. My eyelids grew heavier, and my body grew fatigued. I hated this feeling of needing to wake up to the real world—my timeline.

Kaelun turned towards me and rested his hand on my arm. "It's time to go, my friend."

I nodded and turned to walk towards the small forest. There was no need for a goodbye, as it was a simple 'see you later.' Once I entered the forest, I sat down against a nearby tree and closed my eyes. Meditation was easier as my body was already in a state of peace, present in the moment, and grounded in happiness. As that shift came—waking up and falling asleep at the same time—I felt as though the void was no longer in my future. I was able to jump from my timeline to Troterion successfully.

I woke up in my bedroom, the sunlight shining through my bedroom curtains as I realized it was early morning and time for me to get up fully.

One big meditation, sleep-like cycle—that's what it felt like—the dream world, a different timeline, a deep sleep.

Only I knew in my heart that it was real.

I needed to get some work done today. So, I got out of bed and took a shower before heading to the living room and grabbing my laptop. I decided to write up a few facilitator guides for my team and send out a couple of emails. There were also a few meetings and calibrations on the calendar that I had to attend, as work had not been a priority for me lately.

Some of the memories I gained from visiting Troterion made my current timeline feel futile. In most timelines, either Imani or I were wealthy, wealthier than I was in my current timeline, without having to work. We knew how to manipulate the timelines to become richer than the people around us. Understanding the fundamentals of how certain worlds worked was like a cheat code for living. We were investors and entrepreneurs, creating companies that existed in previous timelines but weren't yet part of our current one. So, as Lanno, since I didn't have my memories of how to gain capital, I lived a humble lifestyle.

I was comfortable, though, but I needed to work so that I could continue to provide for myself in this realm.

After I spent a few hours at work, I made myself some lunch and then listened to a few DJ sets on my music platform app. It was a relaxed day, and I just wanted to successfully get through one day of being complacent by myself, doing my regular daily routine.

Lauren was finishing up her last week of school before the school year was over, so I didn't want to bother her too much during the day.

As the day progressed, I even considered making an appointment with Dr. Ricardo but ultimately decided against it. I was nervous and scared to talk about all the recent events I've been going through.

Instead, I decided to call it an early night and get back to sleep so that I could revisit Troterion and continue my healing process.

Kaelun told me patience was key, but how much was I not remembering, and what kind of effect did it have on my decision-making process? That question lingered in my mind like the plague, only making it harder to do exactly that—be patient.

Chapter 10

When I go to sleep, I have now made it a habit to visit Troterion a lot more often. I felt myself getting stronger mentally and physically. My eyes widened, and I could see beyond the surface—beyond what was merely visible. However, I was sleeping more and spending less time with Lauren. Lauren found it odd that I was going to sleep earlier at night. She would ask me if I felt okay, and I would tell her that I was fine. It wasn't a lie, but it was not the entire truth. I thought, if anyone could do what I could, would they stay stagnant in one world?

It's been six days, and I haven't returned to visit Imani yet. Not seeing her has been rough, but I have been focused on exploring. There was a safety net I felt when I jumped with Imani, so the only place I visited by myself was Troterion. I figured I'd find out why I lost all my memories since Imani wasn't giving me the necessary answers. Unfortunately, I discovered nothing new, but every time I visited Troterion, I remembered more.

Our universe holds so many untold secrets and possibilities. One of the keys to unlocking these possibilities was the ability to tap into a state of consciousness.

I still didn't understand why I lost all my memories or what happened to make me lose them, and this dreamlike world felt like only a couple of hours before I had to wake up again. When I jumped to Imani, I wanted that timeline to be longer than my timeline as Lanno, even though that would mean less time with Lauren. I thought about it, and I didn't want that either. I hated how complicated everything was.

Why did I have to love two women?

Why do they both exist in separate realms to further complicate my life?

It's never that easy, unfortunately. Eventually, I feared that I would have to make a choice.

"Hey, babe, are you ready to go?" Lauren asks me as she puts her hoop earrings in her ears. I turn around with my cell phone and keys and smile at her. In her blue denim jeans and black floral shirt, Lauren looked extra beautiful today. Around her neck was a thin necklace with a crescent moon pendant that she always wore. Her hair was down against her face and curly. She smiled back at me with her gorgeous smile and motioned to head out the door.

I promised Jah that we would link up this week to hang out, and Lauren thought it would be a great idea if we all got together after work, including Fallyn. I wasn't ready to face Fallyn—I knew she wouldn't take it easy on me.

As we left the house and got in my car, I noticed how quiet and uneasy Lauren was. Once we were in the car, I turned to her and stared.

She finally looked back. "What?"

"You're really quiet; what's wrong?" I asked, my voice curious yet concerned.

She smiles and shakes her head. "Nothing, I'm okay."

I could tell she was lying, but I didn't push it. I started the car up, and we headed to our favorite lounge, Sky Lounge. Lauren was extremely quiet the entire ride to the lounge.

When we arrived, it was around six, and Lauren and I got out of the car. I stopped and stared at her across the car as she hesitated. I sighed, gripped my keys, and walked over to the other side, right up to her.

"Talk to me," I demanded.

Lauren starts playing with her fingers as she looks down at them. It was something she always did when she was nervous or feeling uncomfortable. We stood there for a while, and she remained quiet. I looked around and waited for her to talk to me.

"Lauren?"

She sighed and finally looked up at me as I was inches away, locking her eyes onto mine.

Finally, she says, "I didn't tell Fallyn we were back together."

I laugh nervously and then look away. I rub my nose and then look back at Lauren. "This is a whole setup."

"I'm sorry," Lauren apologized. "Fallyn will have to get over it. I mean, she was a little mad and talked a lot of shit when you and I weren't talking, but what's my decision is my decision."

I sigh and then compose myself as I grab Lauren's hand and interlock my fingers with hers. We turn towards the Sky Lounge and slowly walk to the entrance.

Nonchalantly, I responded, "She's going to have to."

Walking inside, we look around the lounge and go to our regular spot in the back. Jah and Fallyn were already there, and as soon as we walked up to them, there was an immediate eye roll from Fallyn.

Fallyn yells, "You have got to be fucking joking, Lauren!"

Jah motions his hands to Fallyn as if to tell her to take it down a bit. Other people in the lounge shift their attention to us to see what is going on.

"It's nice to see you too, Fallyn," I responded sarcastically.

"Shut the fuck up, Lame-o," Fallyn replies sharply to me.

Lauren interjects between us, "Fallyn, seriously?"

Fallyn continues, her eyes locked on me, "Yes, seriously, Lauren. You two are back together? After you cried your eyes out to me over him for weeks!"

Lauren tilts her head back and sighs as she closes her eyes.

Fallyn, still on a warpath, said, "Did all he have to do is dick you down, and you just forgave him?"

Her voice grew louder by the second, and the energy in the room shifted tremendously. I didn't want Lauren or me to argue with Fallyn or have to explain our intentions to her.

"Fallyn, c'mon, easy," Jah says as he reaches out and tries to grab her arm in an attempt to calm her down. Fallyn pulls away and looks back at Jah with a look that could kill.

Fallyn's fiery tongue, as sharp as ever, turned her fury on Jah. "Shut up, Jah. Your boy ain't shit, and I'm not about to let my girl get her heart broken all over again just because this asshole thinks he can do whatever he wants."

"Listen, Fallyn, you have every right to be upset. I fucked up, but I apologized, and I'm sorry." I finally let out. I feel Lauren grip my hand tightly. I looked over at her and shook her hand affectionately to reassure her.

"Lanno Shut the fuck up. I don't care what you have to say. You can't easily sway me like you do Lauren. You can't fool me." Fallyn points at me as she talks.

I see Lauren give her a look. Fallyn looks back at Lauren, groans deeply, and shakes her head. She sits back against the booth and crosses her arms and legs, glaring at both of us.

Lauren finally released my hand, walked up to Fallyn, and stood before her.

"Come, babes, let's go talk. I'm sorry I didn't tell you." Lauren reaches out and grabs Fallyn's hand. She pulls her out of her seat, and they walk to a nearby corner to chat.

I sit across from Jah and take a deep breath. Jah's eyes get big, and he reaches forward and grabs his drink, then sips it.

He clears his throat and looks at me. "Yeah, she doesn't fuck with you anymore. I see why Lauren didn't tell her shit!" He laughs nervously and then takes another sip of his drink.

I run my fingers through my curls and focus on breathing. I can overhear Fallyn and Lauren' conversation in the distance, in a low whisper, but very clear.

"He's fucking mental. Three fucking weeks he didn't talk to you, and you just spread your fucking legs open and forgive him?" Fallyn whispers loudly, as if she wants everyone to hear the conversation.

Lauren whispered back. "He said he was sorry, Fallyn, and I missed him! I'm not going to throw away six months just because he couldn't say, "I love you," back at that moment."

"That's not the fucking point, Lauren. It's him ghosting you after he didn't say, I fucking love you. Are you stupid?"

I rub my neck and sit awkwardly across from Jah.

The waiter comes up and stands next to us. "Can I get you something to drink?"

I looked up at her, defeated. "Yeah, I'll take two shots of your special."

"Two shots? Oh yeah, you stressed. My boy is stressed." Jah jokes. I give him a look and then shake my head. The waiter walks away to get my drink, and Jah continues, "I haven't seen you order two shots at the same time in years, playa."

"Jah, please shut up," I beg him.

Jah doesn't stop. Instead, he continues to run his mouth. "Whew, Fallyn is sexy as fuck when she's angry."

It was hard to focus on not getting upset when I could hear everything Fallyn and Lauren were saying. The music that played overhead was barely loud enough to buffer their very loud whispers back and forth to each other.

Lauren yells at Fallyn. "Look, please be nice. If you care about my feelings, you will go over there and be cool!"

"No, fuck him! You should be saying fuck him too. We've talked about this. You're supposed to be moving on from him." Fallyn snaps, standing her ground.

"Fallyn, I can't. I love him. Can you please just take it easy on him? For me?"

It gets quiet between them, and Fallyn huffs. I try to disengage from their conversation, adjusting myself in my seat while I look at Jah.

I try to take the energy off myself and change the subject. "Have you even asked her out yet?"

Jah rolls his shoulders in a shrug-like manner as he continues to sip his drink. He smacks his lips together and stares at his drink as if examining the taste. I shook my head at him and his goofiness. I knew he would avoid the question because of how hard-to-get Fallyn acts with him. It bruises his ego.

I lean in and whisper, "You're dodging a bullet, my boy. Fallyn is spicy."

"Nah, she just doesn't like you. She's actually a pretty dope-ass person." Jah disagrees and stands ten toes down for Fallyn. He leans back against the booth, stares at me, then continues, "You and Lauren are the toxic ones. You don't want to admit to yourselves that you're always fighting; now you've broken up, now you're back together. Can't keep up with you. Then you ghost her, and I don't hear from you. Are you spiraling again?"

I look around, lean towards him, and whisper, "I'm not spiraling. It's just—"

"It's just what?" He laces his fingers together in his lap and stares at me, concerned.

"I'm just having vivid dreams again, really vivid dreams."

Jah shrugs off my problems and snarls his lip, "Talk to a doctor, man. I don't know what to tell you."

Lauren and Fallyn walked back over to us, and our conversation ended prematurely. Lauren wrapped her arm around my neck, and I reached around her waist and pulled her close as she stood beside me. Fallyn gave me a look and then sat back next to Jah. She crossed her legs and then smiled big—a huge, fake smile.

"Lauren told me that I had to play nice," Fallyn admitted sarcastically as she rapidly blinked her obnoxiously long lashes.

Lauren gives her a look, "Fallyn..."

Fallyn puts her hands up and sinks into her seat, implying she is done being petty.

The tension subsided, and we ordered some appetizers and more drinks as the night progressed.

The appetizers at Sky Lounge were the best. They were your average starters, like mozzarella sticks and spinach artichoke dip. Those were our staples every time we visited, and we never strayed away.

Lauren eventually ordered her a drink—something fruity, like a mixed drink, which was her go-to. She ordered the Tipsy Train, a mix of tequila and sour simple syrup. Something simple, but able to knock you off your feet if you had too many, which she didn't.

Eventually, as it got later, more people piled into the lounge. A few regulars showed and sat in their normal booths. The DJ spinning the music changed the atmosphere, allowing people to come out of their shells and dance to the beat.

I was in my head the entire night after Jah said what he said. I know he has great intentions, but just going to see a doctor about what I was dealing with was not an option. I didn't want to seem crazy or be put on more medication for something I knew wholeheartedly was real. There was no doubt in my mind now that Imani was real and that I could jump to different timelines. I've been doing this for years, and now that most of my memories have returned, I am positive this was not just a dream world but another reality.

It was around nine thirty at night, and Lauren and I finally left Sky Lounge and returned to my place. Once we entered the apartment, we kicked off our shoes, and I took off my shirt and headed to my bedroom. I tossed my shirt into the laundry basket and then let out a very long, much-needed stretch. I felt Lauren following behind me as I started getting ready for bed.

She leaned against the doorframe and tapped on the door. "Going to bed already?"

I turn to her and watch as she takes her earrings out of her ears and rests them on my dresser.

"Yeah, I'm tired."

Lauren walked up to me and rubbed my back as I faced away from her. "You've been tired a lot lately. Are you sure you're ok?"

I take a deep breath in and then exhale through my mouth.

Should I tell her the truth?

I wanted to tell her everything that had been going on with me. However, I was afraid. Lauren was compassionate and reasonable, but this may take her by surprise—this might be the one thing she'd leave me over.

I turned around and faced her. "I'm fine, I promise."

Another lie.

"I don't believe you." She says softly. "You've been distant, moody, and sleeping a lot. Are we good? Did I do something wrong? Please, talk to me." Her voice trembled with concern.

I wrap my arms around her, pull her close, and kiss her forehead. "I promise it's not you. It's just—you wouldn't understand..."

She pulls away from me and crosses her arms, glaring deep into my eyes. "Don't tell me I wouldn't understand.

You don't know whether I would understand or not. Just tell me."

I look away and take off my watch, putting it on the dresser. I flatten my hands together and put them to my lips, thinking. Maybe there was a way I could tell her while withholding some of the details. If Lauren and I could form a soul tie, perhaps she would understand what I have been experiencing lately. I take her hand, lead her out of the bedroom, and sit on the sofa.

I turned to Lauren as I sat and hesitated. "I believe that you and I will be bound for life, like our souls will tie to each other's for eternity,"

She had a look of shock on her face, and then she frowned at me. "Why do I feel like there's a but?"

"There's no but; that's what I believe. I believe we are bound together in this life, and when we die here, we will meet again in another lifetime."

Lauren smiles and exhales, "You scared me for a second. I thought you were starting to break up with me there."

I laugh and then grab her hands. "Nah, that's the last thing I want to happen. I don't want to break up with you." I pause momentarily and think carefully about what I want to say next.

"I feel like there's still something you're not telling me."

I continued, "You know how there are special people like mediums or people who can connect with spirits, right? Or psychic people?"

Lauren scrunches her face, confused. "Um, yeah. I guess."

"Well, I'm special too."

"What do you see, ghosts?" Her face was perplexed and worried now. I could feel her grip my hands tighter in response to what I was saying.

"Nah, so I can't see ghosts, but I can do things you wouldn't believe possible. I need you not to freak out, and I need you to trust me, Lauren. I want to share everything with you, but I need you to believe me."

Lauren nods and stays completely silent. She allows me to continue talking uninterrupted.

So I continue, "So when I go to sleep, I have these vivid dreams. They're so real, and I never understood why that was. But what if I told you that dreams can be real experiences?"

"What do you mean by real experiences?" Lauren asked as she shifted her body on the sofa, visibly uncomfortable.

"Meaning, when you dream about specific experiences, they are real. You can control your dreams and jump to different past, future, and current lifetimes.

She looks at me, confused. So, I explained to Lauren that dreams weren't just dreams but portals to another life.

As we sat in the living room, I told her about my journeys to Troterion and my ancient soul. For the next hour, I laid everything bare—my ability to jump between worlds, how I forgot all my memories, and even telling her my soul's name. I explained to her what soul ties were and the invisible tethered string that bound us to other people. There was excitement in my voice, but it was also shaky and uneasy, reflecting my nervousness about admitting this to Lauren. Admitting all of this felt like walking a tightrope between trust and fear. However, Lauren never spoke a single word. She just listened and let me get everything out into the open. This secret had been a boulder pressing against my chest, and now, with every word, the weight slowly lifted. The one thing I did not mention was Imani. I did not have the heart to bring her up just yet. After I stopped talking, I breathed deeply and exhaled through my mouth for a minute. The silence was loud, and Lauren stared at me. She pushed her hair out of her face, then reached forward and cupped my face.

Lauren looked deep into my eyes and smiled. "Thank you for sharing all of this with me. I love you."

I smile and rest my head in her hand, closing my eyes. I hear her scoot closer as she lets go of my face, and then her arms wrap around my waist. She holds me tight, and we stay in this embrace for a while. It was as if our souls in that moment connected beyond our timeline, tying a knot like a sacred thread only we could feel. The relief felt empowering—I was free from the shackles, the burden of keeping this secret, which I had internalized and caused havoc within my mind.

Finally, Lauren breaks our embrace and the silence. She clears her throat and asks, "So, how do you do it?"

I lay back against the sofa and think for a bit. It was harder to explain that question because not everyone can jump through time and space or shift to a different dimension. At least not as seamlessly as Imani and I can. Even for me, it was not easy until Imani taught me how to clear my mind. She taught me breathing exercises and how to open my third eye and crown chakra. I explained this to Lauren without disclosing Imani, and she seemed interested. I couldn't tell if it was out of concern or pure fascination.

Once again, it became quiet between us. So, I broke the silence. "Are you going to run for the hills now?"

She shakes her head slowly and leans against the sofa as she looks at me. "Not at all. You're stuck with me."

"Do you believe me?"

She pauses, lost in thought, rubbing her nose before letting her head fall back against the sofa. Her eyes closed slowly, as if the weight of everything was finally settling in. I watched her, heart pounding, terrified of what she might say next. So far, she'd been calm, understanding, even, but with Lauren, this moment felt different. She was listening, hearing me out, understanding the gravity in my words. So, why did I fear this would be the end of us? That she'd decide something was wrong with me, something she couldn't fix or understand, and walk out the door without looking back.

After her long pause, she finally speaks. "Whether I believe it or not, you're not hurting anyone by jumping to another timeline, and it's hard for me to wrap my brain around it all. It seems impossible. But it's also fascinating."

Lauren scoots closer again. She leans forward, wraps her arms around my neck, and rests her head against my chest. I wrapped my arms around her and squeezed tightly as she showered me in love, and in that moment, it was everything I didn't know I needed.

I craved acceptance from Lauren.

I needed her not to judge me or think I was crazy. There was a very small but imprinted thought deep inside me that felt as though I was crazy, and I needed validation that I wasn't.

Lauren continues to shower me in affirmations: "Just know that I love you, Lanno. You have a beautiful soul, and you're such a good guy. I support you in everything that you do, and I want you to be able to trust me with anything that's on your mind." Lauren runs her fingers up the nape of my neck and scratches my scalp as she drapes her arms around me. We stayed in this embrace for a few minutes.

"I love you, too."

"So, where are you traveling to tonight?" She asks me curiously. I pull away from her and look at the ceiling as I think. I wanted to respond and say to Imani, but I knew I shouldn't.

"Definitely Troterion again."

"Exciting!" Lauren squeals as she rubs my arms. She stands up off the sofa and unbuttons her jeans. "Well, I'm going to get ready for bed. I'm going to take a shower and then go to sleep. Is it okay if I stay tonight?"

"Of course, babe."

She pulls down her jeans and takes them off, holding them as she heads towards the bedroom. I turn back straight against the sofa and let my thoughts take over.

I felt so relieved that Lauren knew what was happening to me. She took our conversation better than I could have ever imagined, and I was super happy about that. Imani began to creep into my mind as I sat on the sofa. I missed her so much. The last time we were together, our connection was overwhelming. Mentally, I was exhausted and ready for sleep. I got up from the couch, headed into the bedroom, and got into bed.

I waited until Lauren exited the shower and joined me in bed. She lies next to me and cuddles close. After a few minutes of scrolling through her phone, she slowly fell asleep, and I was ready to follow. I lay on my back and focused on my breathing exercises. After a while, I could feel my mind shift into a state of peace. I continued to breathe in, hold my breath, and then exhale through my mouth slowly. I could feel myself drifting into sleep, the transition now peaceful, like slipping into the gentle embrace of a warm current.

Chapter 11

It was Friday—seven days later, and I still had not seen Imani.

Today was an important day for Lauren, and I wanted to remain focused on my current timeline and be present with her. Lauren was having a cookout at her place and invited me and all her family to meet for the first time. This morning she woke up earlier than me and took a ride-share back to her home to prepare for everyone's arrival as I slept in. Once I woke, I quickly got ready and left my condo. I got in my truck and headed to Sunrise Grove while thoughts trickled through my mind like the plague. I was nervous—my palms were sweaty as I gripped the steering wheel, and I couldn't focus on one thought. Meeting Lauren's family was a huge milestone for us, and I wanted to take it seriously. I glanced over at the flowers and bottle of wine on the passenger seat cushion and wondered if these sentiments were good enough. I put my eyes back on the road and continued driving.

A forty-five-minute drive to Lauren's home gave me too much time to sit in my head and think about all that could go wrong. The loudness of the music that played to drown out my thoughts was no help at all, and I was happy when I finally arrived. I sat in the truck and texted Lauren.

I'm here, babe.

About three minutes passed, and there was a ding from my phone. I pushed the mirror back in place after checking myself out and grabbed my phone, reading the message from Lauren.

Coming!

I got out of the car and grabbed the flowers and bottle of wine, then stood awkwardly in her driveway full of cars.

Lauren's home was a beautiful one-story home. It was a brown brick home with navy blue trim and sat quietly on a corner lot. Her yard was a nice size, big enough for her, with a cute shed in the backyard. I slowly walked up to the front door when suddenly it opened, and out came Lauren.

"Hey, baby!" She greeted me with pure excitement in her voice. She looked stunning—her naturally curly hair straightened and her face glammed up. She wore a red romper with white sandals to complement the beautiful, sunny spring day.

She wrapped her arms around my waist, and I hugged her back. "Hey, gorgeous."

We stop hugging, and she takes a step back and opens her mouth, more excitement rushing through her as she asks, "Are these for me?"

I smiled and handed her the flowers and the bottle of wine. "Only the best for you, babe."

Lauren takes the gifts and immediately smells the flowers.

"Mmm, these smell amazing, and they're so beautiful, baby. Thank you so much!"

Lauren grabs my hand and walks me through her front door, and there are so many people inside. Kids were playing video games on the living room TV, and there were people in the kitchen talking. We didn't stay in the home but went straight to the backyard.

"I want you to meet my mom and dad first; the rest are just cousins. Oh, and I think my brother is coming too."

"And your dad's name is Gary, and your mom—Allison?" I asked, my voice wavering as nerves crept in by the second.

Lauren laughed and stopped dragging me through the halls of her home, right before we reached the sliding patio door. She adjusted my shirt and wiped it down. I was wearing a beige cotton polo shirt, matching cotton shorts, and white sneakers.

"Yes, or mom and pop." Lauren winked at me, then giggled, "You smell amazing and look so handsome, by the way."

I grin, "Thank you."

She takes my hands and laces her fingers with mine as we proceed out the back door. More people were standing outside, drinking beers, smoking, and having good conversations. We walked up to a table with an umbrella attached to block the sun. An older white woman sat before us with a wine glass, talking to two other women who sat with her.

"Mom, I'd like to introduce you to Lanno. Lanno, this is my mom, Ali." Lauren interrupted the conversation, and now all eyes were on us.

I held out my hand. "It's nice to meet—"

"Oh, come here, darling." I was cut off as her mom stood up and threw her arms around me, giving me the biggest, warmest hug I'd ever had.

I laugh and hug her back tightly.

She continued, "Nice to meet you, sweetie!"

Ali was a sweet, welcoming woman with a head full of naturally ginger-colored hair. She was a short, thicker woman with freckles all over her face.

"It's nice to meet you too, Mama Ali," I greeted back with a permanent smile printed on my face.

Ali reached and pointed at a chair nearby, "Grab that chair and pop a squat."

I turned around and looked at the chair, then grabbed it, pulling it closer to the ladies at the table. I sat down in the chair, and then Lauren sat in my lap, reaching onto the table where a basket of strawberries sat, and took one. Lauren looked at me and smiled as she bit the strawberry.

"So, you're the infamous Lanno that we've heard so much about. I'm glad we're finally getting to meet you. Lauren has been hiding you away."

Lauren looked at her mom and rolled her eyes playfully. "I haven't been hiding him. You all know I never bring guys home. Unless they're super special." Lauren looks back at me and smiles, then turns her attention back towards the other two women who sat with us. "Oh, and these are my aunties. That's Auntie Linda on my dad's side and Auntie Jess on my mom's."

I wave and look at them both. "Nice to meet you, ladies."

They both wave back and give me welcoming smiles.

"Dad's still on the grill?" Lauren asked her mom as she swayed side to side slowly while sitting in my lap.

"You know he is; that man never leaves that grill." Ali scoffed and then looked towards the grill. "Gary! Come meet Lanno; those burgers don't need twenty-four-seven supervision now."

I turned and looked at her dad on the grill. He gestured with his hands to shoo what she was saying away, then put down his grilling tools to come over.

Lauren stands up and touches my shoulder. "I'll be right back; I'm going to put this wine in the fridge to chill."

I nodded, then my anxiety flared up as I noticed Gary getting closer to our table. As soon as he approached the table, I stood up and held out my hand.

Gary dapped me up and pulled me in, patting me on my back in a swift gesture. He was an average-height man, whom I towered over. He had a muscular build and was completely bald with a very thick beard.

"This Lanno?" He said out loud.

Ali replied, "Yes, this is Lanno, Lauren's boyfriend!"

"Nice to meet you, Gary," I greeted.

Gary grabbed hold of my shoulder and then pushed me back down into the seat. "Sit, sit. Would you like something to drink? Lemonade, beer, or whiskey?"

"Oh, I'll take a beer; it looks like you all are drinking the good stuff." I sat back down in the chair and leaned back to relax.

Gary goes to the cooler and grabs two beers. He comes back and hands me one, then cracks his open and drinks from the bottle. I twisted the cap off the beer and drank some as everybody stared at me.

"So, tell us how you and Lauren met," Ali playfully slurred as she nudged me.

I told everyone how Lauren and I met through her school and my job's career day campaign for the community. Painting a picture of how mesmerized I was when I first saw Lauren, thinking to myself... I must know her name. We talked about our first date, how I took her to see a play from her favorite book, and how immersed I became in theater life from just one night. Everyone at the table had so many questions for me and Lauren. When she finally returned, she shut it down and told everyone to stop grilling me. It was lighthearted, but everyone did eventually ease up, and the conversation turned more into getting to know me.

Turns out, I was nervous about nothing. Her family welcomed me with open arms, warm smiles, and genuine interest in our relationship. They made me feel like I belonged from the moment I walked through the door. Her dad was a character—full of charm and energy, constantly cracking jokes with his wife and sisters, and playfully chasing the kids around the house. He had a vibrant spirit, the kind of presence that filled a room and made everyone feel at ease.

Ali was a true hopeless romantic, the kind of person who lit up at the mention of love stories and emotional reunions. She was utterly captivated by the tales of our adventures—hanging on every word with wide-eyed wonder and the occasional dramatic gasp. After asking me a question, she'd often turn to Gary with a playful grin and say, "Take notes!" causing everyone to laugh. Her charm was effortless, and her teasing came from a place of warmth and joy.

Throughout our conversation, Ali kept glancing over at the bouquet I had bought for Lauren. She complimented the flowers several times, admiring their color and arrangement with the appreciation of someone who genuinely loved beautiful things. Every so often, she'd lean in to smell them, closing her eyes with a soft smile as if their fragrance transported her somewhere peaceful.

When Lauren's brother Amir arrived, I greeted him and was welcomed with open arms by him as well. He was an average-height, gay man who wore a sleeveless graphic t-shirt, black joggers, and sneakers. Draped across his body was a satchel, and he had a septum piercing. Amir had the same complexion as Lauren. However, his hair was more ginger like their mom's, but he bore no freckles. His hair was as messy and thick as my hair, pointing in every direction but straight. In his mouth were retainers, which gave him a cute lisp. Amir also brought his boyfriend, David, and eventually Lauren and I left Ali's table and sat with them.

"You all are so cute or whatever," Amir admitted as we sat down at the table. Once again, I'm in the chair, and Lauren is in my lap. I wrapped my arms around her and laughed at his comment.

"Thank you," I responded. "You and David are cute too. How long have you both been together?"

"Two years and I'm still waiting for a ring!" Amir held up his hand very expressively and pointed at his ring finger, then looked at David.

David rolled his eyes and then looked at us. "It's coming; he's just being a brat."

David was Asian and had short black hair. He was wearing a black shirt and denim shorts. David had tons of tattoos all over his body and gauged ears. Ironically, he had no other piercings.

"You know what," Amir paused and then looked at me and Lauren, "we should go on a double date. That would be so fun!"

"Do people still double date?" David asked as he made a face while looking at Amir. Lauren laughed under her breath, and I looked at her as I tried to refrain from laughing as well.

"Yes, people still double date, David!" Amir snapped back, very sassy.

"Lil bro, nobody double dates anymore." Lauren finally chimed in as she let out a chuckle.

Amir looked at Lauren, and his jaw dropped open, for a moment looking surprised before closing it and speaking again, "Well, I don't care if people don't double date. We will be corny and do it."

"I think it's a good idea." I agreed with Amir.

Lauren looked at me and grabbed my jaw playfully. "You don't have to suck up to my baby bro for him to like you."

I attempt to bite her hand playfully, and she pulls away while laughing. "I'm not; I just think it would be nice."

"It will!" Amir added.

We all agreed to go on a double date to make Amir happy.

While we waited for the food to be done, I quietly observed my surroundings, taking in all the festivities. Lauren's younger cousins were running around, squirting each other with water guns. Her aunties decided to get up and teach anyone who would learn how to line dance. The music was nostalgic—all the tunes I grew up hearing my mom listen to blended into a hijacked playlist from Amir.

An hour would pass, and the food was finally ready, so it was time to dig in and make a plate. Lauren fixed my plate, getting me a nice serving of everything that was cooked so that I could taste her family's recipes. Even her auntie came over to check in on me to make sure the potato salad was good because she "put her foot in it."

Gary did his thing on the grill, making sure the ribs and chicken were perfectly charred, seasoned, and sauced. There were sausages, hot dogs, and hamburgers, and the sides, I admit, were the best part—from the grilled corn to the deviled eggs and greens, everything tasted delicious.

As the house gradually emptied, the energy shifted from lively to calm, settling into a peaceful rhythm. Her mom and dad stayed behind to help with the cleanup, working seamlessly as a team. Her dad collected empty glasses and napkins with playful commentary while her mom wiped down counters, pausing every now and then to chat or offer a knowing smile. It was clear this wasn't just routine for them—it was love in action, the kind that shows up in small, thoughtful gestures.

Watching them move around together, supporting their daughter without hesitation, made the moment feel even more special. There was a quiet beauty in the simplicity of it all—the kind of family dynamic that wrapped around you like a warm blanket and reminded you what real support looked like.

Lauren's family loved her, and I loved that for her. Throughout the day, I often envied her family and its size because my family was small. As the only child of an only child, my mother and I shared an incredibly close bond. Even though our family was small, it was wrapped in warmth and love, creating a world that felt intimate and deeply connected. It was just the two of us, but the depth of our relationship made it feel full and complete.

The house was clear, and finally it was just me and Lauren, sitting in her living room, cuddled up on the sofa. She had changed out of her romper into something more comfortable—a t-shirt and boy shorts.

"So, did you enjoy today?" Lauren asked me, her legs draped on my legs as she sat on the sofa sideways, and I sat facing forward.

I looked at her and smiled, "I did; I had a good time."

Lauren played with my curls and smiled at me. "Thank you for meeting my family. It means a lot to me. I could tell you were nervous, but you did it."

I tilted my head towards her, pressing into her hand more as she began to scratch my scalp. "I'd do anything for you. This was a piece of cake."

"Uh-huh," she smirked and gave me a look.

I laughed, "Okay, okay, so I was a little nervous. But your family made it really easy for me to get comfortable. I was fearing your dad would shake me down or something."

Lauren laughed and let her head fall back. "Oh no, my dad is a big goofball, and he knows I'm a good judge of character. He trusts me." I rub Lauren's thighs as she speaks, and I listen to her. "It was a good little get-together."

I nod and then sink into the couch, getting comfortable.

"So, when do I get to meet your mom?" Lauren asked, her eyes sparkling with curiosity and a hint of playful anticipation. "And your dad, you never really talk about him."

"Hmm," I stated, gripping her thigh as I thought carefully about how I wanted to reply, knowing she was on the edge of her seat, waiting for my response. "You can meet my mom whenever you want to. She works a lot at the hospital. So, when she's free, maybe we can have dinner.

As for my dad, he left when I was a kid. I don't know him or his whereabouts."

Lauren placed her hand over her heart. "Aww, I'd love dinner with Mom, babe."

I took out my phone and pulled up my mom's contact. I showed Lauren the phone as I texted her.

Hey, Ma, we should have dinner soon. I'd like for you to meet Lauren.

"And send," I pressed the send button on my phone and then looked at Lauren, who was glowing and blushing.

She leaned forward and pressed her lips into mine, giving me a deep, passionate kiss. I kissed her back and pulled her closer to me on the sofa.

Lauren pulled away from me quickly. "Oh! We should go to the beach tomorrow. The weather is supposed to be even hotter than today."

"Hey, I'm always down for the beach."

Lauren takes out her phone. "He wants a double date; let's do a double beach date." She texts her brother to see if he wants to go to the beach, and he instantly responds that he is down if he doesn't have to drive.

I read the text and laughed, "I'll drive us; that's fine."

Lauren texted him back that I was cool to drive, and he responded that both he and David were down. Lauren jumped out of my lap and ran into her bedroom. I shook my head and laughed, then stood up and followed her. Her room was cozy, like the rest of her home. Her room had matching white décor throughout it. Her dressers and nightstands were white, and she had a perfectly sized queen mattress with an oversized, fluffy, off-white comforter set. On her bed were so many pillows that they took up most of her bed space. There were multiple windows in her room, allowing for the perfect amount of natural light to creep between the shades. She had art hung up, and there was one specific painting that was her favorite, which was of the different cycles of the moon above her bed. Underneath her bed was a white shag carpet that gave a nice pop against her dark brown wooden floors.

Her room smelled just like her—warm and inviting, coconut and citrus. Lauren was in her dresser drawers, taking out her bathing suit.

She held up two and looked at me. "Which one?"

I easily pointed to the leopard one, and she gave me a devilish grin. I approached Lauren, grabbed her hand, and pulled her towards the bed as I sat down on the edge. Lauren stood between my legs, my arms wrapped around her waist, her aura immediately intensifying. I looked into her eyes, and then she reached forward and cupped my cheeks with both of her hands. She leaned in and pressed her lips against mine firmly, and I kissed her back deeply.

Our kisses weren't just love affirmations but raw, passionate, and nasty. We wanted to devour each other whenever we would be intimate; it was a powerful feeling, one I've never felt outside of Imani until now.

My hands lowered from around her waist, and I grabbed a handful of her ass as I pulled her into me deeper. Lauren laughed, then kissed and sucked all over my lips, adding tongue every now and then to allow us to taste each other. The room slowly began to illuminate as our passion grew more intense between us. Swiftly and with ease, Lauren pressed her hand against my chest and pushed me back to lie against the bed. She climbed over top of me and straddled my hips, not allowing a moment to go to waste. She leaned down and pressed her lips back into mine. Her aura, now heavy, undeniably fueled with love, was activated and pulsating around her—a beautiful red glow against my blue. This red was magnificent—blazing with fire, warm and dangerous yet inviting, welcoming me into her inner soul. It was as if this red was only meant for me, and everyone else would approach with caution.

I pulled Lauren back to look at her, to see her, to admire her. It was breathtaking—being able to see her red aura for the very first time, blending with my blue aura and creating this vibrant purple where our energies mended. A powerful energy surged from us, leaving my eyes glistening just from the sight of it all, witnessing such purity and really seeing her for all that she was. She smiled at me and then blushed deeply just from my gaze, enhancing the already red energy around her.

"I love you, Lauren."

As if she couldn't get any redder, she did. Her face then buried itself into my shoulder, and she exhaled deeply into my shirt. I chuckled and then waited for a response from her.

Muffled into my shirt, she mumbled. "I love you more."

I play with the strands of her hair with one hand, while the other hand rubs her back gently.

"Yeah, how much do you love me?" I asked her.

It was quiet between us briefly as she thought about what she wanted to say and how to respond to my question. I kissed the side of her head, and then Lauren pulled away and looked me in my eyes. Her gorgeous, brown eyes glistened.

"Hmm, I love you more than love itself." She leaned down and pressed her lips into mine again and kissed me gently. It was a different kind of kiss, not as hungry as before, but gentler and more passionate.

I continued to run my fingers against her back as we kissed. Her body felt good lying against mine, and I wanted to stay in this moment forever with her. My fingers went from playing with her tiny hair strands to grazing through her hair, raking against her scalp, and then grabbing a handful of her hair.

Lauren pulled away from me and raised her eyebrow. "Oh?"

I smirked and then pulled her head back slightly and to the side as I moved my lips to her neck and sucked against it gently. Lauren's body seized up as she let out a soft whimper, her hips sinking onto me even deeper, trying to get a rise out of me as I did her. I sucked harder, then carefully sunk my teeth into her skin, not to break skin, but to break her.

"You're asking for trouble, mister," Lauren warned me, her voice low and sultry.

I chuckled evilly, "I like trouble."

I removed my lips from her neck and looked at her again, noticing a small mark against her delicate, light skin. Lauren sits up in my lap and then grabs the hem of her shirt, pulling it over her head and tossing it off the bed. I sit up as well and take off my shirt, then she pushes me back against the bed onto my back.

"Don't start something you can't finish, Lanno."

"Trust me, I can finish it." I shot back at her confidently.

Lauren grabs both my hands and laces her fingers with them. She adjusted herself on top of me and rolled her hips gently. "Finish it then."

In response to what she said, in one swift movement, I let go of her hands, grabbed her, and rotated myself from under her, pinning her against the bed while I was on top of her. Lauren let out a deep sigh and then bit her bottom lip. I grabbed her wrists and pulled her hands above her head, making sure she was barely able to move underneath me. Her legs wrap around my waist, and I go in for a kiss. Our lips intertwine with one another, my fingers rolling down her palm, then back up as I lace my fingers with hers. She tugged on my bottom lip, then sucked on it. It was a whirlwind of emotions explosively igniting between us. Her chest rose and fell against mine as her breathing deepened with mine. I kneeled up and unwrapped her legs from around me, spreading them as I stayed securely between them. I grabbed the hem of her shorts and pulled them off her hips and down her legs, eager to undress her, to see her exposed body before me. She was completely naked now, and I needed to match her vulnerable state, so I took off my shorts and boxers. Lauren's hands moved to my chest, her warm palms rubbed firmly against my skin, and her fingers touched the contour of my muscles.

I rested my body back against hers, completely bare, ready to please her in every way. Naturally, her arms folded around my neck and welcomed me. Her chest pressed deeply against me, warming me and arousing all of my senses. It was electrifying how badly I wanted her—a hungry, charged feeling coursing through me.

I wanted to taste her.

My body quickly lowered itself to her midsection and kissed her belly, gently and delicately. Her fingers rolled through my hair, scratching my scalp, then gently gripping a handful. Once I reached her sweet spot, her back immediately arched beneath me uncontrollably, and her hand tightened in my hair.

As I devoured her, pleasing her first, she wiggled under me but did not dare to stop me. She loved every second of it—moaning, panting, and releasing soft whimpers from her lips every move I made with my tongue or fingers. I stayed in this position for a while, making sure I took care of her as eagerly as she was always willing to take care of me. Until she was ready to erupt beneath me, I went at a steady pace.

"Hold it." I coached her, even though I knew she was on the brink of an orgasm.

I flipped her over onto her knees and grabbed her hips, pushing her face into the pillows. Lauren was breathing deeply, cursing under her breath, and gripping the sheets, awaiting what was about to come.

Thoroughly aroused, I entered her temple and showed her just how much I wanted her, how much trouble I truly was. The room exploded around us as we went at it for hours on end. I turned Lauren every which way I possibly could. Coaching her through her orgasms, then, when they came rippling through, telling her how much of a good girl she was. She loved the aggressive, demanding, yet attentive teasing I engulfed her in. She basked in the dominant attention.

We were sweaty, out of breath, and exhausted when we finally finished later that night. We lie in bed breathing deeply, caressing each other. Eventually, Lauren got up and used the bathroom, then came back and lay in my arms, cuddling up close to me.

Out of breath, I spoke. "So, we can go to my place in the morning so I can pack a few things for the beach."

Lauren nodded and closed her eyes, and I knew she would fall asleep at any moment. I was tired as well and would be following her soon. While I was lying there, allowing sleep to consume me, I thought about where I was going to jump tonight. I didn't plan on jumping to Imani but instead to Troterion to explore more.

A part of me was afraid to see Imani again—fearful because of the promise I made to myself the last time we were together. Our connection was so powerful, so overwhelming, that it left me craving her in ways I couldn't control. The intensity between us wasn't just emotional; it was magnetic, consuming.

Yes, I was in love with two women. And yes, one of them existed in an entirely different timeline—but that didn't ease the guilt. No matter how I tried to justify it, I still felt like I was sneaking around behind Lauren's back. The weight of it all pressed on me—torn between the love I had in my current world and the love that never really left me in the other.

Chapter 12

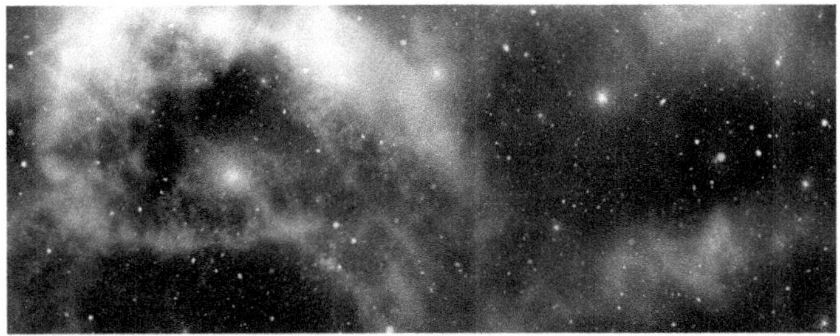

My alarm sounded off early in the morning, and I rolled over in Lauren's bed to silence it. It was time for us both to get up and head over to my place so that I could pack my beach bag. I stretched and then shook Lauren gently to wake her up so that we could leave. Lauren groaned and then looked at me with her adorable sleepy eyes. I kissed her on her nose and then got out of bed. As I got dressed, she finally sat up in bed and yawned. The curtains weren't all the way closed in her bedroom, so the sunrise cast a warm, bright light across the bed and onto the floor, creating beautiful shadows. I got dressed and then grabbed her beach backpack so that I could put it in my truck. Once I loaded the truck, I came back into the house and grabbed my wallet, sliding it into my shorts. Lauren had finally gotten out of bed and dressed.

"Whose idea was this?" Lauren asked as she shifted her body unwillingly through her bedroom and into the bathroom.

I laughed and scrolled on my phone, "It was yours, babe."

After we were both finished getting ready, we piled into my truck and headed to my apartment. Upon arrival, we both got out and headed to the twentieth floor. We entered the apartment, and I walked into my bedroom to get my things together for the beach, while Lauren went into the kitchen to grab snacks and make sandwiches to pack in the cooler.

I changed into something more suitable for the beach and matched Lauren's attire. She was wearing denim shorts and a crop top with sandals over her leopard bikini. Her hair was up in a messy bun, and she had shades tucked into her roots. I figured I'd wear some shorts as well, over my swimming trunks, a sleeveless tank, and slides.

I grabbed my shades and duffel bag and exited the room. "Are Amir and David ready to go?"

Lauren looked up from her phone and gave me a worried face.

I dropped my duffle bag and tilted my head. "What happened now?"

"I invited Fallyn; she's coming."

I sighed and scratched my head. "Fine, I'm inviting Jah then." I pulled my phone out of my pocket and texted Jah.

Beach trip, let's goooo!

There was a ding, and Jah texted back.

Bet, Woodhaven Beach?

I texted him back, yes, and then locked my phone. I shrugged and walked up to Lauren. "Jah's coming too."

Lauren laughed and then stood up from the kitchen barstool and wrapped her arms around my waist. "I should play a little matchmaking today!"

"I'm sure Jah wouldn't mind. Fallyn, though, she's going to kick your ass."

Lauren laughed and finished packing up our lunch, placing the rest of the snacks into the cooler. "Let's go grab Amir and David and hit the road."

Lauren and I left the apartment building and made our way to her parents' home to pick up Amir and David. Ali and Gary lived in Sunrise Grove as well, so I headed there, and Lauren gave me directions as we got closer. Once we arrived, I parked in the driveway, and Lauren texted Amir for them to come outside. As we waited, Ali came rushing outside, not to see Lauren, but to see me. I got out of the car and smiled as she rushed up to me and hugged me.

I hugged her back. "Hi, Mama Ali. How are you?"

"Oh, I'm good, honey; nice to see you again."

I looked back at Lauren, who sat in the car with a grin on her face and the earpiece of her glasses between her lips as she twirled her shades. She was eating up every part of her mom accepting and welcoming me.

Ali left my side of the truck and walked over to Lauren. I got back into the vehicle as they talked and put my seatbelt back on. Shortly after, Amir and David emerged from the house and walked to the back of the truck so that they could put all their stuff in. I popped the trunk, and they packed everything in. Then, they got into the car, and Amir immediately asked to control the radio.

"If I'm going to survive this two-hour trip, I need good music." Amir vented as he leaned towards the front seat and connected his phone to my car.

Lauren's mom backed away from the car and waved as I put it in reverse and looked in my rearview mirror at Amir.

"You're the DJ, I trust you've got this." I joked with him.

Amir nodded, "I got you. I got you."

Lauren waved at her mom as we drove away and made our way to Woodhaven Beach. As we drove, Amir proved himself worthy of being DJ, playing all the latest hits and then switching it over to a playlist that was completely a vibe. After a few hours, we finally made it and parked right on the coastline. The beach had a lot of attractions—hotels, restaurants, and there was even a carnival in town. From where we parked on the beach, you could see the Ferris wheel rotating with distant screams from other carnival rides. We all got out of the car and went to the trunk to unpack and grab everything.

Lauren handed me my phone as I stood behind the truck. "Jah texted you that he's pulling up in about ten minutes, and Fallyn said her ETA is thirty."

I took my phone and put it in my pocket. "Bet, we can set up down there." I pointed to an empty part of the beach. Since it was around noon, the beach wasn't as full yet. Everyone grabbed their belongings out of the car, and we walked across the beach to the perfect spot in the sand. Lauren threw down her bag and then crouched down, unzipping it. She pulled out a nice-sized blanket and then laid it out on the sand. Amir and David also had a blanket, which they placed next to ours, and sat down as well, getting comfortable.

I set the cooler down in the sand, right on the corner of the blanket, so that the blanket would not fly away.

"I don't know what she packed in there, but help your-self to it." I offered it to Amir and David.

Lauren sat down on the blanket and looked back at me. "You had so much food in your pantry and fridge, it's a picnic at this point."

"What can I say? I like food." I sat down next to Lauren and then lay on my back. "Ah, the sun feels so good, and the breeze is even more amazing."

"Yeah, it's so nice out, and it's not even as hot as it's going to be today yet," David mentioned, joining in on the conversation as he put his shades on.

Lauren nudges me and hands me a bottle of SPF to put on her and myself as well. I grab the bottle and open it as she sits next to me. She takes off her crop top and leans over to reach for her bag to put it inside. I made sure I got her back and all the areas she couldn't reach, and then she did the same for me once I took off my shirt.

I lay back down on the blanket and rest my arms behind my head. A few minutes passed, and I received a ding on my phone. I took my phone out of my shorts and noticed it was Jah saying that he had arrived. I instructed him on where to park, then gave him our location on the beach, and minutes later, Jah walked up to us.

"Yo bro, sup man." He crouches down and daps me up, then leans over and hugs Lauren.

Lauren, with her water bottle in her hand, points to her brother, "Hey Jah, this is my brother Amir and his boyfriend David, and you two, this is Jah, Lanno's boy."

Jah nodded his head at Amir and David, and they both returned welcoming gestures to Jah.

He then looked around and stood back up, twisting the cap off his water bottle and drinking it. "So, where's your friend Fallyn?"

Lauren laughed and looked at me, and I looked up at Jah, shaking my head.

"She's on her way and should be here any moment, actually," Lauren told Jah, and he lit up with excitement.

Jah had black swimming trunks and sandals with a black tank top, and he stood next to us. It looked as though he didn't bring a blanket.

I gestured for him to sit down. "You can sit on our blanket, man. C'mon, sit down."

"Oh, nah, I'm good." He looked around more and awkwardly stood there. I knew he was waiting for Fallyn, and he didn't want to admit it.

Jah stood there until Fallyn arrived and joined us on the beach. She was carrying two heavy bags, and he rushed over to her and grabbed them. He set them down next to the cooler, and Lauren stood up to greet Fallyn.

"Hey girl!" Lauren yelled as she hugged her. I sat up and watched as Jah pulled a blanket out of Fallyn's bag and spread it out onto the sand. He then went to the other bag and showed me a bottle of alcohol Fallyn snuck onto the beach before putting it back into the bag. I grinned at him, and he gave me a smirk back in secret.

"Hey Fallyn," Amir greeted her with a lazy wave, lying comfortably on his stomach as he soaked up the sun's warm rays. David followed suit, lifting a hand in acknowledgment. Fallyn smiled and waved back at them both. Nearby, Amir had a small speaker playing mellow tunes, the music drifting through the air as they lounged, creating the perfect soundtrack for a day at the beach.

"Hey, everyone!" Fallyn greeted everyone back and then sat on her blanket. Jah immediately sat down with her and scooted close. "Jah, can you hand me that bottle and some of those plastic shot cups?"

Fallyn was wearing a black sarong around her waist and a black two-piece set. As soon as Jah handed her the bottle, she hid it between her thighs and then placed her bag over it. I observed her as she dug through her purse and took out a container full of pre-rolls. She handed one to Jah, and he quickly lit it and started smoking.

She looked at me and Lauren. "Who wants a shot?"

I raised my hand and one of my eyebrows.

"I will absolutely take one," Lauren said with a grin as she leaned on me a bit to get closer to Fallyn, who was on the other side of me.

Fallyn began pouring shots for everyone, and soon after, the joint made its way into rotation. What started as a casual hangout quickly turned into a much-needed session of release and connection—we drank, smoked, and sang freely as the music washed over us, vibrating through our bodies like a second heartbeat. Laughter echoed, voices harmonized, and for a while, nothing else mattered.

Once the last shot was downed, we all jumped up, full of adrenaline and joy, and sprinted toward the water. The hot sand between my toes made my sensory system burst, sending signals all throughout my body. The waves crashing into each other as I approached the water were music to my ears. And the sun—warming, inviting, beating down on my melanated skin, creating a glow that vibrates around me.

The alcohol had us buzzing, loose, and light, while the weed kept us grounded—just enough to keep us from getting too wild.

When we entered, the water shocked us all. It was cold enough to make us all freeze up, but refreshing once we finally got all the way in. Cooling down the heat from our sun-stained backs and washing away the sand from crevices we didn't even know we had. I would float on my back and allow the waves to carry me as I looked up at the sky—I felt free.

Lauren and I were the first to head back to our blanket on the beach after we spent a while splashing around in the water. Next, Jah and Fallyn joined us as Amir and David went for a walk on the beach. We sat on the blanket, drying off, wrapped in our towels. Lauren went into the cooler and grabbed the bag of sandwiches, then sat between my legs.

"I have the munchies like crazy," she admitted as she opened the bag, took out a sandwich, and bit into it.

Fallyn reached for the bag, and Lauren handed it over. "I will take one of those, thank you."

She took one out and began to eat as Jah looked at her. Lauren and I both looked at each other and grinned.

"So, when are you two finally going to go on your first date?" Lauren cut through the awkwardness and asked a question we all wanted to know.

"Girl," Fallyn responded, mid-chew. "He has to get rid of all those hoes for me to take him seriously."

Jah's facial expression changes as if he didn't know what she was talking about. "Hoes? I don't have any of those." I shook my head, laughed, and then Jah looked at me. "Tell her, bro, I don't know what she's talking about."

Everybody looked at me, and I got anxious. "Wait, why am I being dragged into this?" I laughed and then rubbed the back of my neck awkwardly.

"See, Lanno can't even lie for his best friend." Fallyn laughed and took another bite of her sandwich.

Jah grabbed the bag from Fallyn and took out a sandwich for himself. He aggressively chewed the sandwich while staring Fallyn down, and it made me laugh even more.

"Oh, you know what we should do?" Lauren piped up with excitement. "There's a carnival within walking distance. We should go!"

"I'm down," I responded, putting my shades on and lying back down. "Just need to wait 'til David and Amir get back."

Fallyn took out another joint and lit it. "That sounds like fun."

Jah grabbed the bottle of alcohol, and instead of pouring it into a shot cup, he just tilted his head back and took some straight from the bottle.

"Whew! That was spicy!" He yelled as he swallowed the shot and made a face.

Thirty minutes later, Amir and David returned, and we told them of our plans to go to the carnival. They were both down, so we packed up all our beach stuff, loaded the car up, and made our way towards the carnival on foot. The Woodhaven Strip was a paradise for tourists—lively, colorful, and full of charm. The streets were lined with shops selling saltwater taffy, surfboards, and custom T-shirts proudly stamped with Welcome to Woodhaven. Beachfront hotels dotted the coast, each surrounded by outdoor festivities, busy patios, and lively music.

The area was designed for ease and enjoyment, with pedestrian and bike-only lanes making it perfect for a relaxed stroll or a scenic ride. Toy outlets with quirky, nostalgic treasures sat alongside an impressive variety of seafood spots, each offering fresh catches and oceanfront views. It was a vibrant hub where beach-town charm met endless summer energy.

We almost were distracted as we strolled along the scenic route to the carnival by all the different shops we could enter and explore. However, we finally made it there after a fifteen-minute walk.

As soon as we entered, Lauren's eyes widened with awe as she noticed a ginormous stuffed plushy moon. She loved the moon and everything in space. I had to win it for her, so we stopped, and I popped some balloons with darts. Luckily for me, I had a pretty good aim and ended up winning her the prize.

Jah noticed Fallyn eyeballing a tiger cub plushie, so he decided to play a water gun game to win it for her. She was happy and pushed him playfully when he handed over the tiger cub that he had won. Their body language towards each other was a sight to see, wrapped in each other's charm, they bumped into each other occasionally. It seemed Jah's gesture was loosening Fallyn up in ways I had never seen before. The tough love was still present—she would put distance between them or distract herself by talking to Lauren. Jah was persistent, though, and continued to close the gap. After we played a few games, we made our way over to the Ferris wheel.

"I am not getting on that thing; y'all have fun," Amir, very frightened, said as he backed away from the entrance to get on the ride.

"Amir, don't be a wuss." Fallyn challenged playfully.

Amir rolled his eyes and then sucked his teeth. "I'm good; you all can go." He waved his hands to rush us through the gate as he stayed behind with David. "David has to win me a giant bear anyway."

Lauren and I got into our seats, and Jah and Fallyn went into another car. We had our section, and they had theirs. Lauren sat across from me, and I held my hands out so she could place hers into mine. I held her hands tightly and stared into her eyes. The Ferris wheel started, and soon we were going around and up to the top.

"Thank you for bringing me to the beach, babe, and the carnival. Oh, and thank you for the Croissant." Lauren gripped my hand as she spoke.

I squinted at her. "Croissant?"

"Yes, my moon. I've named her Croissant. Because she's a crescent moon... duh." She laughed as she looked at her giant plushie next to her. "Get it?"

I shook my head and laughed at her, "That's cute... corny, but cute."

Lauren and I both leaned in and kissed. It was a picturesque moment between the two of us, so I took out my phone and snapped a picture of us. We did a few cute and goofy poses together as the Ferris wheel began its descent. After the ride, we walked around the carnival, played more games, and got a funnel cake.

We met back up with David and Amir, who had his teddy bear plushie. There was a mirror maze, and we all smoked before going through it, which was the dumbest thing we could have ever done, but also it was the most fun we had during this trip. We laughed so hard as we bumped into dead ends and couldn't find our way out. Luckily, we conquered the mirrors and reached the end.

We spent some time enjoying the carnival before heading out to explore the outlet shops. As the sun began to set, a cool breeze rolled in, gradually cutting through the warmth of the day. The chill in the air grew stronger, and soon enough, everyone started to feel the cold, bringing our shopping trip to an early close. We quickly made our way back to the cars, hugged each other goodbye as we piled into our vehicles, and went our separate ways. The drive back was a lot quieter than the drive to the beach. Amir, the DJ, and David fell asleep, leaving me and Lauren to keep each other company. Lauren would rub my thigh or my arm to keep me awake and talk to me here and there. We finally made it back to Sunrise Grove and dropped off Amir and David at Ali's.

I looked at Lauren as they exited the car and took their belongings out of the trunk. "Did you want to come back to my place tonight?"

Lauren nodded, "Mhm."

I scrolled on my phone as Amir and David retrieved their belongings from the trunk. I noticed a text from my mother, and she responded that she was thrilled to meet Lauren.

I leaned over to Lauren and smiled, "My mom is inviting us over for Sunday dinner."

Lauren's face lit up with excitement. "Tomorrow?!"

"Yes, tomorrow," I responded.

"I'm so excited to meet her, babe!"

Once Amir and David were finished getting their things, they both waved goodbye and went inside the house. Lauren and I drove back to my place and quickly took the elevator to my apartment so we could get some rest, since it was late.

Lauren undressed as soon as we entered the apartment, she took a shower, and then she got comfortable in bed. I took my shower next and then joined her in bed. We were both beat, and it didn't take long for both Lauren and me to fall asleep as soon as our heads hit the pillow.

Chapter 13

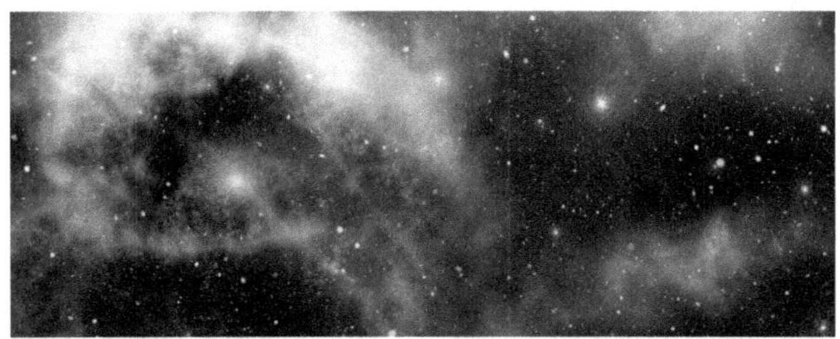

It was Sunday morning, and as I got ready to head out, I thought to myself, I've never brought another woman home to meet my mother; for me, this was a big deal. I rejoiced in my mother's enthusiasm as the day progressed, and she continued to send me text messages.

I got this beautiful centerpiece. Do you think Lauren would like it?

Is Lauren allergic to anything?

I hope Lauren likes shrimp.

Her numerous texts were cute. I could tell she was nervous and trying to prepare herself to meet Lauren. It was almost noon, and Lauren was still sleeping. I needed to run a few errands before we got ready to head to my mom's home. After I finished dressing, I allowed Lauren to rest while I left my condo and headed to our local farmers' market. Libbie Market was located right outside the Holiware Square strip, which added a bit of warmth to the glitz and glamour. My mom loved when I got her fresh fruits and vegetables, so I wanted to surprise her with a nice basket of different varieties. I decided to walk, since it was a beautiful day outside—the weather was hot, without a cloud in the sky. I wore some shorts and a t-shirt with black sneakers. I decided to wear a baseball cap today and paired it with my side satchel as an accessory. As I walked down the street, I passed by a new upscale tattoo parlor that looked to have recently opened. I glanced inside, and to my surprise, I saw Fallyn. Fallyn took one look at me and smiled. The expression on my face was shocked and taken aback as I walked into the parlor with its doors wide open, welcoming all.

The inside of the parlor was exquisite—with brand-new marbled and polished floors and huge vanity mirrors decked out on every wall. There were seats for multiple artists to tattoo their clients, and artwork spread throughout the enormous space. Caterers were serving refreshments, and there was a DJ in the front spinning tunes. Not many people were in the parlor, as it looked as if it were a small event, but it was still lively.

I walked up to Fallyn. "Hey, what are you doing here?"

Fallyn, with a blow-pop in her mouth, raised her eyebrow and laughed. "It's my friend Marco's opening day, and I wanted to come support him."

I nodded my head slowly at her and then looked around the shop. It was inviting; the aroma was scented like fresh soap and paint. Everything was pristine, clean, and had a new and expensive appeal. I looked back at Fallyn, and she was staring me down, so I instantly got nervous.

I cleared my throat. "That's wassup; congrats to him, he has a beautiful shop."

"Uh huh." Fallyn continued to look at me blankly as she sucked on her lollipop. "So, where's Lauren?"

"She is back at my place, sleeping."

"I figured. I tried texting her this morning to come, but... she never replied."

"I was actually on my way to the market to get my mom some things. Lauren is meeting her tonight." I involuntarily admitted to Fallyn.

Fallyn's face lit up, and she looked surprised. "Oh, really? I bet you're nervous, huh?"

"Nah, nah." I lie, nervously gesturing my hands around and then reaching to the back of my neck to rub it.

"Yeah, right!" Fallyn laughs and then crosses her arms. "You look so nervous right now, but you shouldn't be because your mom is going to love Lauren."

"Oh yeah, I'm not worried about that. Everyone loves Lauren; it's just…"

Fallyn squints, "It's getting serious for you, huh?"

"It is, but in a good way, of course. I really do love her, Fallyn." I confess, adjusting my posture in front of her. The atmosphere between us grew increasingly awkward as the tension intensified. Fallyn didn't speak; instead, she just stared at me and sucked on her lollipop. She was studying me, seeing if I'd waver at her intense stare into my soul, trying to make me falter. "And I know that you have your concerns about me, especially because I ghosted her for weeks, but I promise you that I'm trying to make up for that every day."

Fallyn finally spoke, "Well, she loves the shit out of you, and I know you love her." Her eyes rolled, and then a slight smirk formed on her face.

I was finally able to relax, now seeing her smile, knowing she wasn't going to grill me any further. The energy shifted in the room back to a warm, inviting pull over me. Fallyn took out her phone and started texting as she stood before me, with the biggest grin on her face.

"So when are you going to give my boy a chance?"

Fallyn slowly looked up from her phone, her lip snarled with one eye closed as she scrunched her face. "Jah?"

I tilt my head and lift my eyebrow. "What other boy could I possibly be talking about?"

"Me and Jah are cool; I'm actually texting him, and he's about to pull up now." Fallyn laughs and then starts texting on her phone again.

"Just cool, huh?" I shake my head at her. "But look at you all smiling while you're texting him."

Fallyn gives me a death stare and then shoves me playfully. "Shut up, fool! I'm just laughing because he's so goofy."

"Uh huh!" I laugh as I take a step back from her pushing me, "Well, I think you should give him a chance."

Fallyn looks up and rolls her eyes again. "Okay, Cupid." Her tone was sarcastic and short, but hopefully what I had to say would resonate with her. Suddenly, her aura got brighter, and a huge smile formed on her face. Unfortunately, as soon as she noticed that I noticed that she had gotten happier, her presence shifted. I looked behind me and saw Jah walking through the parlor doors. Fallyn pointed at me sternly and then walked away as she went up to Jah and hugged him.

I turned around and approached them both, and when they stopped embracing each other, Jah dapped me up and greeted me.

"Sup, my boy!" Jah called out boisterously and loudly.

"Jah, wassup, man." I pat his back and then pull away from him. "What are you doing here?"

Jah sniffles and wipes his nose. "Oh, you know I had to come see my girl!"

"Oh, your girl?" I look at Fallyn, and Fallyn pushes Jah.

Fallyn pipes up, "Please, not his girl, like girlfriend. You all do too much."

Jah and I both laugh, and I grip his shoulder, holding myself up from peeling over.

Jah shrugs and then touches under Fallyn's chin, but she pulls away. "Oh, come on, you know I had to try."

"Oh yeah, for sure." Fallyn glares at Jah.

I let go of Jah's shoulder and then shook my head, "Well, I'll let you two hang. I need to get to the market."

They both wave goodbye as I head towards the door and exit the shop. I continued my walk down the street, heading towards the market that was only a ten-minute walk away.

Once I arrived, I entered the front of the store, where you were intentionally greeted with an aroma of spices. My mom loved spices, and her favorite was curry, as she crafted many different cultural cuisines. So, I grabbed her some fresh curry spices and then made my way to the fruit section. My mom only enjoyed Ataulfo mangoes, so

I grabbed her a few freshly ripe ones. Libbie Market was charming—its aesthetic matched that of an upscale market, but its roots ran deep among holistic small business owners. Every product in the store was produced locally and provided to the store. It was an opportunity to showcase local organic produce, spices, and herbal remedies, such as soap, tea, supplements, and more. Each section of the store had its own unique smell of either fresh produce, spices, or scented toiletries. The bakery was my favorite because even though none of the baked goods were baked there and were supplied by local bakers, you could still smell the aroma as if you were in their kitchen. There was a lovely bouquet of burgundy lilies from a local florist that I decided to get, and then I went to the checkout. After I checked out, I made my way back to my apartment to wake Lauren so that she could get ready to head to my mother's. Once I arrived inside, Lauren was already up and getting ready. I set the flowers, wrapped in their bouquet wrappers, on the counter, along with the grocery bags. Lauren was sitting in front of a vanity mirror she took from my bedroom and placed against the living room wall. I walked up behind her and stood there as she did some light makeup.

Lauren looked at me through the reflection and smiled, then stopped applying her makeup to gaze at me. "Hey, baby!"

"Hey, gorgeous."

She then continues applying her makeup, "So, Fallyn is right down the street, I hear."

I walk to my sofa and sit down, grabbing the remote to turn on some music.

"Yeah, with Jah."

Lauren stops and looks at me with a huge grin. "I promise you, those two are going to hook up."

I set the remote back down. "Yeah, not if Fallyn can help it. Talk about hard to get."

Lauren laughs and then starts swaying to the music as she sits there. I picked up my phone and saw that I had another text message from my mother.

What time will you be here?

I text her back.

In another few hours.

I scrolled through my socials while Lauren got ready and made a few posts.

"I got a few things for my mother from us. So, you can give it to her once we get there." I yell over the music to Lauren.

Lauren turns and looks at me. "What did you get?"

"Some burgundy lilies, mangos, and her favorite curry spices."

Lauren closes her eyes. "Mmm, curry spices sound delicious. All of that is so sweet, babe, and of course, I don't mind giving it to her." She smiles and then turns back around to finish up.

Fifteen minutes later, Lauren was finally done putting on her makeup, and she got up and walked over to me. She straddles my hips as I sit on the sofa, and I immediately put down my cell phone and grab ahold of her waist.

"Oh, hello." I greet her, distracted by her playfulness.

She giggles and then stares me straight into my eyes, "How do I look?"

"Breathtaking." I immediately responded without hesitation.

Lauren leans in and kisses my lips, and I respond by kissing her back as deeply as possible. She then gets up and steps back, holding her arms out so that I could look at her outfit. Lauren wore a solid blue milkmaid dress, and her hair was still slightly straightened.

"What do you think?" She asked me, curiously waiting for praise.

I chuckle, "You look stunning as ever."

Lauren runs back and climbs into my lap as she wraps her arms around my neck. "Thank you."

I smile at her and then wrap my arms around her waist, pulling her in closer, and then squeezing her tightly as she squealed in my grasp. We lounged around the house for a bit and watched some TV before we left to head to my mother's home.

My mother lived on the outskirts of Metrotown, in a town called Somerville. Somerville housed a lot of middle-class families in their single-family homes or townhouse communities. It was a suburb adjacent to the city, right on the other side of the river. When we finally arrived at my mother's townhouse, I pulled into her driveway next to her black sedan and parked my truck in front of her garage. Her townhouse was a charming brick structure, with black lighting posts on each side of her door, and the grass was freshly cut by her lawn caretaker, Raul.

I looked over at Lauren, who was flattening her dress on her lap, as if trying to brush the seemingly active nerves out of her system. She looked at me and smiled, then grabbed my hand and squeezed it gently. We both stepped out of the car, and Lauren grabbed the flowers and the grocery bag from out of the back seat. I went over to her side and then walked with her to the front door. She inhaled deeply and then let out a deep sigh as we stood in front of the door.

"It's going to be okay; my mom is super chill." I reassured her, attempting to calm the nerves that surged through her.

She looks at me and her eyes grow big. "Yeah, but you told me you never brought a girl home. This is a big deal."

I rested my hand on the small of her back. "Don't get butterflies now." My hand reached for the doorknob, and I opened the front door.

As we stepped into the home, I saw Lauren's eyes open even wider. If they could, they'd pop out of her head and roll across the floor. I knew she was immediately mesmerized by the luxuriousness of my mother's home. The three-story house was beautiful on the outside but even more stunning on the inside, with the most up-to-date modern fixes and strategically placed home decor. While everything looked new and chic, it still conveyed a warm and inviting appeal, with photos of her and me spread throughout the home and my high school and college achievements displayed on intricately placed plaques on the walls or mantel. To the left was the living room, which held a beautiful three-piece sofa set in front of a cozy fireplace. To the right was the kitchen, which had a beautifully crafted island and a chef-style kitchen. Not only was my mother a nurse practitioner, but she was a true chef at heart—that was her passion. Across the floor were freshly polished hardwood floors that led from the kitchen to the living room and down the hallway that led to the stairs.

We stood in the hallway as my mom was in the kitchen preparing dinner. I cleared my throat, and she turned around, her face present with the most enthusiastic and warm welcome.

"My Lanno! Oh my god, and you must be Lauren!" She greets us both as she sets down her wooden spoon and walks up to us. She immediately hugs Lauren and rocks back and forth as they embrace. "Nice to finally meet you, Ms. Boyd." Lauren greets her back, looking at me out of the corner of her eyes.

My mom lets go of her and holds onto her shoulders as she takes a look at her. "Please call me Pauline."

Lauren blushes, her face red and her freckles intensifying. "Okay, Pauline, I can do that!"

My mom continues to hold her. "Ugh! You are so damn gorgeous, girl. My son has great taste."

Lauren giggles and then looks at me, and I nod at her. My mother finally lets her go, then grabs her hand and pulls her into the kitchen. I follow behind as we get to her island barstools, and then we both sit down.

"Oh! These are for you." Lauren hands her the flowers and the bag of mangos and spices. My mom cups her mouth and then rests her hand over her heart. She takes the items from Lauren, setting the bags down on the island and then holding the flowers closer to her as she inhales them. She walked over to her windowsill and grabbed her flower vase, then came back to the other side of the island and started snipping the ends of the flowers on a slant.

"See, now you have to cut them like this, because it helps the flowers absorb all those nutrients you put in the water for them to survive." She takes the included flower packet and looks at us both through the top of her glasses, then tosses it in the trash. "Never feed the plants the stuff that comes with it. You make your own. Sugar water is the trick."

My mom was already trying to school Lauren on her holistic knowledge and green thumb power. Miss Pauline Boyd was an eclectic woman with lots of hobbies that stemmed from holistic wellness. She was beautiful, and nobody could ever guess that she was in her early fifties because she was youthful and treated her body as her temple. My mom also had a brilliant mind, fueled by a deep immersion in her education, which enabled her to become a nurse practitioner. I got my height from my father, because my mother was on the shorter side, standing a bit taller than Lauren. Her hair was in a pixie cut that fit her slim face perfectly, and her attire, whenever I saw her, was always scrubs. However, she knew how to dress up when the opportunity presented itself.

Lauren leaned in, watching my mom cut the stems off the flowers, intrigued by the opportunity to learn and bond over anything my mom had to offer.

"It smells divine in here, Pauline." Lauren compliments as she sniffs the air.

My mom holds up her index finger, pointing behind her. "That would be the Thai coconut curry shrimp that is currently cooking. I'm rendering the base before I add the shrimp."

I tugged on the plastic grocery bag. "Speaking of curry, look what we got you."

My mom's eyes widened, and she opened the bag in a hurry, reaching in and grabbing the curry seasoning.

"Bless your heart, my favorite!" She rushed to open it and then turned around to her pan and opened the lid. "Just a few dashes; I just ran out, so this is coming in handy. Thank you!"

I laughed, "Mom, we got you mangos too."

My mom slams the seasoning on the counter and whips around, turning her attention back towards the grocery bag.

She grabs the mangos out of the bag and holds two in each hand. "Yesss. Ugh. You both are the best!"

Lauren smiles and looks at me as she bites her bottom lip. My mom puts the mangos in the fridge because she loves them chilled and then grabs the shrimp. As she starts peeling them, Lauren intensely watches her, and I watch Lauren, wondering if she was going to find the courage to ask my mother if she could help. Unlike most chefs, my mom enjoys working in the kitchen with others, showcasing her skills and taking pride in her work. She always made me cook with her when I was younger, and I was not the biggest fan of it. I nudged Lauren to encourage her.

Lauren clears her throat. "Would you like some help?"

Pauline smiled and handed Lauren the bowl of shrimp. "I thought you would never ask."

Lauren was glowing as she stood up and went to the sink so that she could wash her hands before assisting my mother in the kitchen. My mom walked to the refrigerator, pulled out a platter, and then walked back to the island, setting it down. She made her famous egg rolls with sweet chili sauce as an appetizer. Without hesitation, I grabbed one and enjoyed every last bite. They both laughed at me as they continued their food prep. I even fed one to Lauren as she continued to peel and clean the shrimp. Mama Pauline then started the white rice on the stove, first rinsing it, and then she added some fresh herbs to it.

While everything was cooking, my mom went to her wine cellar and got a bottle for us all to enjoy. She poured us all a glass in her long-stemmed wine glasses, and we sipped away until the food was ready. Once the food was ready, we sat down at the dinner table that sat in its corner nook, next to a trio of windows.

In each round-plated bowl was a decent amount of rice, mounded in the center, with the curry shrimp surrounding it. There was a drizzle of sauce on the rice and parsley to garnish. It was a simple yet decadent dish—its aroma captivating and warming the inner parts of my soul. The taste was creamy, rich, and bursting with flavor. With every bite, it unlocked a core memory of my childhood and made me realize I had not had this dish in years. This was a Boyd staple, and I melted into its comforting embrace. It made me travel back in time, realizing how loved I was as a child, growing up in a single Black woman's home. Recognizing that, although we struggled at times, my mom prioritized my well-being above all else. Making sure I was well fed and clothed, with a roof over my head. I remembered how every Sunday she would introduce a new dish or revisit a favorite one, realizing that today she did the same thing she would do for me when I was a child. She loved me unconditionally—it was raw, like a mother's love in any timeline. I could tell Lauren was enjoying the food as well, because she would close her eyes and moan with every bite, then compliment my mother. My mother would respond by assuring her that it only tasted this great because she helped.

When we finished our meal, I put the dishes in the dishwasher and then joined Lauren and my mother on the sofa. Unfortunately for me, my mother brought out an ancient, old-school photo album. "People still keep photo albums?" I teased her as I sat down in the accent chair.

My mom gestured with her hands, "Hush, you. Of course, I kept all your baby pictures in here. You were so cute but spoiled rotten!"

She pointed at the book, showing me off to Lauren, and of course, Lauren ate it up. "Lanno always did what he wanted to. Here's a picture of him on his skates. He hated them and didn't want to admit it, so he kept riding them and falling."

I sighed deeply, "Okay! Time to go."

Lauren snickered, and my mom shooed me away again. She pointed at another photo. "Here's him at graduation. I swear this feels like yesterday."

"Aw, babe, you were so handsome!" Lauren complimented me.

I squinted my eyes and tilted my head. "Were?"

Lauren rolls her eyes. "You know what I mean."

I chuckled and shook my head. They continued to look through the album, and I watched as pure joy glistened in Lauren' eyes. She and Pauline were best friends at this point and were bonding better than I could have ever hoped.

I knew my mother didn't want us to leave and was enjoying the company, but a few hours had passed, and it was time for us to get home. My mom packed up some food for us to go, and we hugged her goodbye before exiting and heading to the car. On our drive home, Lauren decided she would stay the night at my place, which she had been doing more since school was out for the summer.

We finally arrived home, and Lauren undressed and stole one of my shirts to sleep in. It was still early, so we decided to watch a movie in the living room. Once the movie was over, we went to the bedroom and got into bed. Lauren was always the first to fall asleep, and I was always jealous of that, up until recently when I learned how to meditate into a deep slumber. I followed quickly after, but not before thinking about Imani. I told myself that it was finally time for me to see her again, and I wondered what my visit had in store for me. It seemed like my next visit was going to be me taking the next step with Imani—it was pivotal. I questioned if it was something I should or shouldn't do.

I had a girlfriend in my current timeline and my soulmate in another. It was a paradox I never imagined I'd find myself in—one that tore at the very fabric of my loyalty and understanding of love. Lauren was real, present, and grounded. She offered me stability, laughter, and a shared future that made sense. But Imani... Imani was something else entirely.

There was an undeniable attraction to her—not just physical, though that part was magnetic and impossible to ignore—but something deeper.

Emotional. Spiritual.

As if the universe had designed her from the blueprint of my soul. With Imani, it wasn't just a connection; it was recognition. It was as though my heart remembered her before my mind even had the chance to catch up.

Being with Lauren felt like building a life. Being with Imani felt like returning home.

I promised that I would devour her the next time I saw her, and that terrified me because I knew as much as I wanted our intimate connection to blossom, it would hurt Lauren. I was fully aware of the choices I wanted to make.

However, I knew I couldn't control the inevitable.

With those thoughts swirling, I finally closed my eyes. And as I drifted off to sleep, I surrendered to the unknown, wherever it was about to take me.

Chapter 14

I stood in front of the sofa in Imani's apartment and watched her sleep peacefully. I wondered what other timelines she was in right now. I could easily find her by connecting with her soul on a deeper spiritual connection, but I figured I'd let her be and wait for her to wake up. I walked around her apartment and looked at the new photos of us she recently put up throughout the home. It was early in the day at her place, and the sun crept through her curtains. The energy in the room felt exhilarating—calm and inviting, with soft jazz playing. It was good to be back. Her black cat, Fizz, jumped up on the console table in front of me, seeking attention, so I scratched his tiny head and rubbed his back as he purred. I continued to explore, noticing her crystals on the table. I picked one up and examined it—clear quartz, helping to clear negative space and energies while amplifying energies in other crystals. It was so pretty, heavy, and expensive, I'm sure. I put it down and looked around more.

There were grunts behind me, so I turned around and noticed Imani was waking up from her nap. I smile and walk over to her. As I got closer to her, the room vibrated more. I lift her head, sit on the sofa, and then let her head lie in my lap.

I look down at her while playing with a loc that snuck out from her headscarf. "Hey, gorgeous."

She smiles big at me and then stretches as her hands playfully hit me in the face. We both laugh as I pull away slightly.

"Hey, handsome," Imani says back, her voice low and sultry. She slides her fingernails across my cheeks and up to my ears. I close my eyes and tilt my head, savoring her touch. A shiver runs through me—it's electric.

Imani wore a black sports bra and grey sweatpants. Waist beads were around her waist, and she always looked stunning, even dressed down.

"I've missed you." She confesses.

I ran the tips of my fingers around her belly button and up her torso. I could feel the warmth of her skin radiating beneath my fingertips. She was also moisturized with scented body oils, so my senses were overloaded with the warmth, the softness, and the tiny bursts of jasmine and vanilla on her skin. A soft haze from the sunset flooded her living room and glazed over her chocolate skin, as if she were the only one in the world to soak up the rays from the sun at this very moment.

Imani lifts her hand and holds it in the air, inviting me. I go to press my hand into hers, but she pulls back a little, making me follow her movements, gliding her hand like a free-falling leaf. I could feel the energy between our palms, a heat I'd never felt, and a connection more powerful than love. I watch as we are inches away from each other's touch, but I can feel her, our auras blending as one.

I look down at Imani, deep into her eyes, as she looks back at me and smiles even bigger. One thing about Imani was that she always loved to smile.

She reaches up with her other hand and runs her fingers through my hair, grabs the back of my head, and slowly pulls me down towards her. Imani's touch rang throughout my body like somebody had struck a tuning fork. Once again, our blue aura began to radiate around us. I leaned down and deeply pressed my lips into hers as the entire room danced around us. Our energy had intertwined since I visited Troterion and regained most of my memories. So this kiss—this was pure, raw, and unfiltered power. My heart skipped a beat as we continued to kiss, both devouring each other. Imani then breaks the kiss and sits up on the sofa. I watch her as she turns and climbs into my lap, straddling me.

I wrap my arms around her body and look into her eyes. "You're so beautiful, Imani."

She smiles as she watches her fingers play with my hair. "My sweet Mahant."

Not only could I feel the energy vibrating around us, but I could hear it roaring as well. My senses were off the charts. Imani was right—had we had moments like this before, it would have sent me into overdrive, and I would not have been able to handle it. I even wondered if we continued whether I would be able to handle it now. She heated me up—with every touch, it felt like I was flying closer to the sun.

"Breathe with me," she says. She must have known I was working myself up. Imani inhales in ten-second increments, holds it in, and slowly releases it through her mouth. I follow her lead, and as I focus on my breathing, Imani wraps her arms around my neck and adjusts herself in my lap. I then move my arms from being wrapped around her, and I grab onto her hips.

After a few minutes of breathing exercises, Imani presses her lips back into mine. Her lips were warm against mine, inviting and encapsulating me as I slipped into pure bliss. The energy between us shifted instantly, vibrating with intensity the moment she let out a soft moan into my mouth. Our eyes remained closed as we melted into the kiss, savoring the taste of each other with a hunger that felt both tender and electric. I held her tight and stood up from the sofa, picking her up and holding her in my arms. She wraps her legs around my waist and holds on as I walk towards her bedroom. Before I could enter the room, I rested her against the console table that sat against the wall. There was a fine line between raw intensity and deep passion as she swept the items off the table, settling herself onto the edge with effortless confidence. Our lips stayed locked, the heat between us rising with every touch and every breath. The light cast as naturally as can be through the room, illuminating around us. Her hands gripped the back of my hair and pulled me deeper into her kiss. Every kiss showed flashes of our past, future, and present lives, outlining every moment we've touched, kissed, or made love. Every moment was more powerful than the one before. I could feel my inner soul escaping my body and slowly becoming one with her.

Imani reaches down to the hem of my shirt and pulls it above my head. She takes it off and throws my shirt to the floor. As she sat back and looked at me, her hands started gripping and touching all over my chest slowly, carefully watching what she was doing. I stand before her, close my eyes, and lick my lips. Her touch felt out of this world—yet familiar. Every time we've made love, it was always this intense. Imani's hands continue to explore my body, going down lower to my jeans as she unbuttons them. I lean forward, bury my face in her neck, and kiss her soft, delicate chocolate skin. Soon after, those kisses turn into me sucking against her skin. Imani releases a small gasp as her hands reach around my neck, holding on. I go back to her waist and grab her as I lift her off the console table and hold her in the air again. She pushes me away from her neck and kisses me deeply again. Slowly, we make our way to the bedroom with my jeans barely staying around my waist.

I slam her against the nearby wall, pinning her in place as our desire ignites into something uncontrollable. My body keeps her pressed firmly between me and the wall, and my hands are planted on either side of her. Her eyes burn with hunger, filled with unspoken want. I dive back in, trailing my lips down her neck before biting gently into her skin. A low groan escapes her lips, but then, just as suddenly, she pulls away again, teasing me with the space between us.

"Stay away from my neck, sir." She demands, then bites her bottom lip as she glares at me.

I smirked at her and then shook my head no. I knew her neck was her weakness, and I wanted to unravel her completely—to have her surrender to my touch, lost in the intensity of the moment. My hand removes her headscarf, then watches her locs fall around her face. I ran my fingers through her locs, then grabbed a fistful. I then make her tilt her head back as I go in again for the kill, ignoring her warnings and kissing her neck again.

Imani erupted with emotions, causing my body to react and sending me into overdrive. It was strange yet euphoric—I could feel everything she was experiencing while still fully immersed in my own sensations. The intensity was almost too much, a whirlwind of emotions and energy crashing over me at once. It was overwhelming, yet somehow, I felt electrifyingly alive.

At this moment, it was just her and me, and nothing else mattered.

I picked her up again and took her off the wall. I walked over to the bed and placed her softly on the mattress. Standing before her, between her legs, I could see her aura as she looked up at me. Blue surrounded her entire body—a deep, priceless blue, like the endless ocean under moonlight or the sky just before dawn. It wasn't just a color but an extension of her essence, a reflection of the depth within her soul. I look down at my hands and see blue as well. Our auras continued to match, and the vibrancy of our colors was fascinating—a blue that seemed to hum, vibrating softly, as if whispering secrets only the universe could comprehend. Vaguely familiar, but still something that took me some time to adjust to—seeing auras.

As I'm distracted, Imani pulls my jeans down, and they fall to the floor. I shift my focus back to her and push her into bed. I grip her sweatpants, pulling them off her hips as I climb into bed with her and hover my body over hers. My fingers lace with hers, pulling her hands above her head and pressing her into the bed.

The passion was exciting, each touch igniting something primal and unstoppable.

At that moment, our worlds didn't just collide—they fused, intertwining into something deeper, something unshakable. I felt beyond words, beyond reason—an intensity so powerful it defied explanation.

Passionate. Slow. Pure bliss...

We made love for hours, moving from one passionate session to the next, exploring every corner of her apartment. We guided each other through waves of pleasure, pausing to laugh, then diving back in with even more curiosity and connection.

Imani and I were completely naked in bed, breathing deeply. The blanket covered the essential parts of our body as it lay sloppily against us. I was on my back, and Imani wrapped her arm around my waist, her head against my chest. I started to feel the energy between us settle. It wasn't as intense as before, but it was still present. Imani grabs my hand and plays with my fingers. We lay in this moment for a while, focusing on our breathing as I watched our fingers intertwine.

The silence felt great between us—soothing, even though the energy between us whispered its secrets, as if we shared the same thoughts. We were both buzzing and on cloud nine—no need to reassure one another how great we felt because we just knew. I closed my eyes and exhaled slowly while Imani rubbed my chest.

Suddenly, Lauren popped into my mind as I lay there in bed with Imani. I was thinking about the conversation Lauren and I had about jumping, and I knew Imani would want to hear about it. It was so easy to talk to Imani about everything because she was not judgmental and always conveyed her thoughts wisely.

I broke through our silence. "I told Lauren about me jumping."

Imani stops rubbing my chest and leans on her elbow as she looks at me. "You did, huh? How'd she take it?"

I see her look over me out of the corner of my eye, waiting for me to respond. I think momentarily, and then a tiny smile creeps onto my face.

"She took it well and was really supportive."

Imani nudges me. "That's good!"

I turned my head slightly to look at Imani. She was cool—sometimes, too cool for me. For as long as I've known Imani, she's always been a free spirit and allowed me to be the same. There didn't seem to be an inkling of insecurity or jealousy in her.

She was very confident, and that was sexy.

I knew I could tell her anything and everything. Sometimes, I wish I had had the same experience with Lauren as with Imani. Something told me that if I brought up Imani to Lauren, I'd not get the same reaction. I needed to tell her eventually. Lauren was very understanding about everything I had already told her. Why wouldn't she accept and be okay with my connection to Imani? Imani was more evolved, though. Of course, Imani would understand. Her mind was open, and she had seen the world ten times over.

Curiously, I asked Imani, "Could I possibly teach Lauren how to jump?"

She thinks for a moment and gets remarkably quiet. Imani walks her fingers across my chest as she's deep in thought. I give her a moment to think and respond.

"I think she must be able to connect with another timeline. If she's new to the universe, there's nowhere for her to jump to." Imani stares at me and then starts playing in my hair. "You're so handsome."

Imani was so affectionate and always showered me with words of affirmation. She always reminded me of how handsome I was in this timeline and that the universe did its thing with my physical body. She always needed to touch me—whether playing in my hair, rubbing my back or my arms, or kissing me, her hands were always on me. And with every touch, our souls would collide and meld into one. It was a powerful expression emitted from our bodies when we were together. It felt so damn good. The moment her fingertips grazed my skin, a wave of emotions shot through me—intense and intoxicating. The sensation was beyond pleasure, sending a surge through every nerve in my body.

"So, are we going to lie in bed all day?" I asked reluctantly. Honestly, I could stay in this moment forever.

Imani gets up, and with her naked body fully exposed, she hurdles over me and straddles my waist. Her hands press into my stomach, and she slowly slides them up to my chest. I could feel the heat pour out of her fingertips, her palms warming my skin.

"Are you complaining, Mahant?" She asks with a snarky tone. "Can't take any more?"

I reach up and slide my thumb across her luscious lips, then slyly push it between them. She sucks on it softly.

I loved it when she called me Mahant. It felt more familiar and personable, as if I were at home with her.

Imani leaned down and lay flat against my chest. I kiss the creases of her lips as I slowly slide my thumb out of her mouth. My arms wrapped around her, holding her tightly against me. Thus, transitioning into another explosive session between us.

For the next few hours, we went at it again, repeatedly. If the universe could collide and separate into two because of the power and strength of love, it would start in this room. The energy that we emitted was insatiable. I rendered myself hopeless when it came to Imani. I was madly in love with her and everything she was.

After our multiple sessions, I felt sleepy but did not want to drift off for the love of me. I wanted to stay with Imani for as long as I could. I wanted to touch her, kiss her, and talk about jumping. I loved asking her questions and how open and honest she had become with me. She wasn't as hesitant as before when she thought she needed to keep things from me for my protection. I understood her wanting to ease me into everything. All the memories that flooded back would have overwhelmed me if it had happened the first night I remembered her. I would have spiraled.

I sat up on the edge of the bed and reached down to grab my boxers, putting them on as I stood up and looked for the rest of my clothes throughout Imani's apartment. I hear Imani chuckle under her breath as I search. I turn around and look at her, giving her a playful grin as I shake my head. I left the bedroom and saw my shirt on the floor. I lean down, grab it, shake it off, and then put it on. I walk to the fridge, open it, and take the orange juice out to have some.

I heard Imani call out from the bedroom. "I don't want to get out of bed! My legs hurt."

I laugh to myself and swallow the orange juice. My body felt good, and my brain was super clear. Usually, my brain was foggy and loud, and I could never think straight. This sense of clarity comforted my thoughts and helped settle me down. I couldn't get the flashes of Imani and our long, passionate session out of my mind. I didn't want to. I saw glimpses of us and nothing more, silently admitting to myself that I couldn't get enough of her.

Fumbling came from the bedroom, and Imani must have finally gotten up and dressed. A few minutes passed, and Imani emerged in only her black bra and boy shorts from the bedroom.

Her body was stunning.

She was wrapping her hair back up in her head scarf, her waist beads were still in place, and they made it through the ride. Imani walked over to me as I stood in front of the fridge. I turn to put the orange juice back into the refrigerator, and she grabs it. As she stares at me, she opens the orange juice carton and sips. Some escaped past the corner of her mouth and dripped down her neck. As she continues to drink, I lean forward, wrap my lips around the orange juice trail on her neck, and lick it up.

She giggles and jumps as she quickly moves away from me and pulls the carton away from her lips. "Listen, sir. Quit it."

"Or what?" I taunted her, knowing she loved every second of my lips on her skin.

I flinch at her playfully and then grab her. She holds onto the carton as she tries to fight me off her.

She laughs more, her voice muffled into my shirt, "You're going to start a part three—"

"Or a part five, or six, or seven." I interrupted while laughing, and then I pulled her closer to me. Her chest presses into mine, and her arms naturally drape around my neck.

Imani looks into my eyes. "You're trouble."

"So are you."

Imani kisses me and then pulls away. She opens the refrigerator and puts the carton of orange juice back in it. I rev my hand back and smack her ass hard, making her jump, then look back at me as she tiptoes away towards the sofa. Imani picks Fizz up off the couch and starts petting him as she holds him in her arms. I walk out of the kitchen and head towards her on the sofa.

I couldn't believe it was already getting late, and it was almost time for me to wake up any minute now. I didn't want to. All I could think about was staying in this moment forever with Imani. I stand before her as she sits on the sofa, sinking into my thoughts. Oh, how these thoughts could take over in an instant. How dark and gloomy they would be—the intrusive thoughts beating away at my brain like a war drum, thoughts that were supposed to stay inside your head. But mine didn't...

"What if I just don't wake up?"

It was word vomit.

I was thinking it, and it casually slipped out of my mouth.

Imani slowly stopped petting Fizz, her gaze lingering on him. She didn't look up at me, and the entire room fell into an uneasy silence. The only sounds were the soft purrs coming from Fizz. The warmth that usually radiated from Imani had faded, replaced by something heavier—something tense and unreadable. The air in the room got thick. Suddenly, it was harder to breathe.

Imani finally sighed and then let Fizz down onto the floor. He walked away slowly and found his cat bed in the nearby corner. She placed her hands in her lap and continued to stay quiet. Imani, calculated to a fault, was trying to find words to say to me.

"I'm not leaving, Imani. Not this time."

She tilted her head and closed her eyes as if she couldn't bear to hear more of what I had to say.

I hated that I was ruining this perfect moment. But if I left Imani this time, I knew for sure that I would not be able to breathe without her. That's how deep this had gotten for me.

Imani finally whispers. "Don't ruin this, Mahant, please. I beg you."

She looked up at me, her eyes glistening in a way that I had never seen before. She looked as though she was on the verge of tears. Her presence seemed weaker, her aura dim. But I needed to stand my ground.

"I'm not leaving," I say again.

"You don't have a choice!" Imani screams at me while she gestures with her hands as if she is squeezing something. She hated getting angry because she immediately retracted herself and looked down, shaking away the tense energy in her hands.

I didn't let up. "Do you not want me to stay?"

"Mmm—don't do that." She looks at me again with this very stern look, her eyes locked onto mine.

Persistent, I asked again; this time my voice was shaking uncontrollably. "Why can't I stay, Imani?"

"I'm not doing this with you. Leave now." She replies to me, emotionless. Imani gets up from the sofa and walks towards her bedroom.

I follow closely, refusing to back down. My voice sharpens with urgency as I ask again, "No! Tell me, Imani. Why can't I stay?"

"I said you need to leave. Go back to Lauren."

"Go back to Lauren? Seriously?"

Imani tries to close the door on me, but I push through it and enter the bedroom with her.

"Do you hear yourself?"

"Yes, I hear myself, Lanno. Go back to Lauren, and just for the love of God, be happy!"

"Lanno?" She doesn't even call me that anymore.

This confrontation was different. I've never seen this side of Imani, not in a hundred years. This feeling was not familiar at all. Why was this such a sensitive topic for her? I stood there behind her, defeated as she fidgeted with her jewelry on her dresser, facing away from me.

I stood there quietly, my heart in my chest pounding, on the verge of breaking. Imani being this dismissive was new to me, and I didn't know how to handle it. She was shutting down, and the worst part about it all was that I could feel how she felt at the same time because we were connected.

This tension hurts. It didn't feel good, and I didn't know what to do or say.

But finally, words escaped me. "Imani, I love you."

Imani sighs and slowly turns around. She leans against the dresser and stares at me. "I love you, too. But I need you to stop these thoughts. I need you to go back to your timeline. Love Lauren, grow old."

"I want to grow old with you."

"We will, babe." She promises. "You must open your mind and realize you have us both, and that's rare. You can always, and I mean always, come to me here, or we can go to other places together."

Imani approaches me and grabs my face to make me look at her. A tear fell from my eyes as I tried to look away.

"Hey, look at me, baby. Look at me. I'm not going anywhere. I promise." She tells me as she holds my face firmly. "I'm not going anywhere, Mahant. We will have so many adventures until we are old, wrinkly, and beautiful. I promise you, but you must let this go. You have to."

Her thumb wiped away my tears as she wrapped her arms around my neck, pulling me into her. My arms fold around her waist tightly, not wanting to ever let go. We embraced each other as we swayed back and forth. The pain was unbearable, crashing over me in relentless waves. My anxiety was through the roof, amplifying the exhaustion and weighing me down. I felt physically and emotionally drained—I was exhausted.

We step back towards the bed, and Imani follows me. I sit down, and she stands before me, her arms now wrapped around me. The side of my face pressed tightly against her stomach.

"Shh. Shh." She whispers as she continues to hold me tight, as my eyes grow heavy.

My time was up, and this was it. I was starting to wake up and tried to fight it as hard as possible.

"I don't want to go, Imani."

Imani, still holding me, responds, "I know, baby. But you can come back every night and see me. I promise you this."

My words slur as I try to keep my eyes open. "I want to fall asleep next to you."

Imani moves from in front of me and pushes me back onto the bed as she climbs into the bed with me. I lay on my side and felt her lie next to me as she pushed my hair out of my face.

She strokes my cheek and whispers, "You can fall asleep with me every night. Just close your eyes and relax your mind."

"No, I don't want to wake up. Please don't make me wake up."

Slowly, the world around me blurs, fading into a hazy, distant fog. My limbs grow heavy, an unbearable weight pulling me down. My vision darkens at the edges, closing in like a curtain falling over reality. A deep, numbing silence takes hold, and before I can fight it, I surrender, drifting off as consciousness slips from my grasp.

Chapter 15

I woke up in my apartment, the morning sun streaming through the curtains, piercing and unforgiving. I squinted against the light, my body heavy with exhaustion. Pushing the blanket aside, I sat at the edge of my bed, staring blankly into nothingness. A strange numbness coursed through me, burning beneath my skin like a lingering ghost of something I couldn't quite grasp.

Imani's scent still clung to the air, delicate yet haunting, wrapping around me like a memory refusing to fade. But even with her presence lingering in the smallest traces, a hollow ache settled deep in my chest.

I felt empty. I felt alone.

There were so many emotions coursing through me that I could not quite understand. I could feel everything—my heart, my blood, and my bones tearing to pieces inside of me. Every time I left Imani, a chunk of me was gone—like an unexplainable force where my soul split into two.

I sat there as it all built up inside. The anger intensified, and I wanted to explode. I needed to rid myself of all this excess energy that I didn't know where to store, so I did.

"Fucccccccccck!" I let out the most resounding, agonizing scream I could summon. My chest tightened, and I grabbed my heart. The tightness in my chest was unbearable, and I couldn't breathe.

Lauren sat up quickly next to me in a panic and got out of bed. She hurried to my side, her movements quick and filled with concern. I stood up and wiped everything off my nightstand, pushing her out of my way.

"Lanno, what the fuck are you doing?" She yells as she gets out of the way.

I had to let it all out. The pain was immeasurable, and I was inconsolable. I reached for my lamp and ripped it off the dresser and out of the socket. I tossed it across the room and heard it shatter against the wall. I then made my way towards the door and ripped it open, slamming it against the wall.

"Lanno, stop!" Lauren screams. She jumps back to clear out of my way.

I continue to slam the door and kick it, bursting a hole right through the wood. I then started pounding away at it with my fist repeatedly. Fury consumed me, raw and uncontrollable, pouring out through every strike. It was an anger like none I have ever experienced.

"What's wrong?" Lauren asks, pleading with me.

A part of me could hear her through the rage and hurt. However, I was spiraling.

I was on a rampage.

I left the bedroom, entered the living room, and headed towards my bar. I grab the bottle of alcohol and pop it open. Without hesitation, I raised the bottle to my lips and took a deep swig, letting the burn settle in my throat.

Lauren enters the living room, looks at me, and rushes over. She grabs the bottle and pulls it away from my lips. She sets the bottle back on the bar and grabs my face.

"Hey, look at me. What the fuck is going on?" Lauren's voice trembled with worry. She examines my eyes, and I try to close them. All I wanted to do was go back to sleep and be with Imani.

Lauren slaps my face gently to wake me up. "Talk to me!"

I quickly fell and crouched down. Lauren crouched down with me and continued to hold onto my face. I fall to my butt and let my head hang low.

"I'm going to call the ambulance." She threatened as she got up. I reached up, grabbed her wrist, and pulled her back down.

"No, don't," I finally break my silence.

"Then fucking talk to me. What is wrong?" She asks again, her voice shaking, begging me to talk to her.

I hesitate and get quiet for a few seconds. Words escaped me, but deep down inside me, I knew I had to tell Lauren the truth. After that performance, there was nowhere to hide anymore. I was tired of hiding anyway. I couldn't keep this from Lauren anymore, and she should have a choice in the matter.

At this point, I was being selfish—keeping a secret from Lauren about another woman in another timeline—a woman I was in love with and wanted to be with.

Finally, words came out. "I wasn't completely honest with you, Lauren."

"I'm listening."

"When I travel to another timeline, I'm with Imani," I confessed.

Lauren gets quiet. The room suddenly shifted, and the tension thickened. I looked at her, and I could tell she was flustered. Her entire face turned red.

Her response was cold and short. "Who's Imani?"

There was no holding back now. I needed to put everything on the table. So, I continued, "We're soul-tied. We have been together for hundreds of years."

Lauren stands up and turns to walk away, but then stops. I get up off the floor and walk up behind her. She lets out a laugh as she turns around and looks at me.

"So, are you trying to tell me that you're fucking someone in your sleep?" She crosses her arms, stares at me, and continues, "Are you crazy? Do you hear how insane this sounds?"

"It's not just about sex," I began to explain to Lauren.

"So, you did fuck her?!" Lauren yells as she swiftly slams her hands into my chest. I step back, lower my head, and don't say anything. I allowed her to take her anger out on me because, at the end of the day, I deserved it.

Lauren throws her hands up, her voice rising with frustration. "What the hell is wrong with you, Lanno? Do you even hear yourself? This is insane!"

She starts pacing, running her fingers through her hair as she speaks. "I tried—I really tried to be understanding when you first told me about this... jumping... whatever the hell it is. Timeline hopping?" She scoffs and spins back toward me, eyes blazing.

"No." Her voice cracks slightly as she shakes her head. "No, that can't be it. You're lying. Imani—Imani is just some girl you're screwing behind my back in this timeline, isn't she?"

Lauren rushes into my bedroom, and I stand there, hopeless. She comes back into the living room with my phone in her hand. "Unlock your phone."

I shook my head and reached for my phone. She pulls away and steps back.

"Unlock the damn phone, Lanno!"

"No, I'm not unlocking my phone, Lauren, because you won't find anything in it. I don't text or call Imani. I can only see her when I jump. I'm not lying to you!" I try to explain, but my voice is low and unsteady when I talk.

Lauren, standing her ground, continues to yell at me. "You are lying, though! You probably have a bunch of girls you're fucking around with, huh?"

"Lauren, I'm not lying to you. I'm not cheating on you with a bunch of girls!"

She wasn't trying to hear me or understand. Lauren was hurt, and she had every right to be. I didn't know what to do or say.

Lauren scoffs, "Oh, I'm sorry... It's just one girl from another timeline. This is so crazy."

Lauren throws the phone at me, and I attempt to catch it, but it falls to the ground. There was a loud cracking sound that rang throughout the room. I suck my teeth and reach down to pick up the phone. Never mind me worrying about a broken screen. I had bigger fish to fry. I walk up and close the space between me and Lauren.

"Get away from me!" Lauren yells as she hits me again in the chest, trying to push me away.

"Stop," I say, my voice sharp and unwavering, fueled with intensity.

Lauren takes a jab at me, her words sharp, cutting through me like a knife. "You're a piece of shit, and Fallyn was right about you. I should have never forgiven you."

I tilted my head and gave her a disgusting look. "Why even bring Fallyn up?"

"Oh, you're going to look at me like that. You're the one cheating on me with some bitch in your dreams." Lauren presses her fingers into my forehead and pushes me again.

"Stop it, Lauren," I warned her again.

"Or what?"

Lauren balls her fists and slams them into my chest. I quickly reacted by trying to grab both of her wrists, but I only successfully grabbed one. She responds by swinging her other hand, hitting my face.

"Let go of me!" She screams.

I grab the other hand as she walks backward towards the sofa.

"Look, I love you, and me being with Imani doesn't change that!"

Lauren looks at me while she's a bit out of breath. "You sound so damn pathetic!"

I locked eyes with her, my grip firm as I held her hands, preventing another strike. My voice was steady, raw with emotion. "I'm not pathetic. I'm telling you the truth. I just wish you'd understand."

Her expression hardened, anger flashing in her eyes. "No, I'm done, Lanno. Now let go of me!" She yelled, struggling against my hold, desperation fueling her resistance.

"Nah, we're not done. I need you to calm down."

Lauren loses her balance and falls onto the sofa. With one foot on the ground and one knee pressed firmly into the sofa cushion, I pin Lauren to the couch, now towering over her.

Lauren yanked her wrist free from my grasp, her movements swift and fueled by frustration. Before I could react, she swung at me again, her fist cutting through the air with reckless force. My jaw clenched as her hand connected to it, making my patience wear thin. I hated when she got like this—when her emotions spiraled so out of control that her first instinct was to lash out physically.

I didn't want to fight her. I just wanted her to calm down, to stop and hear me, to listen instead of letting anger take the lead. But there was no reasoning with her now. Whatever control we had over this argument was gone, and we were full-blown fighting.

"Get the fuck off of me, Lanno!" Lauren screams as she kicks her feet.

"Babe, I need you to calm down!"

Tears streamed down her face, her sobs breaking into sharp, uneven gasps as she thrashed beneath me. She fought desperately, struggling against my grip, her body trembling with frustration and heartbreak. One of her hands had broken free again, but before she could strike, I caught it, holding her down against the sofa with firm restraint.

She kicked wildly, her legs twisting beneath us as she screamed, her voice raw with emotion. Every fiber of her being was trying to break away, to escape the moment, and push me off her. But I couldn't let go—not yet. I needed her to listen, to hear me, to understand. Even if she hated me for it, even if this only pushed her further away, I had to try.

"Don't call me babe. I swear to God I can't do this anymore, Lanno. I can't. Now let me go!" Her voice cracked, tears streamed down her face, each carrying the weight of everything left unsaid. Her chest heaved as she shook her head, her expression caught between anger and heartbreak.

"Are you going to calm down?" I ask her as I look down at her. Lauren tries to pull away and then lies motionless against the sofa after realizing she isn't breaking free this time. She continues to cry as she lies there, finally conceding.

I lean down and press my lips against hers, and for a moment, she kisses me deeply and then pulls away.

Her eyes close, and she shakes her head. "No, I'm not folding this time. Get off of me."

Again, I lean down, press my lips into hers, and kiss her. Lauren kisses me back deeply and then bites my bottom lip, sighing into our kiss. I press my chest into hers and slowly let go of her slightly pink, bruised wrists. As soon as I did, I felt her hands press into my chest and push me as hard as she could.

Then Lauren begins to hit me again, repeatedly. "I said get the fuck off of me!"

I blocked her blows and attempted to grab her hands, but this time was unsuccessful. I've never hit her back and never would. I had to admit it—I brought out this toxicity in every way. I hated it for us. I hated how I was this trigger for her. I looked at Lauren through the blows and wished a small part of her would understand. Unfortunately for me, the blows continued—repeatedly, Lauren continued to swing and kick until we were both now entirely out of breath.

"Okay, stop, Lauren, stop!" I yelled. I finally backed off her, and she sat up and pulled my oversized t-shirt that she was wearing down to cover her panties. She gets off the sofa, looks at me, and then shakes her head.

"You're an asshole. You try to manipulate me by kissing me or pushing this fake-ass love on me."

Lauren wiped her completely red and flushed face, her chest heaving with how out of breath she was.

"I love you, Lauren. My love for you has never been fake. I promise you this with everything that is in me. I love you." I put my hands together as if I were saying a prayer, pleading with her.

Lauren stands before me and expressively uses her hands as she speaks. "Yeah, I hear you, Lanno. You love me, but you love her too. I can barely even wrap my head around you going to sleep and jumping to another timeline. Now you're telling me you've been with another woman and are in love with her. Are you serious? Listen to how this sounds!"

"Yes, it sounds bad. But we are soul-tied. So, no matter our timeline, we will always want to find each other. You don't think it's possible to love two people at the same time?"

"No, Lanno! Absolutely not."

Lauren crosses her arms and stares at me, still breathing heavily. I sigh as I look deeply into her eyes, searching for words, but it is hard for me to explain how I feel. It didn't come out how I wanted to deliver it whenever I said anything. However, I still tried.

"Well, I believe you can because I'm in love with you and her," I admit, not holding back any more lies.

Lauren rolls her eyes and does an eerie laugh as she turns around and leaves the living room, heading to the bedroom. She stayed there momentarily, and I could hear her rustling around. I walk back to the bar and grab the bottle of alcohol, taking another swig before setting it back down.

Once Lauren returned, she was fully dressed and had her keys.

"Lauren, please don't go," I beg, rushing over to stand before her as she tries to exit the front door.

Lauren hesitates and stands in front of me with her eyes closed. She breathes deep, then exhales.

"Lanno, move." Her voice was sharp and stern.

I continue to block her from exiting the door. "No, please don't go. I don't want to lose you, Lauren. Please."

"I'm not doing this with you, Lanno, not anymore. I'm over letting you rip my fucking heart out. Do you really think I want to hear you tell me you love another woman?"

She tries maneuvering around me, but I block her from getting to the door. Lauren steps back, raises her hand to her face, and her fingers pinch the bridge of her nose as if trying to think or calm down.

"Please move." She demands again.

"Can we please just talk this through and figure it out?"

Lauren raises her hands in the air and says nothing. We stared at each other again for what seemed like hours, but only seconds passed. I wanted to get down on my knees and beg her not to leave me. I would have done anything to make her stay.

Lauren finally broke the silence. "Why were you upset when you woke up?"

I inhale deeply and then shake my head, trying to get rid of the thought of leaving Imani out of my head. Whenever I thought about it, it hurt—piercing me like a sharpened blade straight through the heart.

As hard as this moment with Lauren was, I was here with her now and wanted to continue this path of being open, honest, and transparent. I wanted to tell the truth, but I also wanted to lie, not to hurt her any further. I didn't know what to do.

However, more word vomit escaped my lips. "It was just tough for me to leave her this time around."

Lauren closed her eyes, and more tears fell from them. I could feel her heart breaking all over again.

"Wow," she finally says. "So, you'd rather just stay in this fantasy world with someone else? How the hell do I compete with that?"

My chest tightened, and my heart broke. I knew I was losing this battle. However, I tried one more time to convince her. To try to make her see my true intentions. "Lauren, it's deeper than you understand, and I don't want you to feel as though you have to compete with her. But I've been soul-tied to Imani for hundreds of years. I'm also trying to explain to you that I feel like I'm soul-tied to you as well. I'm in love with you both, and if I could—"

"Lanno, stop!" She yells as she balls up her fists. Her breath is shaking even more now, and she continues yelling, "You want your cake and eat it too. But I choose not to be a part of this bizarre-ass polyamorous thing you've got going on in your head. Fine, you're special, and you can jump to other timelines. I'll let you have that. But I can't just be okay with you being in love with a woman who is imaginary to me. It's deranged."

My heart sank, a heavy weight dropping into the pit of my stomach. It was an ache that spread through my chest, tightening like a vise, making it hard to breathe. The last thing I wanted to do was lose Lauren again. But this time, it was different. We were communicating, but it was very hostile and toxic. I knew I was hurting her all over again, and just that mere thought burned me to my core.

"Lauren, it's a lot to understand. But trust me when I say I don't want to lose you. I love you, Lauren. Please don't go."

She hesitates and starts fidgeting with her fingers. Her entire face was redder, and the tears wouldn't stop flowing down her face.

"Do you love me, Lauren?"

She remains quiet and continues to look down. "Please, can you just let me leave?" She begs, crying with eyes full of tears now. Her voice was shaky, and she could barely get the words out.

I sigh and step to the side hopelessly. "At the end of the day, I've told you all of this because I wanted you to have a choice. You're choosing to walk out that door, Lauren, and as much as I don't want you to, I understand. It's your decision. I keep fucking up. I keep hurting you. But Lauren, just know this—" I pause. My lungs were sharp, like I wasn't getting enough air into them. Everything in me hurts. Tears welled up in my eyes as I tried to push through the tightness in my chest. These words were so hard to say, but I couldn't hold back anymore. I had to be honest and vulnerable, even if it hurt. "I am in love with you. If I can't have you in this life, then maybe I will in the next. I've failed you. I want you to know that you mean the world to me, and from the bottom of my heart, Lauren, I am so sorry. But please, if nothing else, please tell me that you love me."

Lauren finally looked up at me, her eyes completely swollen, bloodshot red, and full of sorrow. I hated myself for it. She walks up to me as I stand in front of the door and then attempts to wipe away her tears.

She exhales deeply. "You want to know what the scary part is, Lanno?" Lauren clears her throat and continues, "I love you so fucking much that there was a tiny part of me that considered being a simp and being okay with all of this. But I can't. I just can't do it." Lauren cups my face and then rubs my cheek with her thumb. "I do love you. I am so in love with you, Lanno, and I wish I could be okay with you loving two women. I wish I could say yes because I know that it would make you happy. But I have to be happy too. So, you're going to have to choose. Me or Imani?"

Lauren clutches her keys and leaves the apartment, and there I stand, frozen, devastated.

How could I choose?

Chapter 16

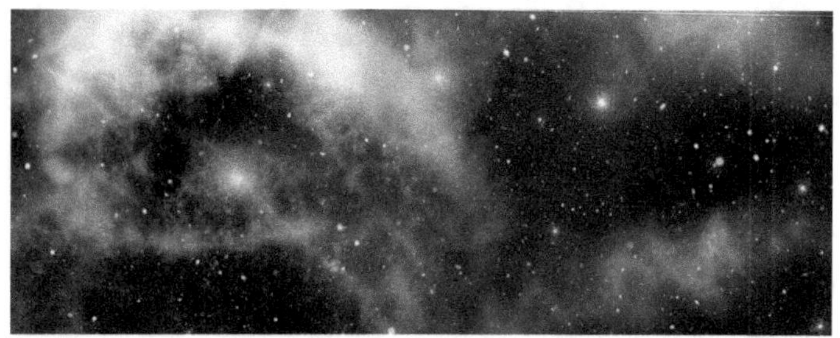

Lauren was gone. Luckily, she gave me a chance to take some time and figure out who I wanted to be with. She didn't force me to make a decision right then and there.

But she left.

I sat in the living room of my apartment with the bottle of liquor in my hand that I had tried to drown myself with earlier in the day. I don't remember how long I sat there. Time stood still, and my thoughts took over me. Lost in them—like a black hole that consumed the universe, they encompassed me. I questioned my entire existence. What the hell had come over me to make me act that way in front of Lauren? It was as if I had no control over my own body or my thoughts—like something deep inside me had snapped. I felt unhinged, inconsolable, and utterly detached from the person I thought I was. At that moment, I had lost myself entirely, and the worst part was that I didn't know how to come back from it.

Every few minutes, I would take a swig of alcohol and then let my hand fall back down. I was pathetic. As heightened as a being as I was, this was low vibrational, but I couldn't help it. I did not care anymore. If I had to choose between Lauren and Imani, I would have to choose neither. There was no possible answer to that equation that I could think of besides not choosing at all.

Who was more deserving of me? Who was I more deserving of?

Lauren's soul was beautiful; she was caring, sweet, and a comfort amid the chaos that sometimes swarmed me. Unfortunately, I hated those fleeting moments when we disagreed or fought, whether physically or verbally; it was emotionally draining for both of us. I knew I was damaging her, fueling a fire that was lowly lit inside of her, gassing it up until she was enraged.

Then there was Imani—a force to be reckoned with. A powerful goddess, lover, someone I was connected to, bound to from the deepest parts of my soul. She was loyal, fierce, and grounded by the universe around her. Imani loved me with every fiber of her being and I loved her just as much. Imani nurtured me in ways I hadn't realized I needed. Where I felt lost, she guided me. When I felt broken, she pieced me back together. She reminded me of who I truly was, pulling me back from the chaos and grounding me in a way no one else ever had. With her, I felt seen. I felt whole.

But I could never choose to be with Imani over Lauren because I truly loved them both.

If I did choose Lauren, I'd still jump to Imani in my meditative state. That part of me would remain, and it was not going away. Even if I wanted to, there was no escaping Imani in this life or the next one.

But who do I choose?

I couldn't choose Lauren, and that was the reality. Even if I did choose Lauren, Imani would always be in the picture.

I take another chug of the liquor and then wipe my lips. I looked at the bottle, and it was almost empty. My vision blurred, and I was exhausted from all the thoughts coursing through my mind. It was later in the day, and I just wanted to fall back asleep so I could be with Imani again. Maybe she could help me figure all of this out. I get off the sofa and immediately trip over my coffee table, crashing to the floor. The bottle flies out of my hand and smashes against the wall, shattering to pieces. I lay there hopelessly, then let out a deep, agonizing groan. I press my hands against the cold, hardwood floor and lift myself, feeling as though I weigh a thousand pounds. I staggered to my feet and tried to find my balance, my eyes half-closed, as my vision faded in and out. Slowly, I walked across the living room and into the bedroom as I stripped off my clothes. I fell into bed and lay there, motionless.

It didn't take me long to fall asleep. I passed out rather quickly.

But then, everything went black. A sudden, consuming darkness swallowed me whole, stripping away every trace of light, warmth, and sound.

There I stood, suspended in the void, utterly alone. The air was thick and heavy, pressing against my skin like an invisible force. My breath echoed, the only sound in the emptiness, but even that felt distant, like I was slipping away from myself. Then came the cold, sharp, and unnatural, creeping into my bones, numbing me from the inside out.

Why didn't I jump to Imani?

I turned and looked behind me, but there was nothing. As far as my eyes could see, there was just an infinite stretch of darkness. Maybe I needed to do breathing exercises to ground myself and get to Imani.

I sat down in this void of darkness, Indian style, closed my eyes, and breathed in deeply, then exhaled. All I could think about was Lauren and our fight. It was hard to center my thoughts when glimpses of us fighting flashed through my mind. But I tried as hard as I could to clear it all away. I sat there for what seemed like hours, meditating. However, there was nothing I could do to focus my thoughts. This darkness crept around me and trapped me in its embrace.

Instead of letting my thoughts drift to Imani, I focused on Troterion—the breathtaking colors, the intoxicating scents, and the crisp, cleansing air that once filled my lungs with peace. But it was all lost on me. No matter how hard I tried to grasp those memories, they slipped through my fingers like grains of sand. My mind was restless, clouded, and unable to hold onto the beauty I once found solace in. I couldn't focus. Not on Troterion. Not on anything. I couldn't jump.

I opened my eyes, and everything was still dark and cold, and at this point, I wanted to wake up. I closed my eyes again and told myself to wake up. But it was silent, and I was still in this cold abyss.

Panic began to settle in, and I got scared.

I stood up and walked around to see if I could find any light or an exit. I ran and saw where it would take me. However, it was just an endless space of darkness. My mind was overwhelmed, and I didn't know if I wanted to scream or cry.

I felt so alone.

Finally, I decided to give this another go. I sat back down, Indian style, and closed my eyes. I hummed for a while to calm my nerves as I rocked back and forth. My body went rigid, locked in place, as I released a slow exhale. Even as I stilled, my mind refused to follow—thoughts raced in endless loops, colliding and unraveling all at once.

Lauren consumed me, her presence running wild through my veins, pulling me toward something familiar, something aching. Then there was Imani—the one I longed to jump to, the one who awakened parts of me I didn't know existed. And beneath it all, a desperate desire clawed at me—I just wanted to wake up.

I needed to ground myself, to latch onto a single thought, a single thread of clarity. But which one? A different timeline with Imani, the present with Lauren, or an escape from it all? The choice loomed over me, heavy and impossible.

This blockage I was experiencing was suffocating—an invisible force trapping me between worlds, between choices, between versions of myself. It was as if my mind and soul were out of sync, tangled in uncertainty, refusing to move forward yet unable to stay still. I was fighting with my inner demon about who I should choose. The blockage was why I could not wake up or jump to Imani or Troterion.

Who would it be if I had to choose for me to get home?

I continued to sit in the darkness, allowing these thoughts to obscure my mind. I was stuck, and there was no way I would get to where I needed to go if I couldn't focus.

I started to think about Lauren and how I did not want to cause her any more pain. If I were to choose her and find a way to suppress Imani again, we could grow old together and be happy. I would seek the help that I needed to allow me to stay in her timeline and do what Imani said: be fucking happy. Maybe that would create a stronger soul tie with Lauren and generate other timelines for us. I wanted to be the best man I could be for Lauren, but I felt guilty for continuously hurting her.

I wanted to choose Lauren.

However, this inner devotion to love Imani was so powerful. Our connection was unreal. I never wanted to be away from her. Her essence captivated and seduced me to give up everything I've built in my current timeline so that I could be with her.

I screamed as loud as I could, and then I screamed again, repeatedly, while being confined to this void. Love's contract was too binding for me to understand. I lived in a world where monogamy was the only way, so this felt taboo. I loved two different women, and I couldn't choose.

I needed to wake up. I wanted to wake up, but nothing I did took me out of this cold, dark space. This empty feeling began to take over, and my mind was foggier than ever.

Why couldn't I wake up?

"Wake up, Mahant," I whispered to myself, repeating the words like a desperate mantra as I rocked back and forth. I was terrified. Fear took over my body—strangling and burning through my entire soul as that feeling of death revisited me.

I sat there and continued to rock back and forth slowly as I told myself to wake up. Hours passed, and no form of meditation was working. Whenever I tried to clear my mind and focus on breathing, distressing thoughts would take over me.

Suddenly, while meditating, I saw a light. It was such a bright light that I held my arm up to cover my eyes to block it. Slowly, I rose to my feet, drawn forward by its force. Each step felt weightless, as if the light was pulling me in, wrapping around me like a warm embrace. I absorbed the light, and everything felt peaceful. It was inviting, almost familiar, and I couldn't resist stepping into it.

The moment I did, a wave of serenity washed over me. The chaos in my mind quieted, the fog lifted, and I could think clearly for the first time in what felt like forever. I felt lighter, more present. But as my senses adjusted to this newfound clarity, one question lingered.

Where was I?

I realized I was back in my bedroom, floating above my bed. Below me was me and—Jah? I was watching myself sleeping in my bed, passed out, as Jah was shaking me vigorously. There was blood on my head and a trail of it out of my room.

What the hell was going on?

I looked at my hands as I floated in the air, and they were translucent. I felt like I was a ghost.

What was this?

Jah continued to shake me as he was on his phone. I could hear him talking, but it sounded far away and unclear. He was on the phone with someone as he left the bedroom, so I followed. There was a trail of blood that led to my living room and ended by my coffee table. Jah was pacing back and forth in the living room as he continued to talk on the phone. As quickly as he entered the living room to observe what had happened, he left and returned to the bedroom. The conversation started to become clearer as I followed him around.

"Yeah, he's still breathing. He must have hit his head and then gone to lie down. There's blood everywhere. I need an ambulance here as soon as possible, please." Jah walks back to my body and grabs my wrists, checking for a pulse. "There's a pulse, and he's breathing, but he won't wake up. I've been trying to wake him up for a while now."

I continue to watch as he tries to remain calm. He was on the phone with what sounded like emergency services. Jah grabs the back of his head and breathes deeply. I've never seen him so serious.

I needed to wake up, but I couldn't.

Jah hung up the phone and sat beside me on the bed. He holds his phone and looks like he's texting someone.

"I'm texting Lauren for you, bud. I don't know what the fuck happened, and I don't know what to do. The ambulance will be here any minute." He continued to talk to me as I lay there.

All I could do was watch. This state I was in was an out-of-body experience I had never felt before. It almost felt like I was astral projecting, but this was different. Usually, I could go back to my body and wake up. Only, every time I would get close to my body, I would feel a vibrating force that immediately bounced me away. It was as if my physical body was blocking my astral metaphysical body.

Minutes passed, and soon after, there was a knock on my front door. Jah rushed to open it, and I stayed in the bedroom, floating above my body, just waiting for them to enter. Again, I tried to get closer to my physical body, but my own energy pushed me back like an ultra-magnet repelling me. Two EMT workers rushed in and began to check me out. They looked at my head, checked my pulse, and then finally turned me over onto my back.

"Lanno, can you hear me?" One of the EMTs opened my eyes and shined a light into it.

After a few minutes of checking me out, they got my body on the stretcher and took me out of my apartment. I followed behind them closely as we all made our way out of the apartment building, and they loaded me into the truck. Jah hops into the ambulance and goes with me to the hospital.

Once they got me to the hospital, they immediately began working on me to figure out what happened. They were hooking me up to IVs, and a phlebotomist came in to draw blood. Nurses were in and out with the doctor as well.

An hour had passed, and I found myself floating around the hospital to find Jah again. He was in the waiting room on the phone. It sounded like it was with my mother he was speaking to. He told her what happened and that she needed to get here immediately.

"Hey, Miss Pauline, Lauren is on the other line. Let me take this, and I will call you back." Jah said, then clicked over to the other call.

Oh no. Lauren was calling Jah, and I knew she would be hysterical. He hangs up the phone and then answers the other call.

"Hey, Lauren—yeah, I don't know what happened." Jah scratches the back of his head as he paces around the waiting room. He walks over to the window and stares out of it as he continues to talk to her. "After you texted me that you all just had a huge fight that got a bit physical, I figured I should go check up on him."

I couldn't make out what Lauren was saying. I could only hear Jah's responses.

"It wasn't right away, no—I had to wait until after work. I grabbed some food for us and went over there because I know how Lanno gets. He won't eat, and he starts drinking."

Jah's voice was shaky as he was talking to her. "There was blood everywhere. He hit his head on the coffee table. There was alcohol and broken glass on the floor, too.

Okay—you're going to come up here? Oh, you're on your way? Bet, I'll see you soon."

Jah hangs up the phone and turns around. He takes a deep breath, exhales slowly, and sits in one of the waiting chairs.

Why couldn't I wake up from this nightmare? That's what it felt like—a nightmare.

As I floated through the hospital, I retraced my steps. The last thing I remembered was falling to the ground in my apartment when I got up to head to bed. I must have hit my head on the coffee table as I fell and didn't realize it. I then got up and went to my bedroom to fall asleep. Instead of jumping to Imani, I entered this void, trapped for hours. Now I'm astral projecting through a hospital and can't wake up. Maybe I needed to center my thoughts and align my third eye and crown chakra. I needed to focus on my breathing exercises and do everything that Imani taught me without distractions. I floated back to the room my body was in and sat on the floor in front of the bed. I close my eyes and try again to clear my mind of impurities.

My body began to tremble, a deep, uncontrollable vibration radiating from within. My aura, once vibrant, now flickered and dimmed like a dying flame. A searing heat spread through my head as if my very mind was on fire, consuming every thought and fragment of clarity.

There was no possible way to realign my chakras in this state—my energy was too scattered, too unstable. But despite the overwhelming chaos, I refused to give up. I pressed forward, desperately trying to regain control, to find even the tiniest sliver of balance.

I closed my eyes and sat in that moment for over fifteen minutes, but nothing worked. I sighed and stood up, automatically floating in the air. I tried to get closer to my body again, and the gravitational pull pushed me backward. I tried to push through the pain, forcing myself to endure, but it only intensified. The heat grew unbearable, a searing wave that felt like ten suns bearing down on me all at once. I screamed as I closed in on my body, but the pain was excruciating. I finally stopped and was pushed back across the room. I let out another scream of frustration.

Footsteps approached, and I turned around to see Lauren and my mom come through the door with the doctor. I moved out of the way as a reflex, as if they could see or touch me, and listened to their conversation.

"So, there was some head trauma resulting in some stitches. He hit his head pretty hard, which explains why he is not waking up. His AST levels were extremely high due to the traces of alcohol found in his test results. We will continue to monitor him in hopes there is no damage to the liver and run more tests." The doctor explains to them both as Lauren walks up next to my physical body while I lie in bed.

She rubs my cheek and then my forehead. Her eyes were extremely red, and she began to cry while she stood next to me. My mom came up to her and hugged her.

Lauren was always an emotional being, but I've never heard her wail the way she was. She couldn't stop crying and let it out in my mom's arms. My mom was always a strong woman. I don't ever recall seeing her cry. She was the type of person who bore other people's pain. She was tough. But even her eyes were full of tears.

My mom tells Lauren she needs a moment, and she leaves the room. I'm sure seeing her only son under these conditions was overwhelming for her.

Lauren pulled a chair next to the hospital bed as I floated off into a corner, watching. She sits down and rests her hands on my stomach. "Please wake up, babe." Tears continued to fall from her eyes in streams.

"I'm so sorry we fought, but I love you, Lanno. I need you to wake up. Come back to me." She continued to talk to me. Her voice cracked as she spoke. She rubbed my stomach and then moved her hand back to my face. Lauren stroked my forehead, her fingertips touching the head wrap as she traced along it. She then rested her head against my chest and sniffled as she tried to calm herself down from crying.

At this moment, there was nothing I could do. I wanted to console Lauren and tell her everything would be alright. A part of me wanted to wake up and tell her I chose her. If I could wake up from this hellish nightmare and go back three months to when it was just her and me, I'd be happy. It all now seemed too late.

It was getting late by the hour, and Lauren stayed beside me the entire night. My mother went home and said she would return in the morning, but Lauren never left my side. She would doze off for an hour or so, and then when the nurses entered, she would wake up in a panic to check on me. Lauren would get out of the way and let the nurse do their thing, and then once the nurse left, she would climb into bed with me. Her arms would wrap around me, and she would rest her head on my chest. Tears would fall from her eyes as she lay there, and then she would drift back off to sleep again. I knew Lauren had to be exhausted mentally.

Occasionally, I sit Indian style and meditate. Watching Lauren and my physical body together gave me a sense of ease. It helped calm my nerves, and I knew that no matter what happened, Lauren had my back. She would always be there for me, even if I were no good to her.

She loved me even when I hurt her and made her feel less than worthy—I didn't deserve her. I stayed in this meditative state for hours and attempted to clear my mind. For hours, all I thought about was Lauren and what our lives would be like if I had chosen her. I cleared my mind of all things Imani, in hopes I'd return to my body, but nothing worked.

So, then I thought about simply waking up. I reminisced about the smells, the taste, and the desire to be in my timeline. I begged and pleaded that I would be a better person to myself and all my loved ones if I could wake up. I thought about the smell of the river outside my apartment and the sound of the city. No matter how hard I tried to focus on specific thoughts, I stayed in this spiritual state.

Finally, my mind wandered back to Imani. If anyone in the universe could pull me from this chaos, it was her. I imagined her, wherever she was right now—did she sense what I was going through?

Did she know?

I pictured her apartment, the soft glow of the lights, and the way her space felt like home, no matter where we were. I replayed our conversations in my head, the quiet moments we shared, the unspoken connection that spanned across all the timelines we'd explored together. The thought of her brought a brief sense of peace, a fleeting moment of calm that I desperately tried to hold onto. I thought about jumping to her, begging for her help, for her warmth, for her strength. I imagined her smile, the way her laugh could fill any room with light. It was all I wanted—just a taste of that comfort, of the safety she brought. Anything that could keep me grounded, I brought into my mind. I got a familiar feeling when I was about to jump that took over my body. Instantly, I got happy, and I started my breathing exercises.

I breathed deeply, held my breath, and then exhaled through my mouth slowly. The meditation lasted five minutes before I felt my body begin to shift. The void scared me, but I remembered what Imani always told me. I had to hold onto the memories and continue to breathe through them. My mind stayed focused, and I did precisely that. I continued my breathing exercises as everything went black again. However, it was not for long. From the darkness emerge brown walls, a brown sofa, and a huge bay window behind it. The realization that I was back in Imani's living room brought a smile and warmth throughout my body like no other.

I stood there and looked around. It was quiet.

"Imani?" I called out.

Imani emerges from the bedroom, confused. She had a towel wrapped around her locs and a T-shirt with panties on.

"Hey, is everything okay?" She asked, concerned.

I rushed up to her, grabbed her face, and kissed her deeply. The copious amounts of joy I was feeling exploded around us.

Imani kissed me deeply, then pulled away. "Hey, baby, what's going on?"

I wrap my arms around her waist and pull her close, burying my face in her neck. I wanted to stay in this moment forever. Just touching her again made me feel alive, overwhelmed with happiness, and a surge of excitement. I wasn't stuck in the void anymore or in that out-of-body state. I needed and wanted to know some things, but I was just content with her being in my arms. Imani wraps her arms around my neck and holds me tight. Her nails stroked up and down the nape of my neck. Tears began to fall from my eyes, and I sniffled.

Imani pulls me away and looks at me as I try to look away so she can't see me crying.

"Mahant, talk to me."

I wipe my eyes, then speak, "I, uh—I crashed out when I returned to my timeline. I crashed out badly."

Imani takes my hand and leads me to the sofa. We sit down facing each other, and she holds my hands tightly.

"I'm so sorry. I know leaving here last time was rough for you after what we did. That's my fault because I should have known you weren't ready for that." Imani explained.

"What do you mean?" I ask as I look into her eyes.

She clears her throat. "Soul ties are bonded by energy that expands across the universe. It grows more intense when we are together. So, any physical activity like that can be like two stars colliding. If you're not used to it, it's a lot to handle, so I should have explained that to you." Imani rubs my hands as she holds them and then continues. "How did you crash out?"

There was always a calming presence about her, a quiet assurance that made everything feel steady. But this time, something was off. When she asked me that question, there was a noticeable hesitation in her voice, a momentary pause that I hadn't heard from her before. Her usual calm demeanor felt strained, and I could feel it in the air. Her aura, typically soft and grounding, now pulsed with tension, a subtle but undeniable shift, like she was holding something back, something she wasn't ready to share.

"Um—I uh—I got into a big fight with Lauren. It got physical because I told her about you. Because I had gone on a rampage." I admitted as I looked down, embarrassed.

Imani got extremely quiet for a while and didn't say a word. It was awkward in the room—the tension in the air was so thick it felt like you could cut it with a butter knife—heavy and impossible to ignore.

"Mmm," Imani finally let out. She exhaled deeply and got quiet again.

"Lauren told me to choose you or her," I told Imani hesitantly.

I finally looked up and watched for a response from Imani. Her eyebrows frowned a bit, and she tilted her head. I could tell she was thinking.

But what about?

"I can see the dilemma," Imani says as she nods and locks her eyes back on me.

"Can you?"

"Mmm, yeah. You can't choose Lauren, and that bothers you. Because even if you choose Lauren, I will always be in the picture."

She was very intuitive, Imani—intelligent and beautiful inside and out. In less than twenty seconds, she could see how terrible the ultimatum Lauren bestowed upon me was. Imani leans forward and wraps her arms around my waist, giving me a big hug before sitting back up straight on the sofa.

Imani pats my knee to reassure me. "I've had you for hundreds of years, and I can wait for another hundred to sync up in another timeline with you. It's hard, but I will manage. It may be hard for you, but you can do this."

"No—that's not all. Something is wrong, Imani, and I'm so scared." I finally confess.

Imani looks at me, "What, Mahant?"

"I can't wake up."

Imani's entire demeanor changes, and her eyes get big. Her breathing starts to deepen as she stares deep into my eyes. "What do you mean you can't wake up, Mahant?"

"After Lauren gave me that choice, I drank. I drank a lot of alcohol, Imani. I, um, drank so much that I fell and hit my head. I went to sleep thinking I would jump to you but went into this void instead. I don't know what happened, but—" I stop explaining mid-through. Imani stands up, grabs her head, and walks away from me.

She begins to whisper to herself. "No, no, no."

I stopped talking and watched her. Her mood and aura shifted. I've never seen or heard Imani so afraid, but I could feel the energy she emitted.

Imani turns around and looks at me with concern. "Did you astral project out of your body?"

"Yeah..." I responded to her, confused. "Wait, how did you know?"

Imani rushes back over to me and sits back down on the sofa. "Listen, you must go now and return to your body, Mahant."

"What are you not telling me?"

Imani, waving her hands, yells at me, "No matter, you need to go now!"

Enough was enough. I needed answers, and I needed them now. There was no more withholding the truth and not explaining what was happening to me.

Imani grabs my hand and begs me. "Mahant, please, listen to—"

"No, you listen to me, Imani!" I snapped, my voice low and forceful, raw with frustration. "I can't go back to my body. I've tried! So, tell me what's going on!"

Imani's eyes begin to well up with tears as she stares at me. Once again, the room gets quiet. Tears fall from Imani's eyes, and her chest rises and falls quickly. "You're dying, babe."

I stared at her in disbelief.

Did she say I was dying?

I felt completely numb, as if my body was frozen in place, incapable of movement. My breath quickened, and a wave of panic rose within me, flooding my mind with urgency. The tightness in my chest intensified, and I could feel myself spiraling.

Then, Imani's hand pressed gently into my chest. The warmth of her palm seeped through the panic, grounding me and offering a sense of calm in the chaos. It was as if her touch was the only thing that could anchor me in that moment.

I whisper, "Explain."

"The longer you stay outside your body in the astral projection state, the more your physical body weakens. It doesn't take long before your body shuts down and—" Imani stops talking and looks away.

"And?" I asked.

"And you start all over. You end this timeline, and you enter a new one."

I would lose Lauren if that were to happen. Was my soul tied to her strongly enough to create another timeline with her? Where would I go?

So many questions entered my thoughts and raced around my mind. Imani was so transparent with me during this time of need, which I appreciated.

"If I end that timeline, can I come to this one and stay?" I asked Imani.

"No, you can't," Imani responded very shortly.

"Why not?" I asked her.

She shakes her head and looks at me sternly. "Stop thinking like that. You need to go back to your timeline and finish it."

I persisted with my questions. "What happens if I don't finish it?"

"Mahant, please—I just answered this. You will go to another timeline. Not this one because—" Imani hesitates again and gets quiet. She looks away and covers her face, her elbows on her knees. She lets out a small sigh of frustration.

"Stop holding back and tell me the truth," I demanded sternly.

"We've been down this road before, Mahant. More times than I can count. No matter what I do or say, you always seem to disregard the rules." Imani says, muffled in her hands.

"What rules, Imani?"

She sits up and looks at me again. "The rules of the universe, Mahant. Whether we are together or apart, you can't seem to handle certain things in every timeline, and you self-destruct. I thought maybe if I eased you into it this time around, it would be different. I've tried so many different ways. Telling you the truth, destruction. Not telling you the truth, destruction." Imani breathes in deeply, then continues. "You've got to concentrate. You have to want to be with Lauren in that timeline to get back. It's going to be so hard, and you are probably not going to want to. But I told you that you needed to trust me. Mahant, you seriously must trust me if you want to get stronger and see me again. Go back and live out that timeline, and stop trying to bend the will of the universe."

"I need your help getting back," I confess to Imani.

Imani takes my hand and leads me off the couch onto the floor. We sit in Indian style, facing each other, and hold hands. She immediately closes her eyes and starts her breathing exercises without a word. I follow her as I breathe in deeply through my nose and exhale through my mouth. I clear my mind and release all negative thoughts. My hands suddenly felt clammy, and I was super nervous. Some thoughts escaped me, but there were also thoughts that tried to sneak in. I blocked them to the best of my ability and continued to focus on my breathing.

"Always focus on staying in that present moment you want to be in and harness the healing powers from Troterion." She continued whispering small, detailed affirmations to me. Imani and I sat in this moment for a long time. After a while, neither one of us spoke a word. We simply breathed in and out. Her energy felt vibrant, while mine seemed dimmed.

I was tired.

But I continued to focus on Lauren and getting back to her. I thought about our adventures, visiting our favorite lounge, or eating out with friends. I held onto the good moments and felt a sense of warmth take over my body. Not being able to wake up was scary, and I was terrified even though I was with Imani. I didn't want to leave Lauren like this. But I didn't allow fear to take over me like I had before. I let the warmth of those memories surround me.

Suddenly, there was darkness again, and Imani was gone. I was back in the void, still sitting Indian style. I could not allow this void to distract me from returning to Lauren. I continued to hold onto those thoughts as a glimpse of light slowly formed in front of me, and as I floated towards it, I found myself back in the hospital in my room. Unfortunately, I was not back in my body but astral projecting outside of it again. I was off in a corner, and tons of nurses and doctors surrounded me. It was a chaotic scene. Jah was pulling my mother and Lauren out of the room as they resisted leaving. I couldn't hear much because everyone was panicking, but it didn't look good.

Even though I couldn't physically feel any pain, I couldn't bear to watch. My entire body felt empty as I watched over my lifeless body. I was helpless as the team of doctors worked on me. I didn't understand where this took a turn. I know Imani said the longer I was away from my body, the harder it would be to return.

Did I even want to return to my body in the state that it was in?

As I watched, I grew colder. The commotion died down as the medical professionals stood around me, and I could faintly hear them talking.

"The EEG is coming back flatline. He's stable on the machine for now." The doctor announced.

I didn't understand what they were discussing and how quickly I declined. How long have I gone with Imani? I left the room and looked for Lauren. Lauren was a mess as Jah attempted to console her. Her face blushed, her eyes were bloodshot red, and she was crying in his arms. My mom talked to a nurse, and the doctor came out. I shook my head to hear, but the conversation was too low. Everything felt faint; even my energy was fleeting, slowly slipping away even in my metaphysical state. I floated back to the room and tried to get close to my body, but there was that re-pelling feeling again. I sat down and began to meditate, this time telling myself that I could and would get back to my body so that I could put a stop to all these emotions my loved ones felt. I blocked out everything around me and focused on my breathing. I concentrate on Lauren, my mom, and Jah. Imani told me that even if I returned and it looked like it was too late, it never was. She reminded me to harness the energy of Troterion and its healing abilities and to remember that I needed to want to be here.

There I sat, completely still, focusing every ounce of my energy inward. I blocked out everything—the beeping monitors, the murmurs of nurses passing by, and the sterile chill of the hospital air. I didn't allow a single distraction to break my concentration. An hour passed, and I was still there, meditating on the cold tile floor in front of my lifeless body.

Not a shift. Not a flicker. Just silence and stillness. A growing weight of frustration settled over me.

Nothing worked.

Chapter 17

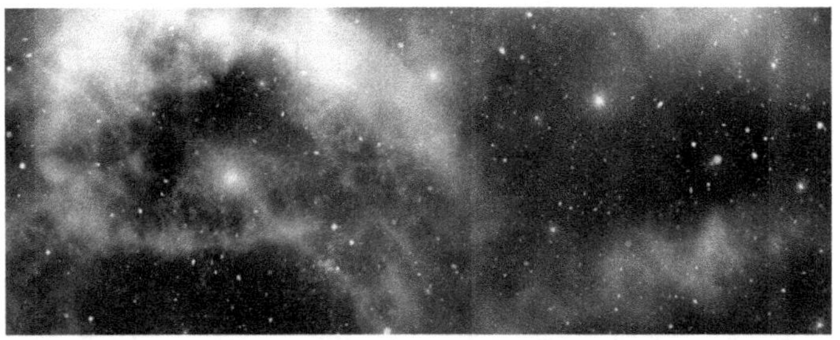

Days blurred into one another as I remained locked in my meditative state, unwavering in my focus. I had never pushed myself this far before—never had to concentrate with such intensity for so long. But no matter how hard I tried, clarity remained just out of reach, slipping through my grasp. Frustration settled deep in my chest, heavy and suffocating. Eventually, I exhaled sharply and let it go. I couldn't keep fighting a losing battle. I had to surrender. I stood a few feet in front of the hospital bed and watched as Lauren slept in a chair next to my body.

Her head rested on my chest, with her phone almost falling out of her hand.

She never left my side.

I overheard a conversation the doctor had with my mother earlier. They informed her that the fall and the hit to the head caused severe swelling. There was no longer any brain activity, and I had been hooked up to a machine to keep me breathing. There were also tough conversations about how much longer my body could stay like this and what the best possible outcome was.

Imani was right. I was dying.

As much of a mess as my head was, it seemed easy to jump to Imani if I wanted to. But I have concentrated heavily on reconnecting with my body over the past few days. I started to think that maybe I could not return to my body because, deep down, I didn't want to. The possibility of my timeline ending here and continuing with Imani intrigued me. Even if she said it wasn't possible, I was hopeful. If I couldn't get back to my body, maybe I could be with Imani now. It was a stupid and selfish thought. Though it was undeniably present in my mind.

I sighed deeply and shifted my thoughts to Imani. It was time for me to revisit and update her on everything happening. I closed my eyes and felt my body shift into peace, a seamless transition.

When I opened my eyes, I was back in Imani's apartment. She was sitting on the sofa, watching me as I came in, and once everything came to, we stared at each other in silence for a while. The next thing I knew, a single trail of tears trickled down her cheek. I walked over to her as she slowly stood up and wrapped her arms around my neck. I hugged her waist, and we held each other tightly.

She whispers, "My Mahant."

Tears formed in my eyes, my voice cracking as I spoke, "I'm so sorry. I tried as hard as I could."

My energy was weaker than it had been in the days before, as hers felt warm and inviting towards me.

"What happens now?" I asked Imani.

Imani stays quiet and continues to hold me in her embrace. She sighs into my arms and then pulls me away. "Let's sit." She sits down and pats the sofa next to her. I sat down and turned towards her, waiting for a response. Imani wipes my shoulder and fixes my collar. I could tell she was trying to avoid eye contact with me. To comfort me, her hand rested on my chest, and she rubbed softly.

"Do you remember Scotty's Bar?" Imani asks as she clears her throat, attempting to keep her composure.

I thought about what she said, and memories came slowly.

It was 1994, a different timeline, and I had just left a place called Scotty's Bar. As I walked past the alley, I heard a woman screaming. I remember contemplating whether to keep walking and mind my business or intervene. However, I decided to help. Walking down the alley, I saw a man with a gorgeous woman. He had his hand around her arm and pulled her deeper into the alley towards a door. The guy and I went back and forth until he finally decided it wasn't worth the fight and left her alone. I came to her aid, and she thanked me by offering to buy me a drink. We headed back into the bar and talked for hours. It was as if I knew her already, but I couldn't pinpoint the connection.

After that night, we stayed in contact with each other. I realized I hadn't gotten her name on our second date, so when I asked her, she told me it was Imani. I remember the eerie feeling that I had back then. Inexplicable memories swept over me, and I didn't understand them. Later, Imani would explain what it all meant to me. The emotions that surged through me in those moments were beyond comprehension—intense, raw, and almost surreal. I struggled to process the flood of information Imani had poured into my mind. It was too much, too fast—an overwhelming surge that left me reeling. My chest tightened, and a wave of anxiety crashed over me, drowning out any sense of clarity. Fear crept in, whispering that I wasn't ready and couldn't handle the weight of it all.

"1955 in Dubair," Imani whispers to me. The tips of her fingers ran through the side of my hair. She continued to play with my curls as I sat and listened.

Another memory took over, another timeline. I remembered that Dubair was a planet in our universe that favored Earth. This time, however, I was much younger. A friend who lived close to me would always come to get me so we could go outside to play—her name was Soleigh. There was a nearby park that we frequented and played ball in. Some days, we would play with our toys or get milk ice, our form of ice cream from the corner store, or Nooklax, a kind of snack jerky. We did everything and went everywhere together. Our bond was inseparable.

Unfortunately, one day, she and her mom packed up and moved away. The bond we shared was unbreakable, and when she left, it shattered me. She was my only true friend, the one person who understood me, and without her, I withdrew into myself. As time passed, our connection faded. High school came and went—I grew taller, stronger, and more independent. Then came college, where the nights blurred into endless parties, heavy drinking, and fleeting moments of pleasure that never truly filled the void. No matter how much I indulged, the emptiness lingered, a constant shadow. In this memory I was reliving, I saw myself spiraling—losing myself with substance abuse and meaningless encounters.

Well, one day, out of the blue, I thought about Soleigh. So, I decided to look her up and see what she had been up to in life. I felt like a stalker, but just thinking about her made me happy and hopeful that we could reconnect. I decided to look her up on Exo, a platform where people connect with others.

Everyone had an Exo account, and since her name was so unique, it didn't take me long to find her. I was so upset with myself for never having thought of doing this before and for not rekindling our friendship much sooner.

Soleigh grew up to be so beautiful.

It was a much different Soleigh than I remembered.

For days, whenever I typed her a message, I would stop myself. There was so much anxiety and nervousness that I had built up.

Would she even remember me if I were to reach out?

For the next few days, I studied her account, checking her recent posts or her daily stories, seeing if there were any updates. She didn't live too far away and only posted a couple of times a day. Her aesthetic was that of a quiet girl who loved books. She would post cute images of small items thoughtfully placed together—photos of objects with the same color palettes in slightly different shades or pictures of a fresh manicure set. Amidst these, there would always be a glimpse of her—a subtle, endearing presence. She held a book in most photos, lost in its pages, while in others, a steaming cup of coffee rested in her hand, completing the cozy, intellectual allure she embodied.

Finally, on day four, I decided to send her a message.

You probably don't remember me. The last time we saw each other, we were kids. But it's me, Rally.

I sent the message and waited—anxious, with sweaty palms, impatient for a response. I was such a scrawny kid the last time she saw me. However, puberty did a number on me in this timeline. I was very athletic and of average height. I had traditionally done rite-of-passage tribal markings covering my body, and my hair was jet black.

I reminisced about the gut-wrenching feeling of waiting for Soleigh to message me back. It wasn't long after I sent the message that I would hear a ding on my phone.

OMG, Rally??

More dings came through.

I can't believe it's you! We have to meet up.

I was so happy at that moment to receive those messages from her. We exchanged numbers, and a couple of days later, I found myself driving an hour away to meet up with her. When we finally got together, she was even more stunning in person—a short, beautiful woman with the most amazingly gorgeous smile. Her hair was naturally dark brown and curly, and her eyes were dark brown to match. I noticed she also had her rite-of-passage tribal markings as well. This timeline was unique, like Troterion, because we were all the same human-like beings. However, some beings didn't get their markings and were outcasts, completely segregated from the rest of the world. They would have their own schools, stores, and laws. I was happy to see she had her markings on her hands.

The first time we met, we ended up at a local bar near her home and talked for hours on end. She told me why her mom moved them away and that she looked for me for a long time after. She expressed how sad she would get when no results showed up. I couldn't help but blame myself because I joined Exo recently. Soleigh told me she had stopped searching but had never forgotten about me. Hours had flown by that day, and soon, it was time for us to leave. This powerful rush came over me, and I didn't want to leave her. We stood outside the bar for a while, waiting for public transportation so she could get home. It was quiet and unsettling before she finally popped the question, asking if I would like to go back to her place.

I, of course, said yes, and we headed to her home, but before we could get into her house, our lips collided. We stumbled through the doorway, kissing passionately, stripping each other out of our clothes until we finally made it to her bedroom. Our bodies intertwined, touching, kissing, caressing one another until we erupted beneath the moonlight. After an explosive session, we would laugh, talk, and then repeat the process all over again. Once finished, we'd cuddle up next to each other, tangled in the sheets as we conversed the remainder of the night away.

We discussed everything, from the universe and how it works to life beyond our own planet. She confessed that she had something to tell me and didn't know how I would take it. However, what she confessed made all the sense in the world to me. She told me we were soul-tied and got lucky to end up in the same timeline again. She also confessed that her true soul's name was Imani, and she withheld this information when we were kids to protect me until I was older. In both moments, now and then, a rush of memories swarmed me, finally unlocking core memories that were stored away. Whenever Imani would relinquish information about my past or say our soul's name, I would remember. Whenever we were close to each other and bonded, my core began to restore. My mind healed in ways that I didn't understand. She had the power to mend my broken mind. But she could never do it alone and restore my memory to its full extent. With every memory and every timeline, we would have to visit Troterion.

I looked at Imani, and she smiled back. She never stopped stroking my hair, and as we sat there, more memories and lives we once shared filled my mind like missing links.

"Why am I remembering everything now?" I questioned Imani.

Imani sighed, pushed my hair out of my face, and then took my hands. She rubs them as she sets them both in her lap.

"Shh. You will understand soon. Close your eyes and remember the beginning." Her words wrap around me like a gentle embrace, urging me to surrender to the moment. Imani closes her eyes with me, and we hold hands on her sofa.

I started to get a vision of what seemed like the void, but this time it was different. The void was usually pitch black, empty, and cold. This darkness that engulfed me was warm and vibrant. Instead of it being completely black, tiny stars surrounded me and Imani. Those little stars were small forms of light illuminating around us in a massive space that seemed as though it were alive. I reached out and touched one—it was cool to the touch and inviting, dancing around my fingertips, then going on its way.

Finally, when I turned back to Imani, she was shifting—her form unraveling and morphing before my eyes. She no longer looked like herself but something otherworldly. My breath hitched as I glanced down at my own hands, only to find them transforming as well. My skin flickered between shades, then rippled with the sudden appearance of scales, only for them to vanish just as quickly. My body warped unpredictably, growing taller, then shorter, expanding and contracting in an endless cycle of change.

These changes were all me—different beings I have been across the timelines with Imani. Every time I would change, the memories took over me, and I would remember. It was refreshing to remember, but with every memory came sorrow, and with every birth came death. All the times I have been with Imani across time and space, my death was always bizarre.

In 1944, Scotty's Bar, Imani had found me, and six days later, I shot myself in the head from the overwhelming truths bestowed upon me. When the vision swept over me of that timeline, I let go of Imani's hands and clenched my chest as I crouched, pain sweeping over me in a quick, gut-wrenching force. There was immense sorrow that led up to that breaking point, and there was even deeper pain when I pulled the trigger. The coldness of the steel gun caressing my fingers and the thoughts that crept through my mind were unsettling. The confusion that hovered over me had me in a state of panic.

Dubair, 1967, twelve years after Soleigh moved and we rekindle our friendship, I would be found dead in my dorm from an overdose. Only weeks after Soleigh had revealed to me who she was and the powerful abilities I had. Once again, her revealing who she was sent me into a spiral, emotions clashing into me like a jagged wave in a storm.

Memories continued to take over my mind as I was there in this new space with Imani. She crouched down and rubbed my back as I experienced this everlasting pain.

Whether we were in the same timeline or Imani jumped to me, it caused an eruption in the universe that set off a recurring chain of events. Repeatedly, I saw different lives that I was born into, different evolutions and timelines, and I experienced the same pain—from breathing life into my soul to creating death. It seemed there was no hope that these events would course-correct themselves to create an alternate outcome. However, as all the dark memories came in, there was also light.

"Allentown and Utopia," Imani whispered as she knelt beside me.

At the same time, both of those timelines rushed over me. I recalled Imani and I were much older when we died in both timelines. Allentown came first, and when I died, I was 94 years old in human years and 829 in soul years. In Allentown, I successfully regained all of my memories because Imani restored them, and then I lived out the entirety of my life as Tony. Fast forward to the next timeline after I passed away peacefully in my sleep as Tony—I was born as Thomas in Utopia, with all my memories from every timeline I ever lived in. Thomas was who I was in my previous timeline, before I became Lanno in my present timeline. I died at 92 years old in human years and 921 in soul years as Thomas.

So many questions ran wild through me—how did I remember as Thomas, and why didn't I remember as Lanno?

I looked up at Imani, still crouched down, and shook my head slowly. "I still don't understand, though. I remembered all my past, present, and future lives as Thomas. This has never happened before, Imani. How's that possible?"

"Because you finished your timeline in Allentown as Tony, Mahant," Imani explained, then continued, "Whenever you are the cause of your death in a timeline, you don't get to remember the next. Not unless your soul tie finds you. You lived your life to the fullest as Tony. As Thomas, you did not."

I closed my eyes and let the memories continue to flow through me. As I focused, bits and pieces of Thomas's memories came back to me about how I died.

I remembered.

"I was sick, and I kept visiting Troterion. I was losing my memory and didn't understand why. Troterion would restore it, but I was sick all over again when I woke up. My human body was corroding my brain." I held onto the memories as I thought it through. Imani steadily rubbed my back and comforted me. "I couldn't bear the pain of it all, so I took a handful of pills and fell asleep so I could stay in Troterion and heal. My mind couldn't remember at that moment that it would affect my memory in the next timeline. I fucked myself."

I opened my eyes to Imani's big, beautiful eyes, blood-shot red. She sighed and started to wipe her tears as they fell down her face.

"Mmm—that makes sense. Which is why you've forgotten again in this timeline," Imani murmured, her voice unsteady. A sharp inhale broke through her words.

"You're right, Imani. I'm the catalyst."

Imani remained quiet and continued to listen to me. My body grew weaker, but I didn't want to admit it to myself or her. I sighed and finally plopped down on my butt from crouching. I was exhausted—my arms resting on my knees as I sat there, my head draped low and my chest shallowly rising.

Imani scoots closer to me and grabs onto my shirt. "Hey, listen to me, Mahant. You made the right choice to come see me before…" She gets quiet for a while, trying to collect her thoughts. I grew fatigued as the seconds passed. "Before you start all over, I've gotten the chance to see you again. To help you piece this all together. Hey… look at me."

Imani shakes me a little, and I attempt to lift my head and keep it up. I stared into her eyes. Her voice and spoken words so beautifully danced between my ears. She placed her hand back on my chest, as she always did, and rubbed slowly. All the while holding me up. "I've made you promises, okay, Mahant? Promises I damn sure am willing to keep. No matter what timeline, year, universe, or beings we are, I will always find you. I will always love you. If we must do this repeatedly for as long as we live, that's the sacrifice of immortal love, a love stronger than its creator, the universe. I choose you over and over again."

I mumble and slur my speech. "I love you, Imani."

Imani finally sits down on her butt as well and pulls me in between her legs. The side of my head rests up against her chest as she wraps her arms around me and locks her fingers. She rocks side to side, and I close my eyes. Tears streamed down my cheeks as I opened myself to the flood of memories I had lost. Each one crashed into me like waves of static, sharp and relentless, piercing my mind like a thousand needles against my skin. The air around me buzzed with an electric charge, crackling with the weight of everything I had forgotten—and everything I was about to remember.

But then, finally, this warmth that I had always experienced while being with Imani crept in. Her energy soothed away the anxiety and fear that incapacitated me. Our bodies connected as one again, and her aura cleansed my spirit.

"I love you too, Mahant," she whispers as she starts stroking my hair again, consoling me. I just wanted to lie in this moment forever, for the rest of eternity, with her. If time passed by, whether slow or fast, this is where I truly wanted to be. I looked up at Imani, and her eyes were full of tears. I was so tired of causing pain to those who mattered the most.

"I'm so sorry, Imani. I keep messing up." My voice staggered, and my energy was depleting.

"Hey, hey, no. Listen to me. You're such a beautiful soul. None of this is your fault. Our minds sometimes are just a mess, and we will heal yours. I promise." Imani grips my face as she holds me and locks her eyes on me. "Ugh," she lets out, frustrated.

I very weakly lifted my hand, pushed her one long precious loc out of her face, and then wiped away her tears. "Talk to me."

Imani looks up and inhales deeply, holding back more tears. She hesitates before speaking again. Then she looks down at me. "I need you to do something for me. It will be hard, but I need you to do it."

"Anything, Imani," I responded, my voice raspy and low. It was getting harder to breathe.

Imani sniffles and then clears her throat. "I need you to go back to Lauren when you pass. Go be with her and your body. You must go back. And I know you want to ask why, but remember, she and your family love you, and you love them too. Those are ties you may never see again."

I stay quiet for a few seconds, and then I nod my head.

"I'm so scared," I confess.

"I know, baby, I know. But listen, I promise you, Mahant. I will find you again. I always do." Imani leans down and presses her lips into mine, and I kiss her back deeply. We stay in this embrace for a while, illuminating the dark space around us even more. I could barely feel my body heat or energy, but hers kept me warm.

"I love you," I tell her again as I pull away from her lips briefly. Her damp face pressed against mine as her tears fell on my face. She presses her lips back into mine, and we have the most passionate kiss we have ever had. She didn't want to let me go, but she had to. There didn't seem to be much time left for me.

Imani finally pulls away and clears her throat again. She adjusts herself. "Okay, go. Focus on Lauren, your family, and friends. Focusing on them will lead you back now."

I sat up and attempted to cross my legs in the Indian-style position. However, everything to my core was on fire. I focused my thoughts and cleared my mind of the pain. In my meditative state, I thought about Lauren and waited until my body shifted back to my timeline.

The transition from Imani back to the hospital was, for the first time, unbearable, but I made it.

Chapter 18

My mom decided to pull the plug on me sometime today, as I was showing no signs of improvement whatsoever. My brain was completely dead. It's been a week since I've been in the hospital, and whatever glimmer of hope my mother had for me was gone. She was making the hardest decision of her life later today, which was to allow me to pass. I floated in the hospital room for a while, watching over my body.

I hated how I was leaving Lauren, and there was a piece of me that longed to be with her again before I was gone. I wished I could hop back into my body one last time to say goodbye. Somehow, though, through the midst of it all, I felt at peace. I held onto hope that I would see Lauren again in another timeline, and I also had my promises from Imani. She promised to find me wherever I landed in the universe—beyond the stars, across the galaxy, we will be together again. It was hard ending this timeline, and however hopeful I was, dying was scary.

My circle was small, so not many people had to come to pay their respects. It was just my mother, Jah, Fallyn, and Lauren.

I had never seen Jah cry before. However, these past few days, he has been choked up. On this day, he would sit in the chair next to me and talk to me.

"I don't know what to say to you, Lanno. I don't know if you can hear me, but I will pretend you can. I'm going to miss you, big dog. I'm sorry I didn't get to you sooner that night. Maybe then you would have had a fighting chance. But look, I've got something to tell you." Jah would scoot closer and lean in as he whispered the next part. "I level-set with Fallyn and told her that I would give up all these girls if she gave me a chance. I told her I really liked her and wanted to make her my one and only girl. You know what she said? She said she would give me a chance. I wish you were here to see how I will treat her. But I promise our love will be strong like yours and Lauren's."

Jah continued, his voice steady as he reminisced about our shared memories—growing up together, the hardships we faced, and the victories that followed. He sat there with me for hours, his words flowing nonstop, filling the space between us. Floating off in the distant corner, I couldn't help but laugh at him because he always knew how to talk.

His last promise warmed my heart as he spoke. "I'm going to look after Mama and Lauren for you, too, I promise. It will be hard for us all, but mostly for them. I got your back, brother. I love you."

Jah would sit with me, finally, in silence for a bit. He placed his forehead against mine, then stood and left the room.

The next person who came into the room was Fallyn. She sat in the chair next to me and got extremely quiet. She pushed my hair out of my face and rubbed my forehead before saying a word. I had never seen Fallyn in a sensitive or emotional state, but even her eyes were as red as can be.

Fallyn spoke, "People make mistakes, and I won't hold that over you because I know your love for Lauren was real. I also know that Lauren's love for you is undeniable. I've never seen someone love another human being with all that they were until I saw how much Lauren was in love with you. She could never stop talking about you and how happy you made her. She thought the world of you. I don't think she will ever stop beating herself up about you guys' fight before all of this happened, but…" Fallyn wipes a tear from her eyes and clears her throat. She adjusts herself in the chair and composes herself. She looks around the room and then back at me in the hospital bed. "Look, I promise to get her through this the best I can."

Fallyn's last few words were short and sweet, a form of tough love she concluded with when she got choked up that I could appreciate. It was her in her brutal, undeniably raw self. I appreciated Fallyn coming to see me and being a huge support system for Lauren. It brought me happiness in my final moments, knowing that the people I loved would be okay.

A warm, soothing energy enveloped the room, drawing me closer to my body. The resistance I had once felt, the force that kept me from returning, slowly faded. Though I still couldn't fully settle back into myself, I could feel myself gravitating towards my physical form that was lying in the hospital bed. The pull was gentle, like an invitation, and with each passing moment, it became more inviting and comforting. Despite the distance, it was as if my body was calling me home, offering peace and renewal.

My mom came through the door next and sat down in the chair. She began to caress my face. My mother was a strong and stoic woman. But even she looked defeated. Her eyes were red, and around them were extremely puffy. Her body language was completely different from the woman I once knew. She always kept herself well-groomed; however, her shirt seemed a little wrinkled and rushed this time around. She was wearing a flowery blouse and black pants, accompanied by white loafers. My mom took in a deep sigh before proceeding to speak to me.

"My handsome man," she started while caressing my cheek. There was a heart-wrenching pause before she continued, "I'm going to miss you. A parent is not supposed to bury their child, and here you are, defying the odds. You always did what you wanted, even as a young boy. You'd have your mind set on something and wouldn't let it go. I loved that about you, though, my son. You worked hard for what you wanted and went above and beyond to earn it. Such a brilliant mind you had with such a big, beautiful heart."

My mom sat beside me, her gentle hum the only sound filling the room, yet laced with sorrow. Her tears fell steadily, streaming down her face as her hand rested softly on my head. She rocked back and forth, her movements slow and rhythmic, as if trying to soothe both of us in this unbearable moment. I could feel her heart breaking, each tear a reminder of how much she loved me, how much she was losing. Watching her like this—vulnerable, raw, and helpless—was a pain that sliced through me in ways words couldn't capture. It was as if every drop of her grief was a reflection of my own, and seeing her finally cry after years of her being my anchor was a pain so deep it felt like it could swallow me whole. "I wish you'd wake up, baby boy. But I know soon you'll be at peace. I love you."

Those were her final words after many she spoke to me. She stood, leaned down, kissed my forehead, and left the room.

My physical body began to pull me in, and my energy became much stronger—my mind became more peaceful and quieter. Finally, with clear consciousness and calmness, I floated above my body while it lay in bed. The repelling energy that once emitted around my body was gone. I closed my eyes and hovered, slowly sinking back into my almost lifeless body. I could now feel the pain that surged through my entire body like sharp icicles, the feeling of death at the center of my core. I settled in and continued to focus my mind. The room was eerily quiet, with only the machines' soft beeping and birds' distant chirping outside the window breaking the silence. The faint sounds of voices and footsteps from the staff passing by drifted in from the hallway, but inside, everything felt still—dark, like time had paused. Then, out of nowhere, a familiar voice cut through the silence. It was gentle at first, as though unsure if it could reach me, but I knew it instantly. My heart skipped a beat as the voice I recognized echoed through the shadows.

Lauren was here with me.

"I wrote these words down because I knew I wouldn't have been able to say all of this to you without structure. First and foremost, Lanno, I want to tell you that I love you, and I am so sorry that we fought. I can't help but blame myself for leaving you vulnerable enough to drink away your sorrows and cause you to hurt yourself. I should have stayed and talked things through with you. Though this is nobody's fault, it's hard to bear this pain alone. Fallyn keeps reminding me that destiny and fate are unmatched, and things happen for a reason. This all made me think about what you told me about soul ties and how we could possibly be bound for life. This resonated with me because I want this to be true so badly."

There was silence for a few minutes. I could hear Lauren controlling her breathing, sniffling, and crying. She then continued speaking. "I really wish there was this miracle that would make you wake up, and you would be all better again. But if you don't, Lanno, please promise me that you will find me in the next timeline if we are bound for life. Promise me that you will search for me beyond the stars.

And as much as I promise you right here and now that I won't ever stop loving you, will you promise me the same? I will cherish our time together in this world and keep your memory alive until we meet again. Just know that you were the best damn thing that has ever happened to me. Even in this short amount of time we've known each other, I feel as though I've known you forever. You were able to be real with me, open and honest. Even when you thought I would 'run for the hills,' were you still vulnerable."

Lauren paused one last time, and as it remained dark, I could hear and feel the presence of other people coming into the room. The energy shifted, and I knew my mom, Jah, and Fallyn were present. The doctor and their team surrounded me as they were finally ready to end it all.

Lauren kept talking, her voice shaking as I heard someone come up and mess with a machine nearby. "I love you, babe. I'm holding your hand as you go so that you will know you are surrounded by nothing but love in the end."

There were a few beeps and then silence. My entire body was warm, and I couldn't breathe. Darkness still encompassed me, and a faint, distant memory of Imani came to me. She reminded me to focus on breathing when I felt I couldn't breathe. It was painful, but I controlled my thoughts as best as I could. Seconds passed, and I continued to think of affirmations, reminding myself repeatedly to breathe.

Finally, a glimpse of white light emerged from the darkness, calling to me and pulling me in. My entire body surged forward, pulled into the light with incredible speed. Soon, there was no more darkness, and I soared at light-year speeds. I was flying fast through the universe—speckles of colors began to flash as millions of stars and planets passed me by. As fast as I was soaring, my breathing leveled out quickly, and I was at peace. I let this phenomenon take me as I was, allowing it to encapsulate my body and orbit me through time and space.

Suddenly, I stopped in what seemed to be the heart, maybe even the center of the universe. I stood there in this quiet space and listened.

"Hello?" I called out.

"Hello, Mahant," A voice sang back to me.

It was just me in this vast universe alone. I turned around as I floated to see who was speaking, but nobody was there.

"Where am I?" I asked the voice.

The voice answered. "You are in the middle of where the universe breathes. Where it whispers and creates life."

The voice sounded majestic, like a melody to my ears. Neither man nor woman, the voice was neither and both at the same time. Its tone was soothing and powerful, carrying an ancient depth as though it had existed long before time itself. It wrapped around me, filling the space with a presence so vast that I felt both insignificant and deeply connected, as if it spoke directly to the core of my being.

"What happens now?" I asked with an eerie familiarity about the power of this realm.

"That depends on you, Mahant." The voice responded to me.

"I'd like to go back," I confessed.

"You can go back. You can always go back. Things can be the same or different, your choice." The voice explained.

There was silence for a moment between us, and I noticed that, once again, I was shifting into different life forms. I was no longer Lanno but other beings—a dolphin, an owl, and more, constantly evolving into intelligent forms. This time, I didn't know if these were beings I've experienced or beings I could be. I just assumed it was my Mahant form.

The voice finally broke the silence. "When you go back, you will take the life form of a species and promise that no matter how hard, you will see it through." The voice was transparent, and it seemed that this was my opportunity to get answers.

"Do I get to choose what I want to be regarding the species?" I asked curiously.

"Yes." The voice responded quickly.

"I'm starting to remember now. I remember being born into the universe hundreds of years ago. I remember living multiple lives, whether past, present, or future. I remember my soul tie, Imani, and you birthed us at the same time. I also remember you, universe. There's only one thing I don't understand. Why can't I remember when I'm reborn again? Is what Imani told me correct?" There was passion behind my voice when I asked this question. I wanted to understand the ins and outs of everything I did, even if I couldn't remember it afterward.

"Imani was right. She has never had to experience a loss of memories and can restore memories, just like any soul tie, because she has always lived every single lifetime through. You, on the other hand, Mahant, have not. However, even so, it is still not that simple. I only birthed hundreds out of billions of souls who remember. You are special and have potential. Now, go ahead and ask me the question you ask me every time you are about to be reborn again."

I thought momentarily about what the universe meant by that last part. Then, I finally found another question to ask. "So, I won't remember this time then?"

"Ahh, there's the question. Precisely." The universe responded, wise and knowing, as if it had anticipated my thoughts.

Whenever I died, I had always asked the universe the same questions initially. It was as if my mind was foggy and slowly catching up to all the memories I had once lost.

However, being in this space, trading secrets with the universe, every single memory eventually came back to me, and there was nothing that I couldn't remember from my previous lives now. I wished there was a way that I could remember once I was reborn, but I knew there was not—unless I finished my previous timeline. My knowledge was vast and powerful at this moment. I remembered and cherished all my prior conversations with the universe whenever I came to be in this space.

How was I supposed to remember not to be the reason for my own demise if I'm not able to remember thoroughly? This rule was confusing and upsetting. But no matter what, I was determined to solve this problem.

"I'd like to go back as a human, and I'd also like to look the same," I informed the universe. With all the memories coming back, I knew my request was obtainable.

"So that body did you well..." The universe responded.

"And what about Lauren? Can she be soul-tied to me as well?"

"Yes," The universe responded quickly again. "For you, my son will return with no memories of this. Allow yourself to rejoice in the evolution of the universe. Take me not for granted and live out this precious life. Other souls wait longer to be able to go back. You should be grateful."

A bright red star started to glow even more brightly in the distance. Slowly, it floated closer towards me.

"Lauren's light is among the hundreds of souls that will remember. You are lucky, Mahant. Not many are tethered to each other as strongly as you are to two souls."

The red star danced around me as I turned with it, mesmerized by its beauty. It reminded me of Lauren—it was so bright and illuminated my palm as I moved my hand around it. It was a small star, but its energy was powerful. Another shining star, slowly floating off into the distance, started to drift towards me. This star was blue, next to Lauren's red star.

The universe continued, "Imani and you have one of the strongest connections I've ever seen—a beautiful story celebrated with song and dance across the universe. We will also see how your story and Lauren's evolve, another melody to unfold. Do you want an easy life again, Mahant, or one with challenges?"

I made a face in disbelief. "You call Lanno's life easy?"

"Yes." The universe responded.

"If that was easy, I need an easier life, universe!"

We continued to discuss me going back as a human being. The universe asked me how many kids I wanted, whether I wanted some struggles or no struggles at all, how old I wanted to live to be, what year I wanted to live in, and what timeline was best. I was helping to build my next life, which always fascinated me.

The universe and I had a long conversation to prepare me for what came next.

After our conversation, the universe around me shifted. The stars twinkled, growing brighter as they swarmed around me. The energy surged, and there was an increasing pull of my inner self. My form felt lighter as I transitioned into a blue round star, glowing tremendously against the black space. As I transformed, Lauren's red star, and Imani's blue star merged with mine. I could feel them both, the universe's core and everything around me, as a black hole opened up before me. I was being pulled into this black hole, no longer having any control to resist.

I expected darkness inside the black hole, but I encountered an overwhelming light—a blinding yet comforting white light that surrounded me in every direction.

And through that bright white light, I went.

Chapter 19

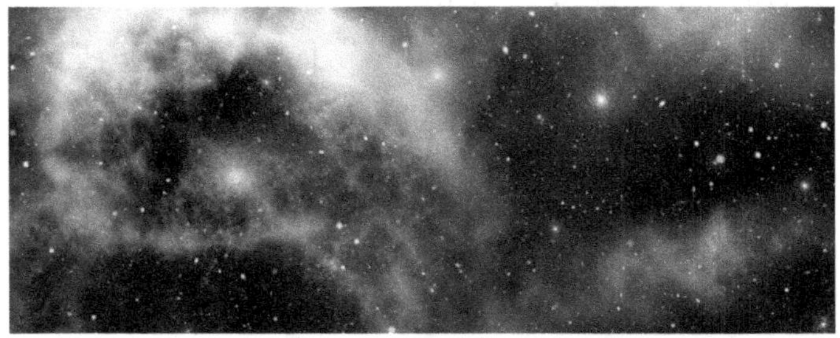

My eyes opened as I was lying on my platform bed. I did a big stretch as my auto-dim lights turned on in my bedroom. I turned over and picked up my phone to check the time, which was 3:00 a.m. Why did I always wake up around this time, and then I would never be able to fall back asleep? I got out of bed and walked to my kitchen to grab some water. My bare feet were cold against my hardwood floors as I tiptoed to the kitchen. I had to be quiet not to wake my roommate up because he was a grouchy man when he didn't get enough sleep. He had to get as much sleep as possible because he spent his days streaming online and playing video games. He would say it was 'exhausting' and he needed his 'beauty sleep.' Kaje was eclectic—a nerdy, tall, slinky South Asian with glasses, but all in all, a decent guy who went by KJ.

It was a rainy summer night. I looked out the patio door, and the rain came down hard, swiftly falling in all different directions. When it rained, it poured in Bluepoint City.

I took another sip of my water and walked to the counter to put the glass in the sink. I started thinking about my dream before waking up—it was always the same one of these two beautiful women whose faces were so vivid. However, I've never seen them before. As a security guard in retail, I've come to know many faces. My dreams were always so strange. But this one dream I've had since I was a kid has never faded or changed. I would see them, and they would just smile at me. The only thing that ever changed was that they weren't always together. Sometimes, it was in different places, and it was one of them. Often, it was both the same place and the same time.

I walked to the bathroom and lifted the toilet seat to pee. Standing there, I looked to my left and into the mirror. My face looked so tired from lack of sleep and because I had recently broken things off with my girlfriend of two years. I was only twenty-four and felt I needed more than relationship goals. The problem was that I didn't know what I wanted. I was a six-three, naturally athletic-built guy who loved to write. Whether it was song lyrics, poetry, or short stories, that was my passion. I wasn't into sports, and no, I didn't play basketball. I was more into tattoos and anime, with tons of tattoos covering my entire body. KJ always called me a walking conundrum. I just liked my peace. I've always had women throw themselves at me, but I was never truly interested. Yeah, I've dated around, but usually, it ended as fast as it started. Dating Courtney was my longest relationship, and I didn't feel fulfilled. It always felt like there was a piece of me that was missing—a daunting feeling of a connection more profound out there for me. I flushed the toilet, washed my hands, and returned to my bedroom.

If I were going to be able to perform my job duties at work tomorrow, I would need to fall back asleep. I lay back in bed and covered myself with my blankets, getting nice and cozy.

The sounds of the raindrops tapping against the window put me at ease, and after a while, I slowly started to drift back to sleep.

I prepared myself for work when I woke up a few hours later. My favorite color was black, so I wore a black crew neck, black jeans with a belt, and some boots. I grabbed my phone, security badge, and keys and left.

I didn't have a car, but we had excellent public transportation. Bluepoint City was a huge city that was still under development every day. I worked as a security guard at Blue City Mall, a local mall, for one of the stores, a beauty store called QT Beauty, that many teenagers would frequently visit and shoplift at. I got to work and stood outside the store, watching people pass. I have always wondered what the timeline of events was for a specific person on that day.

What exactly did they do in their daily routine?

Did they wake up and brush their teeth? Did they shower? What did they have for breakfast? It was very intriguing to me that billions of people had their own personal daily patterns that I knew nothing about.

I also saw people strolling along with their families, which was always painful for me to watch.

I always thought I had a good memory and could remember my earlier years up to birth. I remember being born into this world to a couple who did not want me. I was a young kid when they finally decided their lives were better off without me. So, they would give me up to foster care. And as much as I was in and out of foster care, in different housing, and with various people, I never was the type of person to have that define me. I wasn't angry like the rest of the kids. I stayed to myself, read my books, and kept quiet. I wasn't the smartest in school, but I pushed through it. Growing up without parents was challenging. There was a void there that made it hard for me to understand what love truly meant.

That probably was the ultimate reason I broke up with Courtney. She would often discuss her love language and how words of affirmation and acts of service were her top two preferences. I never understood what she meant by that. She would explain it to me, and I'd hear her, but I never took the initiative to do it. She deserved better.

"Hey Brandon, are you going to that slam jam tonight?" Stacy asked me, her voice cutting through my thoughts and dissociation while I watched people walk through the mall.

I turned around and saw Stacy standing next to the entrance of the beauty store. Stacy would always come out and casually talk to me during her lunch break. She was a short, chubby girl with a heart of gold, with brown wavy hair and brown eyes. She was endlessly curious yet undeniably caring, constantly checking in on me, asking how my day was going, and if I had eaten. And if I hadn't, Stacy made sure we got something together. There was a warmth in the way she looked after me, a quiet attentiveness that made me wonder if she liked me.

"Yeah, I'm definitely going to Dustin's Lounge tonight. Slam Jam is my favorite. You know I can't miss that." I responded to Stacy.

She smiled big at me and then looked down. "Well, maybe we can go together?" Stacy blushed and turned extremely red. I wanted to say yes but didn't want to give her the wrong impression. So, I was honest. KJ always tells me I'm too honest.

"I mean, we can for sure. But you know it's just as friends, right? I just got out of a relationship, and I'm just trying to chill, ya know?" My tone may be a little too stern and honest.

Stacy's face looked puzzled and embarrassed. She took a step back and threw her hands up. "Hey, I wasn't asking you out or anything. Ha, a guy like you with a girl like me? No way. You're too, uh,—" She pauses and turns to rush away.

I grabbed her arm to pull her back as I towered over her. "Don't say it like that. You're a super sweet girl, and we can definitely go together and enjoy Dustin's. I'll meet you there."

Stacy smiled big again and then nodded her head. I let her go, and she walked back into the beauty store. Wow, that was beyond awkward, but I knew Stacy would have been devastated if things had played out differently. She was a lovely girl and deserved someone to be nice to her. I saw how people looked at her in the beauty store when she would come up to help. People can be so cruel.

After work, I got home, and KJ was on his PC. He was gaming on a popular battle royale game.

"Hey KJ, sup man?" I call out as I walk to the fridge and pull out some dinner and a water bottle.

KJ responds, "Sup, Brandon. How was work, my man?"

I heat my food in the microwave, then take a sip of water. "It was work. How's streaming?"

KJ shoves his mouse and keyboard and then talks into his microphone on his desk. "Be right back, ladies and gentlemen." He turns around from his desk tucked off into the living room's corner and sits in his gaming chair, looking defeated.

I burst out laughing when he didn't say a word. Just his reaction spoke volumes.

Finally, he says, "Streaming sucks right now, dude. I'm getting my ass kicked left and right in this game. Got these little-ass kids hawking the servers."

"That's tough," I say back. "So, look, you promised to come to Dustin's with me tonight. I invited Stacy."

"Stacy?" KJ asks, forgetting about Stacy, whom I've mentioned to him before.

I look into the microwave, impatiently waiting for my food to heat as I continue talking. "Yes, Stacy. Thick, short Asian from work, Stacy. I need you to come so this does not look like a date."

KJ spins in his chair like a child and yells out to me. "You know I hate leaving this apartment, man."

"Yeah, no shit, KJ, that's the problem. Get out and get some pussy." I tease him.

KJ stopped spinning and looked embarrassed. "Hey, I get pussy... vagina."

"If you're calling it Vagina, KJ. I can't see how you're getting it." I take another sip of water to quench my thirst. I look at KJ, and he stares back at me and then shrugs.

He turns back around to his desk and turns on his mic. "Apparently, I have to go and get some pussy, ladies and gents, so that is all for the night. See you all tomorrow!" He shuts down his PC and takes his headphones off. KJ turns around in his chair and looks at me again. I raise my eyebrow and crack a smile. I mouth the words thank you to him.

"Yeah, yeah," KJ arrogantly says as he stands up and enters his room. The man always walked around in boxers, a t-shirt, and fuzzy slippers. He was a goofy guy.

After I ate, I decided to dress up a bit nicer. I kept the black shirt and jeans on, but I also put on a black, striped button-up shirt over top with a wide-brimmed fedora hat. I put my dangling cross earrings in my ears and sunglasses on. As for my shoes, I decided to wear dress boots.

KJ and I left the house and took city transportation to Dustin's. Once we arrived, we noticed how packed it was, and I was thankful I had purchased my tickets in advance. Slam Jam was an event that Dustin hosted a lot, but they also did events across other locations in the city. They showcased artists who sang, wrote poetry, and danced. I have always wanted to build up the courage to showcase my talent. Either way, I always loved showing up to support the performers.

I texted Stacy.

Hey, where are you?

Moments later, there was a loud ding on my phone as we stood outside the lounge in the damp weather.

Just found parking, walking towards Dustin's now.

I grip my phone and then begin to look around for Stacy. From the corner, I saw her appear. She wore an oversized jacket that hung off her shoulders, paired with a crop top and blue jeans, and completed the look with boots. Her hair was flowing down past her shoulders. Stacy walked up to me and KJ, clenching her purse in one hand and her phone in the other. I looked over at KJ, and he was staring her down, his mouth slightly open. I nudged him, and he closed his mouth, cleared his throat, and looked at me.

"Sup Stacy, this is KJ. KJ, Stacy." I introduced them.

Stacy goes in for the hug, wraps her arms around KJ, and KJ hugs her back.

"Nice to meet you, Stacy." KJ greets her, his voice crackling.

Stacy smiles, then giggles, "Same, KJ, nice to meet you too."

Stacy then comes towards me and wraps her arms around me. I hugged her back, and then we both let go.

"Sorry, I'm a hugger." She confesses.

I smile at her. "Oh, you're good, no worries."

We moved towards the line as we took out our tickets. Once we got to the door, we showed the bouncer, and he let us all in. There were many people here tonight, but thankfully, there was still a lot of seating left. We found a table close to the front of the stage and sat down. A hostess immediately came over and took our drink orders.

"I'll have a Rolo and soda," KJ said. "Put everything on my tab."

A Rolo was a brand of one-hundred-proof liquor that packed a punch. I guess KJ needed some liquid courage. He handed the hostess his credit card and gave Stacy a nod. Not only was KJ a privileged guy, but he also earned a substantial amount of money from streaming. He was one of the top players in his division, and it paid for half of the bills. He was always generous when we went out and never asked for anything in return.

Stacy sat up in her seat and pointed at the drink menu. "I'll take the Blue Sweetheart."

"And for you, cutie?" The hostess asked with a flirtatious look on her face. She gave me a wink.

"Oh, I don't drink. I'll take some water." I responded nonchalantly.

The hostess nodded and then walked away. A few minutes later, she returned with our drinks and set them on the table. It was a round table, and I was sitting on the far left facing the stage. Stacy was in the middle, and KJ was to her right.

Dustin's was cozy, warm, and inviting—a true gem nestled into the roaring nightlife in the heart of the city. It was big enough to accommodate a crowd but still maintained a controlled and relaxed atmosphere. The main floor had tables perfectly spaced apart, with a massive stage situated in front of the seating area. To the right was a medium-sized bar that didn't seat many since the flooring compensated for seating.

Not only was Dustin's a place for local artists to showcase their work, but it was also a restaurant that served the most delicious food. Waiters passed by, handing out food while we waited for the show to start. The aroma filled the space with a blend of hearty spices and fresh ingredients.

"We got a nice spot," Stacy says as she leans over and whispers to me.

KJ texted me as people started filling in and the space got more crowded; my phone dinged.

Dude, Stacy is hot.

But she's into you.

More dings after the next.

Maybe you can hook me up. You know I'm not good at this stuff.

I continued to look at my phone, and then, out of the corner of my eye, I looked at KJ and laughed.

"What's so funny?" Stacy asks me.

I smile even bigger and look at Stacy. KJ leaned back and motioned as if telling me not to say anything.

Honest and blunt, I said, "KJ thinks you're hot."

Stacy immediately gets red and blushes all over. She looks over at KJ and smiles. "Really?"

KJ was red as well, and he began to nod.

From that moment on, those two were inseparable. Stacy and KJ talked endlessly, her hand constantly finding its way to his arm in playful touches. He, in turn, would flash a wide grin every time she spoke, his eyes locked onto hers with undeniable interest. They hit it off effortlessly. Stacy had completely forgotten about me, and honestly, I was okay with that.

The show started, and a performer came out to sing. Her voice was beautiful as she performed a rendition of a popular song that was currently out, and I can honestly say it sounded better. Then, the next performer that came out did a poetry slam. The way she told her story was breathtaking. I resonated with it a little because it was about someone who couldn't find love. There were a lot of cheating aspects in the poem, so not everything correlated with me, but it was a lovely poem.

It was a big show featuring a lot of fantastic talent, and it was enhanced by the addition of a DJ during the intermission. I had a lot of water to drink tonight, so I excused myself from the table and went to the bathroom. The roaring sounds of the DJ playing his tunes reached into the back of the lounge where the restrooms were. There were no complaints from me because it was a good-ass DJ. I bobbed my head as I opened the bathroom door and walked in. I went to the stall, used it, then went to the sink and washed my hands. I looked into the mirror and stared at myself for a moment. I fixed my hat and then turned and left the bathroom.

As I left the bathroom and headed to my table, it felt more crowded than it had five minutes prior. I pushed carefully through people, apologizing and excusing myself. I took my phone out of my pocket and saw another text message from KJ.

I just asked her out on a date, and she said yes!

I smiled at the text. I was so happy for KJ. I don't believe he has had too many girlfriends, if any, so I'm glad he got out of the house and met Stacy.

As I stood there reading the text, a sudden rush came over me—an anxious, eerie feeling. I looked around, and it felt like I was having an out-of-body experience. It felt almost too perfect, as if this moment couldn't possibly be real. Happiness like this always seemed fleeting, and a part of me braced for the inevitable crash. A wave of dizziness washed over me, my thoughts spinning faster than I could control. I took a step forward, but my legs trembled beneath me. I stumbled slightly, catching myself just in time, my heart pounding with joy and unease. There was a hand that reached out to me and grabbed my arm.

"Hey, are you okay?" A familiar, soft voice cut through the room's noise, gentle yet sharp enough to pull me back to reality.

I looked over, and my heart immediately stopped. There before me was the most beautiful woman I had ever seen.

She had long, wavy, dark brown hair and brown eyes to match. She was a short girl with freckles and perfectly pink lips. This woman was light-skinned like me, with long manicured fingernails. She was holding a serving platter in her hand and dressed in all black. There was no way that this could be possible. How could this be one of the women from my dream? I was lost for words and couldn't catch my breath. It felt like I was choking on the air and unable to breathe. She came closer and rubbed my back.

"Are you choking?" She asked me frantically.

Finally, words escaped me. "No! I'm not choking. Sorry, I uh."

She pulls me towards a nearby empty seat and makes me sit down. She puts her serving platter on the bar, and one of her coworkers grabs it and takes it to the back room.

"I was watching you come out of the bathroom, and then next thing you know, you just stopped and stumbled." She explained to me as she pushed a curl out of her face.

I look down between my legs and then lean over to catch my breath. How is this happening? The only explanation is that I've seen her here before, and then I started dreaming about her. No, that wouldn't make sense because I have been dreaming about her since childhood. She has the same face as in my dreams. Then I remembered—the necklace. In my dreams, both women wore necklaces. One woman had a crescent moon, and the other had multiple layers. One day, I researched the necklace, which featured various layers, including a rose quartz crystal, the Eye of Horus, and the evil eye.

When I looked up at her, I could feel the energy radiating from her—it was intense, almost overwhelming. It pressed against me like a silent force, demanding my attention, pulling me in.

It was the same rush that came over me when I left the bathroom. How could I feel another person's presence this strongly? The heat from her skin was unexplainable, and her aroma was a fresh citrus mixed with a hint of warm coconut, creating a grounding presence.

I looked around her neck and noticed a gold chain tucked into her shirt.

"That's a pretty chain," I said to her, almost out of breath.

She looked down and smiled, then grabbed her chain and pulled it out of her shirt. "Oh, thank you. I've had the crescent moon pendant since I was a little girl. I never take it off."

I was in even more shock than before. I needed to know who she was and why she kept appearing in my dreams.

"Are you sure you're okay?" She asks again.

"Yeah, I'm fine. I'm sorry. I don't know what's happening, but I'm getting hot."

She fanned herself as she spoke. "I'm getting hot, too. You emit a lot of heat. I can feel how overwhelmed you're getting."

I tried to compose myself and sit up straight. Something deep down inside me told me to relax my mind and breathe, so I did.

I took a deep breath, inhaling as much air as possible, slowly holding it in, and letting it out through my mouth. I shake the energy off and then turn and look at her.

"What is your name?" I asked, my voice unsteady while trying to catch my breath.

She smiles at me big and then plays with her fingers as her eyes lock on mine. "My soul's name is Aeries, but you know me as Lauren Lanno."

Suddenly, vivid flashes of memories surged through me, crashing like waves against my mind. Were these just more dreams or fragments of real-life memories resurfacing? I couldn't tell, but they consumed me. The intensity was unbearable—I clenched my head, groaning in pain as the overwhelming flood of images threatened to drown me.

And with those words spoken, I remembered Lauren, Imani, and vast timelines of the reincarnated. But most importantly...

I remembered myself.

Welcome back, Mahant.